Forbidden Woods

Adventures in Norlandis

Jason B. Whittier

Howling Wolf Press

ISBN: 978-1-961703-13-1

DEDICATION

*To Mom and Dad: May you rest in the
glory of Heaven.
To my beautiful and amazing wife:
Your unwavering support and love made this book possible.
To my daughter Savannah:
Your resilience and strength give me
hope.
And to Emily, Hannah, Abbigail, Oliver, Benjamin,
and Gracelynn:
Your laughter and love bring endless
joy to my life.*

Contents

Prologue

As the sun descended beneath the horizon, desperate screams for help echoed from deep within the forbidden woods. Two black ravens shrieked from their perch on a jagged tree branch, their penetrating eyes fixated on Ashley who had been trapped at the bottom of an abandoned well for several hours.

"Help!" Ashley wailed into the crisp autumn air, her warm breath lingering about as the ravens disappeared into the burnt-orange sky.

Only a speck of light remained inside the crumbling well. The damp walls had a strong earthy and musty smell. The temperature continued to drop with every passing minute. The silence inside the dark well was beyond eerie, making Ashley's spine tingle. A chill in the air sent goosebumps up and down her arms. With nightfall approaching, the darkness began to overwhelm her senses. Even at the age of fifteen, Ashley was still very much afraid of the dark and hated being in tight spaces like this. Her claustrophobia was unbearable at times. It probably didn't help that several years earlier, she got locked in a closet by her babysitter and ended up passing out with a panic attack. At least then her babysitter let her out of the closet at the end of her time-out. But this time, she had no one to help her.

In front of her friends, Ashley always pretended she wasn't claustrophobic or afraid of the dark, but now she had no one to impress. There was no one to laugh at her, mock her, or call her names for being petrified.

"Please help," said Ashley, barely above a whisper, rubbing her forearms for warmth. She had kicked and screamed for hours, to the brink of utter exhaustion. Unfortunately, no one came to her aid, and she seriously doubted that anyone would. Nobody went into these woods anymore except foolish and rebellious kids like herself.

Ashley had reached her breaking point, sobbing into her hands uncontrollably as her wavy brown hair dangled in front of her dirt-covered face. "Why did I say dare?" Ashley muttered to herself. "What is wrong with me?" Her raspy voice bounced off the old brick walls. She should never have played that stupid game with her friends and should have just gone home. Then, instead of being stuck inside this disgusting and slimy well, she would be safe in her warm home, having a delicious dinner with her family. Her mom and abuela were planning to make steak and shrimp mofongo with a special sauce tonight. It was one of her favorite Puerto Rican dishes. Her family had an amazing recipe that had been in their family for generations. Every time friends came over, they begged Ashley's mom and abuela to make it for them.

Ashley's mouth began to salivate at the thought of the spicy garlic sauce drizzled all over the mashed plantains with steak and shrimp. The thought of food made her stomach rumble beyond belief. She couldn't bear the thought that she might never get to have dinner with her family again or ever see them.

Playing *Truth or Dare* always made her do crazy and questionable things she was not very proud of. Ashley never picked *truth* because she honestly feared what questions her friends might ask her, and she hated being judged and made fun of by them. Instead, she always picked *dare*. She personally loved the rush it gave her and all the attention she got, especially when they filmed her and posted it on social media for everyone else to see. One of these times, she hoped her *dare* videos would go viral and she could become an influencer and start making some money on the side.

For some reason, when they played the game she had an overwhelming feeling that she should have picked *truth,* for the first time ever. Her friends all had strange and suspicious smiles on their faces when it was her turn to pick. She never would have guessed that they would dare her to go into the forbidden woods. Did they think she would chicken out so they could tease her about it? Or, more importantly, did they secretly want her to disappear like all the other kids? Had they only pretended to like her? What kind of friends would do this to someone? Of course she could have refused to venture into the forbidden woods. Technically, she wasn't forced. But who could handle the ridicule she would receive for being weak and afraid?

Ashley stood up, enraged. She had to get out of this well and the woods before it was too late. "Help! Anybody! Help me!" She yelled repeatedly until her voice became hoarse. Ashley kicked the wall a few times, but that did nothing to calm the storm brewing inside her. She could seriously strangle her friends for what they had done to her. They knew she was never going to come back if she entered the woods. They truly wanted her gone. Even her boyfriend did nothing to try and stop her. Did he not love her like he claimed? Ashley felt so foolish for falling in love with such a horrible person. She would never have done this to him or any of her friends. She cared about them. But they preyed on her weakness and knew she would never say no to a *dare*.

"Someone, help me!" Ashley tried to grab onto the slippery sides of the well, but she couldn't get a good grip on anything. Dirt and tiny rocks crumbled down on top of her, causing her to scream in frustration. Her body shook with rage.

Ashley had to calm herself, or she would never get out of this nightmare alive. She leaned her back against the cool and moist wall, taking a few deep breaths. She could die from dehydration or hypothermia. Getting herself worked up wasn't going to help her one bit.

She tried to settle down and find some sort of peace. From the corner of her eye, she noticed a loose brick a few feet above her head. She barely grabbed onto it with her fingertips and reached for another brick that was sticking slightly out. When she tried to lift herself up, one of the bricks came loose and smashed her shoulder, while the other one grazed her upper lip.

Ashley wailed as metallic-tasting blood filled her dry mouth. She brushed the back of her thumb against her lip and wiped the blood onto her pants. As she stared at the opening above her, anger and frustration surged through her again. How could she have been so careless, oblivious to the well? She should have noticed it when she ran through the woods. Of course, it was entirely covered with leaves, but she still should have seen it. There was no excuse.

The light above Ashley slowly faded into complete darkness. "Help me," she whispered. There was no point crying for help anymore. No one was there; no one would ever find her. Ashley doubted her friends would even bother to come looking for her. They were all too afraid of the woods themselves, even though no one ever mentioned it. She knew her friends feared the punishment they would receive for provoking her into entering the forbidden woods. It was an unwritten rule that no child should ever enter the woods without an adult, and no one should ever force a child to venture there. Ashley also knew none of her friends had the guts to tell the police or even let her mom or dad know. Her family would suffer and never know how she had vanished.

Tears streamed down her face at the thought of never seeing her parents or siblings again. The black ravens reappeared, landing on the crumbling bricks of the well. They squawked and gazed down at Ashley.

"Go away, you filthy birds!" she yelled. A faint light coming from an opening on the opposite wall of the well caught her attention. Why hadn't she noticed the hole before? Maybe the bricks and rocks that fell on her had somehow opened up the wall. But why was there now a mysterious light coming from it? Without another thought, Ashley poked her head inside the hole. "Hello," she called timidly.

She paused, her heart racing with adrenaline. Would she finally be rescued? "Hello," she said again, almost whispering. The light grew brighter, filtering into the well. But where did the light come from? Impulsively, Ashley squeezed herself through the opening in the wall, disappearing inside. Instantly, the stones to the well magically sealed the hole shut behind her, trapping her inside. The light faded away, leaving it pitch-black.

Ashley's voice trembled, her body shaking with dread. *What just happened?* She kicked her feet against the solid wall behind her that was once a hole. But she couldn't budge it one bit. Ashley turned back around, trying to manage the tight space. She crawled forward through a narrow tunnel, the darkness suffocating her as the earthy air filled her lungs. Ashley had no idea where the tunnel led, but she had no other choice at this point. If only her friends had let her bring her cell phone, she could have used it as a flashlight. Even if she didn't have cell service here in the middle of the woods, she longed for some sort of light.

After crawling only a few more feet, the faint sounds of children's laughter drifted to her from farther down the tunnel. Ashley froze, and her voice shook. "Hello?" How could anyone else be in the tunnel? She had been trapped inside the well for hours and hadn't heard a single voice or noise, except for the birds. Her imagination ran wild with thoughts of ghosts, monsters, and strange creatures that could be lurking inside. Ashley had seen way too many horror movies that never seemed to end well with characters like this.

The children's laughter grew louder and louder until it echoed back and forth between the walls of the tunnel. Ashley's heart raced as she inched forward. Was she starting to lose her mind?

"Hello! Who's here?" Ashley crawled as fast as she could. The laughter was beckoning her like some kind of magical force. Ashley stopped to catch her breath, waiting for it to continue. The silence was almost deafening. She couldn't take it any longer. Ashley crawled another foot forward, and the ground beneath her collapsed. Her body became numb, and her mind went blank as she fell through a chilly, never-ending abyss.

Chapter One

At the end of a winding gravel road, an old, weathered farmhouse towered ominously on a hill by the edge of the forest. Tall pine trees cast shadows, shielding the house from the blazing summer sun. Long grass and colorful wildflowers swayed back and forth in the gentle breeze as the faded shutters tapped against the abandoned house. It was the first home ever built in town before the area was eventually settled by other immigrants, and it had loomed mysteriously over the small town of Sturbridge for almost three hundred years.

Countless families had come and gone over the years, typically moving out as quickly as they moved in. Some claimed that the home was haunted or possibly even possessed. Locals argued that it was not the house at all, but the terrifying forest behind it. Most referred to it as the house next to the forbidden woods.

Stories were passed down from generation to generation to instill fear in any child's life. It was said that, at night, you could hear the faint sound of children's voices drifting from deep within the woods. Their laughter and screams were like Sirens beckoning other children from the community to join them. Sadly, since the house was built, hundreds, perhaps even thousands, of children and teenagers had vanished into the forbidden woods without a trace. Not a single piece of evidence was ever found of their whereabouts, and none of them were ever heard from again. The police conducted numerous investigations into their disappearances over the years but were unable to uncover any explanation for all the missing children.

Adults in the community warned every child that they should never enter the forbidden woods for any reason. It was ingrained in them at school, at home, at church, and from local authorities. Multiple efforts were made to protect children and teenagers from the dangers of the woods at all costs. Recently, the town considered building a wall to surround the forest due to kids vanishing after a series of social media challenges that went awry. But the vote was not approved, most likely due to the huge cost of building a wall and the lack of resources. Regardless, police officers had patrolled the edge of the forbidden woods, day and night, for many years. Every effort was useless because children continued to disappear without a trace.

Karina hoped more than anything that she would never be one of those kids. The woods both fascinated and terrified her, which led to frequent nightmares and vivid dreams which felt as if she were there. Of course, it didn't help that her bedroom window faced the woods, and she lived right next to the peculiar house on top of the hill.

Kids from school, including her brother, claimed she was obsessed with it. Maybe she was, but she didn't see it that way. Unfortunately, she was bullied relentlessly for her strange fascination. Karina had read practically every newspaper article and story ever written about the forbidden woods and couldn't seem to get enough of it. Her curiosity was overwhelming, and she felt strangely drawn to it.

Due to her unusual obsession and quirkiness, Karina didn't have many friends. She had more acquaintances than anything, and no one really wanted to hang out with her after school. Karina was not your ordinary teenage girl, preferring to keep to herself most of the time with her head often buried in a book. Even though Karina had just turned fourteen a few months earlier, she looked older and more mature than the other kids her age.

Like other young teens, she was very self-conscious about the way she looked. Karina had long black hair and glasses that framed her beady brown eyes. Her parents often called her "Sunflower" because they said she was the prettiest flower in the whole garden and towered above the rest. But she never understood what they saw. Honestly, what parents would call their own children ugly? They were always trying to boost her self-esteem, which she absolutely loved about them. Either way, she tried not to care too much about what people thought of her.

All summer long Karina tried to distract herself from thinking or reading about the forbidden woods. She spent most of her time reading fantasy and sci-fi novels, listening to music, drawing or painting, gazing up at stars through her telescope, or playing games on her phone. However, no matter how much Karina tried to keep herself distracted, her mind always seemed to wander back to the woods.

During previous summer vacations, Karina usually hung out with her older brother, Oliver. But this summer he had a job working at the movie theater and spent the rest of the time with his annoying girlfriend. Karina barely ever got to spend time with him anymore, which frustrated her beyond belief.

Each summer vacation day seemed longer than the next. Karina was starting to get stir-crazy. She was glad middle school was far behind her, and she couldn't wait until high school. The summer felt like it was never going to end. Her dad kept bugging her to find a new hobby, and her mom told her to spend some time outdoors. But who was she supposed to hang out with? No other kids lived in her neighborhood, and most of her classmates were either away at summer camp or on vacation somewhere or another. It's not like any of them wanted anything to do with her anyway.

Finally, the house next to the forbidden woods had been sold. It had been on the market ever since Ashley had vanished without a trace a few years earlier. Karina's mom was the realtor who sold the house to the new family. Luckily, Karina discovered that a few kids her age were moving in. She anxiously peered out the window now and then, knowing they should arrive any minute. The anticipation was killing her. She felt kind of like a creep, peering out her window every couple of minutes. But she couldn't focus on reading or anything else right now.

Karina stared up at the K-pop posters on her wall in a trance, bobbing her head to the beat of one of her favorite songs. Kids at her school didn't understand how she could like music in a different language. But she didn't care if she didn't always know what the lyrics said, as long as she enjoyed the music. If she liked a song enough, she would usually translate it. She had actually learned an impressive number of Korean words and phrases purely from listening to K-pop.

Karina nuzzled her head into her pillow, feeling her eyes getting heavy, when a loud rumbling noise began to shake the walls around her. Startled, Karina jumped to her feet and hurried over to her window, trying to get a glimpse of what was happening. A thick cloud of dirt filled the hot summer air, making it nearly impossible to see through. Once the dust settled, Karina's eyes lit up with delight. A large rental truck and minivan rolled into the driveway of the house on top of the hill.

A little girl no older than six jumped enthusiastically out of the minivan as soon as it stopped. She straightened out her pigtails while a chocolate Labrador jumped from the van, barking with excitement. The dog dashed around to the moving van with an enormous smile. A teenage boy about Oliver's age got out of the rental truck and threw a tennis ball far up the hill.

"Go get it, Bash," yelled the boy as the dog chased after it.

A tall, slender woman with long, wavy red hair stretched her back and gazed up at their new house. A balding man with glasses struggled to get out of the minivan and walked up beside her, wrapping his arms around her. "I know it needs some work, but we will make do with it," said the man.

"I know, we always do," replied the woman, leaning her head against her husband affectionately.

Two girls hopped out of the backseat of the van. The older one, who appeared to be Karina's age, skipped over to her parents with a wide grin. The younger girl, who looked about twelve years old, kicked the gravel as she approached them with the biggest frown in the world.

"Is this it? It looks so old," the younger girl said.

"You're going to love it, Molly. I promise," the dad replied.

"Doubt it. It looks like it's going to fall apart any second," replied Molly. She spun around and locked eyes with Karina, who was still peeking through her bedroom window.

Karina jumped back from the window. She felt like such a creep and stalker but hadn't thought any of them would notice her. There was no escape. Molly had clearly seen her. Karina wasn't sure what to do. Should she pretend like no one saw her and keep watching them, or should she work up the courage to go meet her new neighbors? Karina peeked back out through her window. Molly's eyes were locked on the window as she pointed Karina out to her older sister. Karina ducked back down and slithered away from the window. Once she was far enough away, Karina leaped to her to her feet. She rushed out of her room and down the stairs, nearly tripping on the last step.

"Karina! No running in the house," yelled her mom. But her comments went in one ear and out the other. Karina stumbled into the kitchen, nearly bumping into her mom. "Slow down, Sweetie," said her mom, handing her a blueberry pie from the kitchen island.

"I'm not hungry," said Karina.

"It's not for you, silly. Can you please take it over to our new neighbors?" asked her mom.

"Sure," replied Karina as she took the pie and left the kitchen in a hurry. She clumsily bumped her shoulder into the door frame, almost dropping the pie all over herself.

"Be careful!" chuckled her mom, straightening out her new dress for work.

"Yeah, yeah, yeah," replied Karina. The screen door slammed shut right behind her.

Karina strolled across the crispy lawn, the hot sun radiating down upon her. As she trudged up her neighbor's driveway, she had to pause to catch her breath, which was even more challenging due to the humidity. Every breath she took was like drinking soup. When she finally made it to the moving van, there was no sign of any of her new neighbors.

The gravel driveway crunched beneath Karina's feet as she made her way toward the front of the truck. She stopped in her tracks and glared up at the old farmhouse. Time seemed to stand still as she became lost in memories of all her former neighbors who had lived there and all their children who had vanished. Tears began to fill her eyes. She tried her best to push the thought of

Ashley's disappearance out of her mind, but it didn't help. Tears streamed down her cheeks.

Karina glanced up at the forbidden woods but had to avert her eyes right away. Her whole body began to tremble, and anxiety consumed her.

Suddenly, Molly appeared from behind the truck's hood, causing Karina to jerk her arms awkwardly to the side. Before she knew it, the pie slipped out of her hands and plopped upside down on the ground.

"Shoot!" said Karina.

"Was that for us?" asked Molly rudely.

"Yeah."

"Great! We haven't eaten anything all day."

"I'm sorry. I didn't mean to drop it."

"Whatever," snapped Molly as she stormed away and pulled out her phone. Hurrying to the house with her eyes glued to her phone, Molly was completely unaware of her surroundings, causing her to stumble up the stairs. She nearly tripped on the last step but kept her balance and continued scrolling. Seconds later, she slammed right into the glass door. Her phone bounced away from her.

Karina burst into laughter, unable to look away.

"Be quiet!" yelled Molly. She scrunched up her face while picking up her phone.

"I wasn't laughing at you," lied Karina. She couldn't help but smile.

"Yeah, right." Molly stormed inside her house.

She reminded Karina of all the kids at her school who walked around the hallways and everywhere like they were zombies. They couldn't stop staring at their phones. Everyone was completely addicted and oblivious to the world around them. While Karina had a phone, she wasn't nearly as obsessed as other kids her age.

Karina turned to head back home when the older sister practically bumped right into her. Karina gasped for air, letting out a shrill noise.

"Sorry about my sister," the girl said.

"It's okay." Karina released a loud sigh.

"Did I scare you?"

"No! Well, maybe just a little."

They burst out in laughter simultaneously.

"Hi, I'm Hannah. I guess I'm your new neighbor."

"I'm Karina."

Hannah had long, dirty-blond hair and a nose ring that sparkled in the sunlight. She looked exactly like her sister, Molly, as if they were clones, except Hannah was obviously older and taller.

"Where are you––" Karina started to ask but was cut off by Hannah's father and mother rushing down from the hill toward them.

"Have either of you seen Abby?" asked Hannah's father frantically.

"Who?" asked Karina.

"Our youngest daughter, Abby," replied the father impatiently.

"No," replied Hannah.

"Me neither," said Karina.

"We haven't seen her since she got out of the car," said Hannah's mother.

"Please go look for her," said the dad as he and Hannah's mother darted away, calling for Abby.

Panic-stricken, Karina and Hannah sprinted toward the truck.

"Abby!" yelled Hannah as they quickly poked their heads inside the front of the rental truck, but there was no sign of her. "Maybe she's in the back."

"Hopefully," muttered Karina.

They rounded the corner to the back of the truck, which was wide open. Abby's small pink backpack lay discarded on the ground next to it.

"Abby!" Karina cried out, peering into the truck filled with boxes and furniture. A cold fear gripped her as she and Hannah climbed into the truck. Karina's heart pounded in her chest as she tried to squeeze past a few boxes and furniture. There was no way Abby was in the truck, and she truly hoped she hadn't already ventured into the one place no kid ever should. Karina hadn't even had a chance to warn them.

"Abby, are you in here?" asked Hannah skeptically.

"I doubt it," said Karina.

The girls craned their necks, desperately hoping to catch a glimpse of Abby.

"Let's go," said Hannah, jumping out of the truck.

"We should probably go check inside the house," said Hannah as she helped Karina out of the truck.

"Agreed." Karina felt a knot tighten in her stomach. She glanced back up at the forbidden woods. The trees loomed ominously against the darkening sky, their gnarled branches reaching out like skeletal hands. Could Abby have already wandered in there?

"Come on," said Hannah, tugging on Karina's arm. Hannah's dog began to bark from the edge of the forbidden woods.

"She must be in there," said Karina, pointing up the hill.

"You think?" asked Hannah.

"Why else would your dog be barking?" replied Karina, approaching the hill with trembling hands.

"Maybe Bash heard or saw something."

"Possibly."

Hannah's parents rushed frantically over to the two girls, making their way up toward the woods.

"Any luck?" asked Hannah's dad.

"No," replied Hannah.

"I think she's in the forest," said Karina, pointing up at Bash. He continued barking and pacing around but seemed apprehensive about entering the forest.

Hannah's brother, Noah, rushed out of the house with Molly. "I couldn't find her inside," he said, breathing heavily.

"Me neither," mumbled Molly.

Their words fell on deaf ears. Their parents' eyes were transfixed on the forbidden woods, and Bash was barking uncontrollably by the edge of the woods.

"What's wrong, Bash?" Hannah's brother yelled.

They all lumbered up the hill in a daze. Bash whimpered and backed up against Karina's legs.

"I've never seen him act like that," said Noah.

Karina nervously glanced down at the ground, petting the dog's soft fur for comfort. She couldn't bring herself to look into the woods. There were too many painful memories.

"Abby!" shouted Hannah's dad.

"Where are you!" yelled Hannah's mom.

Bash whimpered and took off down the hill toward the house.

"You two go search every inch of the house," said Hannah's father.

Karina moved a few steps back. Hannah and her brother bolted away, yelling out Abby's name. Hannah's parents brushed past Karina, who stood frozen as if her feet were cemented into the ground.

"Abby!" called Hannah's parents, approaching the path that led through the forbidden woods.

"Don't go in there." Karina's voice shook. She could barely breathe. Her vision began to blur. All she could hear was her heart beating faster and faster. It seemed like the whole world was spinning out of control. She staggered backward and fell to the ground.

"Stop, please," cried Karina.

Hannah's mother and father barely flinched, plunging deeper into the forest, screaming out Abby's name.

"Please don't go in there," Karina said, her vision blurring until everything was completely black.

Chapter Two

Tall oak trees creaked in the wind, swaying back and forth ever so slightly. The strong smell of pine filled the air. The sky drew darker much faster than Karina had hoped for. She leaned her back against the jagged bark of a tree in the forbidden woods. Her mind was on overdrive as her heart beat out of control. She felt like she was having another panic attack, but she couldn't let another kid disappear into these woods. Karina knew she had to get over her fears once and for all. They always say the best way to get over your true fears is to confront them head-on. Perhaps all the stories about the forbidden woods were fabricated and merely urban legends designed to scare children. No one had actually ever found any dead bodies or a single shred of evidence that they were even in the woods. But then the question remained: Where did they go? Where were Ashley and all the other neighbors who never returned home?

Karina couldn't keep wasting time. Precious daylight was dwindling with every passing second. She pushed herself off the moss-covered tree and made her way through the dense forest undergrowth. Small pine saplings covered the area, making it difficult to navigate through them. Karina used her cell phone flashlight to guide her through the thick brush. The dim light of her phone barely did anything, but somehow it still brought her a sense of comfort.

"Abby," said Karina timidly, inching her way along the path.

Suddenly, the sound of faint laughter and giggling came from the near distance. Karina stopped dead in her tracks. Her body became as stiff as a board. Her eyes surveyed the area, while her neck and head remained motionless.

"Abby, is that you?" whispered Karina into the eerie and ominous woods. "Abby?" she repeated.

Time remained still. Every second that passed without a response felt like an hour. Her spine and head began to tingle. She could feel the presence of something or someone in the woods. A gust of cool wind came, grazing against the many hairs that were standing up on the back of her neck and her goose-bump-covered arms.

Gentle laughter and giggling echoed beyond the pine trees. There was no way it was only Abby. It sounded as if there were many children nearby. But how could there possibly be any children in the woods this late? Had Abby found all the missing kids? Were they hiding out or trapped somewhere? Maybe her mind was playing tricks on her, or perhaps the forest was truly haunted or possessed, like everyone said they were.

Karina's phone beeped, letting her know she only had five percent battery power left. Her cell phone flashlight instantly shut off. "Shoot," said Karina softly, stumbling forward. She caught her foot on a tree root and fell to the ground. Karina landed face-first in a pile of dry leaves and pine needles. Her phone bounced away, disappearing underneath some brush.

The children's laughter stopped as Karina sat on the ground in fear. All she wanted to do was crawl into her bed, pull the covers over her head, and pretend like this wasn't happening. The silence was overwhelming, making her almost wish the laughter would continue. Karina reached around on the ground, brushing dry and crunchy leaves to the side with both arms like a maniac, desperately hoping to find her phone. Then perhaps she could call her parents or brother to come help her. But it was only wishful thinking, because she couldn't find her phone anywhere.

The next moment, an eerie child-like voice whispered Karina's name from not too far away. It grew louder and louder, repeating "Karina, Karina." She covered her ears, leaning her back against the jagged bark of the tree. She closed her eyes tightly, hoping this would end. "Karina, Karina," the voice chanted as Karina shook her head from side to side in frustration.

"Stop it!" screamed Karina at the top of her lungs.

The whispering stopped immediately. Karina waited a few moments before opening her eyes. She scanned the still and quiet forest, removing her hands from her ears. Her chest rose quickly up and down until she was able to regain control of her breathing. Nearby, a twig snapped from behind Karina. She turned her head quickly back around, scanning the calm and peaceful woods.

"Hello," whispered Karina. Fear consumed her as a chill ran down her spine. She could feel a presence lurking out in the dark reaches of the forest. But there was no response. "Somebody," Karina cried out. An unnerving silence seemed to amplify every rustle of the leaves and creak of the trees bending in the wind.

"I'm not afraid!" Karina called out into the darkness, her voice shaky and not at all convincing. She wasn't sure who she was trying to convince more: herself or whatever was out there.

A quiet ding from Karina's phone broke the silence. A faint light illuminated a pile of pine needles, revealing her phone just inches away from her feet. She scrambled toward it, snagging it from underneath the brush. Her fingers fumbled clumsily over the screen. She didn't have long before her phone would die. Karina started to dial her brother's number when she heard a child-like giggle, and then another. Her heart sank. Children's laughter erupted again in the distance. Karina rose to her feet and ran in the direction of the laughter. "Abby," Karina called out.

There was no response. Only giggling. It grew more intense as if thousands of kids were now playfully laughing at her. "Karina, Karina," they taunted. She hoped, the faster she ran, she could get out of this nightmare.

Karina stopped next to a large rock to catch her breath, nervously scanning the woods. The giggling and laughter had subsided to a soft murmur. At the bottom of the hill were several objects hanging from trees, but she couldn't quite make out what they were. Her body began to shake, making her feel like she was going to collapse or vomit.

Suddenly, the eerie voice screamed out Karina's name, beckoning her. It had this strange force over her that was magically pulling her toward the objects hanging from the trees. "Karina, Karina," the voice chanted.

Karina covered her ears to block out the noise, pushing herself off the rock. She tried to hurry down the hill to find out what was hanging from the trees and where the voices were coming from. Karina had only made it a few feet down before she lost her footing on a couple of slippery rocks. She slammed down hard onto her back and slid all the way down to the bottom of the hill.

Karina wailed and clutched her lower back on the cool, damp ground. The rough texture of the tree root pressed up against her back, adding to her discomfort. Patches of sunlight filtered through the canopy of leaves above her. Thankfully, the voices had stopped. The forest was quiet now, except for the sound of Karina's exacerbated breathing and the occasional rustle of leaves in the wind. Karina took a few deep breaths, anticipating what was about to come.

The children's laughter ramped up again, louder than ever. The voices were no longer in the distance but directly above Karina's head. She honestly didn't want to open her eyes, fearing the worst. All she wanted to do was find Abby and go home, but the laughter and giggling intensified to the point that Karina's eardrums hurt.

"Stop it, stop it! Stop it!" screamed Karina at the top of her lungs. The laughter abruptly stopped. Karina slowly opened her eyes and was astonished to see hundreds of strange plastic and porcelain baby dolls hanging from tree branches above her head. She stood up in bewilderment. Karina reached out to touch one of the dolls right above her head, feeling its cold, smooth plastic surface and delicate features underneath her fingertips. She pulled a few pieces of crumbling leaves out of the mangled red hair and gently brushed it back into place to smooth it out. The doll seemed to be staring right back at her, practically piercing her soul.

Karina strolled around the tree, examining the dolls in complete awe. She didn't realize that every tree, as far as she could see, was adorned with countless dolls hanging from their branches. The dolls softly giggled as if they lived in another world or were stuck in time. Some of them were brand new, while others were many years old and were covered with dirt and grime.

In unison, the dolls began to whisper her name. At first, it was just a few, but then one by one, the dolls chanted her name in unison.

"Karina, Karina," whispered the dolls.

Karina took off through the sea of dolls, who flailed their arms about, crying out Karina's name. She screamed in fear, sprinting as fast as she could through the never-ending cluster of dolls.

"Help us," cried one of the dolls.

"Karina, Karina, we need your help," cried another doll.

She stood frozen in the middle of the swarm of dolls, letting them engulf her as they repeatedly called out her name louder and louder. They seemed to be closing in on her. Karina was trapped. She would never make it out of the forbidden woods like everyone else before her. Karina covered her ears and muttered, "Make it stop, make it stop, make it stop."

"Karina," whispered a soothing and familiar voice. "Karina."

Chapter Three

Karina lay disoriented and motionless in the tall grass at the top of the hill by the edge of the forbidden woods. Her face was ashen white. Through shallow breaths and blurry eyes, the warmth of her mother's touch on her cold and clammy hands seemed to bring her back to reality. The dolls were not real, but merely another vivid nightmare of the dreaded woods that her mind could not escape from.

"Karina, are you okay?" asked her mother.

"I don't know. I think so," replied Karina.

Her mother handed her a bottle of water, helping her sit up. "You will be all right," said her mother.

As Karina gulped down nearly the entire bottle, she realized her mother was surrounded by all her new neighbors, staring at her, worried and speechless. Molly pointed at Karina, laughing and mocking her under her breath. Karina felt utterly embarrassed. She could not believe she had fainted and made a fool of herself yet again. How long had she been unconscious? Talk about making a good first impression!

Abby appeared from behind her parents and approached Karina innocently with a popsicle. "This will make you feel better," said Abby, handing it to Karina. "It always helps me when I'm sad."

"Thank you," replied Karina, staring at Abby in bewilderment. She thought for sure Abby had disappeared into the woods, especially with the way their dog was barking. Now she felt even more foolish.

Abby ran off toward her house with Bash barking playfully along the way.

"Come on. Up you go," said her mother, reaching down to help Karina stand up.

"Thanks," said Karina.

"Well, that's enough excitement for today. Do you want to come home with me?

"No, I'll hang out here for a bit, if that's okay," replied Karina.

"Fine with me. Just be home before dark."

"Got it."

Karina's mother shook the hands of Hannah's mother and father. "I hope you love your new home. Come on by or call if you need anything."

"Thank you so much," replied Hannah's father.

"We really appreciate it," said Hannah's mother.

"Of course," replied Karina's mother. She strolled down the hill, glancing back over her shoulder at Karina with a comforting smile.

"Are you hungry? We were going to order some pizzas," said Hannah's mother to Karina.

"Yeah, that would be great," replied Karina.

Hannah's parents walked away toward their house holding hands. Noah smiled at Karina and then followed his parents.

Karina glanced up at the woods and then had to avert her eyes. Molly passed by, bumping her shoulder into Karina. "Watch out, freak," said Molly.

Karina groaned in pain as Molly pranced away toward the driveway.

"Molly, stop being such a jerk!" screamed Hannah.

"Why don't you?" replied Molly, storming away, kicking a small stick in her way.

"She's such a pain," said Hannah, shaking her head. "Sorry again about her."

"What's your sister's deal?" asked Karina.

"She's just mad that we moved here. She pretty much hates the world right now."

"I see, and what about you?"

"I'm used to it. We've moved around a lot."

"That stinks. I wouldn't know anything about that. I've always lived here," replied Karina. Her face became somewhat solemn at the thought of Hannah not living in Sturbridge for not that long. "Why do you all move around so much?"

"My dad's job."

"That's cool."

"Yeah, I guess so. It's frustrating to have to move after you've made new friends and adjusted to a new school. It gets annoying."

"I get that," replied Karina, as they continued down the hill.

"Wanna check out my new house?"

Karina wasn't sure what to say. Did she really want to go inside? What if the stories were true? What if something happened to her? What if the house drove her crazy and she ended up in the forbidden woods?

Hannah eyed Karina curiously. "What's wrong?"

"I've never actually been inside before," replied Karina.

"Do you not want to then?"

"No. I mean, yes," replied Karina with a nervous laugh. "I'd love to."

Hannah led the way toward her house. Karina hesitantly walked behind, looking back over her shoulder at the woods. Her nightmare had felt so real and vivid, almost like she was actually there. It was very weird because she could feel the dolls' pain as though they truly needed her help. Karina wished her nightmares would end, but they kept getting more intense, making her wonder why they were becoming so strong now.

Inside, Hannah's home was nothing like Karina would have ever imagined. She always had this crazy image of blood-stained floors and walls, dark rooms with weird statues and paintings, spirits and ghosts haunting the halls, and other bizarre things you might see in a horror movie. But, to her surprise, the house was actually quite amazing.

In the foyer, the girls stood under an antique chandelier that had hundreds of intricate crystals sparkling from the natural light pouring in from the large windows above. The walls were covered with faded wallpaper and had intriguing designs you certainly wouldn't find in a modern store. Elaborate wood carvings adorned the door frames, while several rustic lanterns hung from the walls. The air was a bit musty, mixed with the scent of aged wood, which was not surprising considering the home had been empty for the last few years. Karina couldn't help but think that her house seemed so boring and ordinary compared to Hannah's.

"Want to find my room?" asked Hannah, breaking the silence.

"Sure," replied Karina as Hannah led the way toward the staircase. The wide hardwood floorboards creaked beneath their steps, echoing throughout the empty room.

Along the staircase were old black-and-white photos and oil paintings, covered in cobwebs. Karina studied the first painting very closely. Five teenage girls were sitting on the steps of Hannah's house, but strangely, no one was smiling. Four of the girls had striking blond hair, and the oldest had midnight-black hair and looked like she could shoot daggers from her piercing eyes. Karina had seen this image once before in a newspaper article about their horrible tragedy. All five sisters had vanished one day, and their aunt and uncle, who were their adoptive parents, were never able to find any traces of them. Apparently, they were the first girls who had ever disappeared into the forbidden woods, or at least that's what Karina believed.

As the girls climbed the staircase, the pictures became newer and in color. Karina recognized many of the pictures from her research on the forbidden woods and knew some of the families who used to be her neighbors. It was peculiar that these pictures were still on the wall after all these years.

"What's with the pictures?" Karina asked.

"Beats me. The other family must have left them here," replied Hannah.

"All of them?"

"Yeah, I don't know."

"Weird," muttered Karina, becoming lost in thought of all the various stories she had read about the different families and kids who had gone missing. It was beyond strange that, with the number of families who had lived here over the years, the older pictures remained on display. You would think that the pictures from previous families would have been taken down by someone new.

As they neared the top of the stairs, Karina gasped at the very last photo of her old neighbor, Ashley. She felt a lump in her throat, remembering the day Ashley had disappeared. She had watched helplessly from her bedroom window when Ashley vanished into the woods, while her obnoxious friends cheered her on. When she never returned, her friends left and never even bothered to look for her. Karina spent weeks observing Ashley's parents, police officers, and search parties enter the woods and return without finding Ashley or any evidence of her. Every day, Karina regretted not running up the hill and stopping her from entering the woods. Even though Ashley was a few years older than her, they still had a very close friendship, and Karina always looked up to her. Ashley acted like a big sister and often gave Karina advice or stood up to bullies on her behalf. A piece of Karina was ripped apart the day Ashley vanished.

"You okay?" asked Hannah, interrupting Karina's thoughts.

"Yeah, I'm fine. I was just looking at this picture of my neighbor who used to live here." Karina tried to clear the lump in her throat and keep herself from not getting too emotional. "I wonder why her parents left it here."

"Who knows? Maybe they were in a rush when they moved out."

"I guess," mumbled Karina, thinking about all the months Ashley's parents had spent searching for her and the countless nights Ashley's mother had spent crying in Karina's family room with her mom. Even Karina's brother was heartbroken when Ashley disappeared. Karina knew he secretly had a crush on her, even though he would never admit it. Oliver brought her up once in a while, and you could tell he had feelings for her.

Karina and Hannah crept up the last couple of stairs as the lights flickered on and off a few times. They both glanced at each other in fear, while a soft tapping noise radiated throughout the walls.

"Did you hear that?" Karina whispered, her eyes wide with apprehension. Hannah nodded slowly, scanning their surroundings. The lights flickered again as they reached the last step. The air was certainly heavier on the second floor. The scent of the old house grew stronger. The flickering lights cast eerie shadows on the faded wallpaper, while the tapping noise got louder and louder.

"What is going on?" asked Hannah.

The lights flickered on, while the tapping sound ceased. Laughter suddenly echoed from the bottom of the stairs.

Hannah rushed to the railing and yelled, "Molly, you're such a brat!"

"I got you idiots," laughed Molly, running out of sight. Her laughter lingered, echoing throughout the house.

"I cannot stand her sometimes," said Hannah.

"She seems nice," Karina replied sarcastically, trying her best not to laugh.

"You want a sister?"

"I think I'm good."

Hannah couldn't hold back as she burst into laughter, which then made Karina laugh uncontrollably. They playfully strolled down the dimly lit hallway, snickering until they reached the room at the end of the hall.

"I think this is it. My mom said it was at the end of the hallway," declared Hannah.

"Let's check it out," replied Karina.

Hannah tried to turn the antique brass doorknob, but it refused to budge. She twisted it forcefully, while pushing her shoulder hard into the door, but it still wouldn't open. "It's stuck," said Hannah, trying to give it another push.

"Let me try," replied Karina, giving the door her best shot. But it didn't budge an inch. "It's probably warped from all this heat."

"Maybe. Let's both try." Hannah turned the doorknob while both girls pushed with all their might. The girls grunted, leaning their shoulders forcefully into the door. It moved ever so slightly at the top and bottom but remained stuck in the middle.

"Come on, you little bugger," said Hannah as both girls continued to push without much success.

"I got an idea. You keep your hand on the doorknob and keep pushing, and I'll slam my body into it," said Karina.

"Okay," replied Hannah, while Karina backed a few steps away.

"Ready. One, two, three," said the girls in unison. Hannah twisted the doorknob while pushing her head and shoulder into the weathered door. Simultaneously, Karina took a few quick steps forward and slammed her shoulder and side into the door. It finally jarred open, with a loud popping noise from the friction, and smashed against the wall. Karina and Hannah almost fell to the floor as they plunged into the room, laughing hysterically.

Hannah staggered toward the light switch and flicked it up and down a couple of times, but nothing came on. "Welcome to my room. Isn't it wonderful?" laughed Hannah.

"It's actually pretty cool. You probably just need some light bulbs," said Karina as Hannah backed into an enormous spider web in the corner of the room.

Hannah made a disgusted noise. "And a good dusting," shrieked Hannah, running her fingers frantically through her hair, trying to get the cobwebs out. She danced around, attempting to free herself from the sticky webbing.

"And you have your own pet spider," Karina joked, peering at the wall where a daddy long-legs spider scurried up to the ceiling.

Hannah squealed, "I hate spiders," and took a few steps back.

"It won't hurt you at all," replied Karina.

"I know. But I still don't like them one bit."

When a soft thud came from another room, Karina and Hannah exchanged terrified glances.

"Did you hear that?" Karina asked, her face turning white as a ghost.

Hannah nodded. "It's probably Molly again."

"Maybe."

"She usually stays committed to her pranks until a fight between us breaks out."

"Right, so we should stay here then?" asked Karina skeptically.

Another loud thud from right outside Hannah's room made the girls jump. They both held their breath, listening intently with their ears up against the wall, right next to the doorframe. The floorboards creaked beneath Karina's feet as she shifted her weight. Hannah motioned with her finger for Karina to be quiet. Karina could practically hear her heart beating. But after a couple of silent minutes, there were no other noises. Only the eerie silence of the old house.

Hannah gathered up enough courage and poked her head out of the room. "Molly? Is that you?"

A muffled giggle echoed throughout the house.

"See what I mean," whispered Hannah.

A shrill scream echoed from down the hall, gripping the girls with fear. With their eyes bulging, both girls stared at the door.

"Are you sure she's only pranking us?" asked Karina.

"We should probably go check on that, like right now."

Hannah and Karina rushed out of the room and down the dark hallway. At the very end, cobwebs covered the ceiling, clinging to the old light fixtures. Molly stood motionless in the hallway, her back pressed against the wall, eyes wide with terror. Her gaze was fixed on a room before her with the door slightly ajar.

"What happened?" Hannah stuttered, trying to control herself.

"I saw something," mumbled Molly, pointing to the room. "In there."

Karina felt her stomach plummet. She glanced at the slightly opened door that Molly was pointing at with a shaky hand. If she was pranking them, she was an excellent actor. Karina inched forward right behind Hannah. A shiver of dread ran down Karina's spine.

"Don't!" Molly whimpered as the girls poked their heads inside the room.

With a deep breath, Karina pushed the door fully open and peered inside. The room was empty except for an old, weathered wardrobe in one corner and a broken mirror on another wall. The wallpaper was very faded, and portions of it were peeling off the wall, much like the rest of the house.

"See? There's nothing here," said Karina, trying to sound brave. She exhaled deeply, inhaling the lovely musty smell of the wardrobe.

"I wonder if it goes to Narnia," joked Hannah.

Karina nervously laughed. She was a little surprised Hannah was familiar with one of her favorite book series of all time. Almost no one at school had ever even heard of the famous book and movie series.

Suddenly, a loud thud came from inside the wardrobe. All three girls screamed.

"Wh-wh-what was that?" Hannah stammered, wrapping her arms protectively around Molly. Karina swallowed hard as they all slowly approached the wardrobe. A dull thumping noise rattled the wardrobe doors.

"Maybe some sort of animal is stuck inside there," said Karina.

"Only one way to find out." Hannah reached her trembling hand toward the handle. "One, two, three," she counted, and she jerked open the wardrobe door.

"Boo!" screamed Abby, springing out towards the three girls. Karina and Hannah both yelped. Karina practically jumped out of her skin, while Molly clutched her gut from laughing so hard.

"I'm going to kill you two!" screamed Hannah.

Molly and Abby sprinted out of the room and down the stairs, giggling the entire way down.

"Gotta love siblings, huh?" joked Karina.

"Do you have any?" asked Hannah.

"Only an older brother."

"Lucky! I'll trade both my sisters for him then," laughed Hannah.

Karina forced a laugh. The girls went back to Hannah's room in silence, the old floorboards creaking beneath their steps. As they entered the room, Karina felt a strange force compelling her to look out the window. A sliver of light filtered into the empty room. Karina approached the window in a daze. Hannah's room was directly facing the forbidden woods. Less than a hundred feet away from Karina was her worst nightmare.

Hannah stared at Karina quizzically. "So, how do you like living here?" asked Hannah, trying to break the awkward silence.

"It's all right. It can be kind of boring, though." Karina kept her eyes on the woods as if she were anticipating something would happen any second.

"Is there anything fun to do?"

"Huh?"

"I asked if there was anything cool to do around here?"

"Not really," replied Karina, snapping out of her trance and trying to direct her attention to Hannah.

"There's got to be something."

"I mean, there's this pretty sweet lake."

"Cool."

"At night, teenagers usually hang out there."

"Seriously? We should go then."

"I don't know."

"Come on. Please, please, please," begged Hannah. "I don't know anyone else here."

"Okay, fine."

Hannah squealed with delight as Karina moved closer to the window, transfixed by the woods. The sun was beginning to set, which meant the voices would start soon.

"What's wrong?" asked Hannah.

"Nothing," replied Karina.

"Why do you keep looking up at the woods? Is there something in there?"

"No. I mean, maybe. I'm not really sure."

"I'm confused," replied Hannah with a quizzical face.

"It's kind of a long story," Karina said, looking down at the wooden floor and purposely avoiding eye contact.

"Tell me," replied Hannah, shifting closer to the window.

"You wouldn't believe me even if I told you."

"Sure, I will."

"Everyone always says that."

"I promise."

"Yeah, okay."

"I'm serious."

"You sure?"

"Cross my heart," replied Hannah, jokingly crossed herself with both of her hands.

"Okay, okay, okay. So, the forest behind your house is pretty much called the forbidden woods by everyone around here."

"Why?"

Karina stared blankly at the woods as Hannah anxiously waited to hear what she had to say. "The woods are haunted or cursed. I know it sounds crazy, but they truly are."

"Yeah, okay. Heard that one before," replied Hannah.

A faint and muffled voice came from downstairs.

"What?" yelled Hannah, marching across her room and opened the door.

"Pizza's here," yelled Hannah's mother.

"Okay. We'll be down in a minute," called Hannah.

Karina rushed over and slammed the door shut. She kept her hand firmly on the door and stared Hannah dead in the face. "I'm being serious. Terrible things have happened in those woods."

"Yeah, like what? Let me guess, a monster or maybe a werewolf. Better yet, a spooky ghost," replied Hannah jokingly.

"Nothing like that at all," replied Karina, relaxing her hand from the door.

"Then what?"

Karina stared into Hannah's eyes. She was so frustrated and angry that no one ever listened to her.

"Once kids go into the woods, they never come out again. Not a single kid who has gone in there has ever been seen or heard from again," said Karina.

"No way!" replied Hannah.

"It's the truth. I don't know why, but it's been happening for a long time."

Hannah burst into laughter. "Yeah, okay. Nice try."

"I'm not joking. The last four neighbors who lived here have all had kids disappear in the forbidden woods. No one even found their bodies or any traces of them. They basically vanished from existence. Then, after months of searching, each of their families moved away and have never returned to our cursed town. My last neighbor, Ashley--"

Just then, Hannah's father angrily stormed into the room. The door bounced hard off the wall.

"What kind of nonsense are you telling my daughter?" he yelled.

"I, uh... " mumbled Karina.

"I want you to leave right now."

"Why? For telling her the truth?"

"I think it would be best if you left Hannah alone. In fact, don't ever talk to her again."

"Dad! Stop it! You're embarrassing me!" screamed Hannah.

"Stay out of it," snapped Hannah's dad. "Karina, please go home."

"Fine. No one ever listens to me anyway."

"Just get out of our house now!" he demanded.

Karina left the room without saying another word. Hannah's father slammed the door shut behind her. Tears streamed down Karina's face, while she trudged down the dark hallway.

Hannah and her father screamed back and forth at one another. "You are so annoying! Why do you always have to do this!" yelled Hannah, her voice permeating the bedroom wall.

Karina began to hyperventilate from crying so much. A few feet away, Molly stood in the middle of the hallway holding a candlestick, illuminating only her face as she stared at Karina approaching.

"You are crazy," laughed Molly.

Karina felt like shoving her down the stairs but held back every temptation she had. Instead, she squeezed past Molly without saying a single word.

"Bye, freak!" said Molly.

Chapter Four

A dusty box fan rattled back and forth on top of Karina's nightstand, attempting to cool her hot and humid room. Moonlight filtered in through the windows as she tossed and turned. Uncomfortable and unable to fall asleep, she slammed her hands down on top of her bedsheet and let out an enormous sigh of frustration.

Karina picked up a mystery novel lying next to her, hoping it might help calm her down enough to put her to sleep. She wanted this day to be over with and to forget everything that had happened. Unable to focus, she kept reading the same lines over again, not understanding a single word that she read. It wasn't like her at all to not grasp what she was reading, because she was probably the best reader in her entire grade. All she kept thinking about was how angry Hannah's dad had gotten at her. He had clearly overreacted, but there was nothing she could do about it, especially at the moment. Her friendship with Hannah was over before it had even begun. Karina didn't understand why he yelled at her and kicked her out of their house. She was only trying to be a good friend and protect Hannah from the dangers of the woods. At the very least, he should have thanked her for it.

The words began to blur, while Karina's eyes became heavy. Hannah's dog, Bash, barked several times, sounding like he was right outside her window. Karina opened her eyes, and she let out an enormous yawn. She scanned the room, waiting for the dog to bark again. As she dozed off, her book fell from her hands and tumbled to the floor.

"Karina," whispered a voice, causing her to jolt awake. Did someone say her name, or was that in her dream? Karina's eyes darted around her room, confused, debating whether she should go see if someone was at her door. She often heard random and weird sounds or voices right before falling asleep but never knew if it was normal or if she should ask her parents. Maybe it was all in her head, or perhaps the forbidden woods were playing tricks on her mind.

Karina tried to dismiss the thoughts of her own insanity until the voice whispered her name again from right below her window. Karina slipped out of bed, tiptoeing over to the window. She peered out into the darkness, but all she could see was Hannah's dog pacing around. The light outside Hannah's house flickered on and off, while the smell of a campfire filled the air. Karina took a deep breath, letting the scent of smoldering firewood fill her nostrils and lungs. She had always loved the smell, which reminded her of the summers she spent camping with her cousins.

A stream of light came from below, shining directly into Karina's window. She cautiously lifted the screen and poked her head outside. The light beam went right into her eyes, practically blinding her.

"Karina," called Hannah, while straddling her bike and pointing the flashlight.

"Hey. What's up?" said Karina, trying to sound as cool as possible.

"Get dressed and come down."

"Why? Where are we going?"

"Just come down."

"Give me a second," whispered Karina. She quickly changed out of her pajamas and slipped out of her room without making a sound. But as she closed her door, it creaked very loudly. Karina stood still for a moment, expecting her parents or brother to emerge from their own rooms. Fortunately, her parents were sound asleep by now. Deep sleepers, they could sleep through pretty much anything. It always amazed Karina how thunderstorms would keep her up all night, but her parents would never wake. She joked with Oliver that a marching band could parade through their room, and they wouldn't flinch one bit.

After a few tense minutes of anxiously waiting, listening to the humming vibrations of all the house fans and rattling air conditioners, Karina decided to try her luck. She crept down the hallway on her tippy-toes, stealthily past her parents' room, trying to move her feet to the rhythm of the grandfather clock ticking away at the bottom of the stairs: *Tick, tock, tick, tock.* Time was passing too slowly. Karina needed to hurry. Hannah was waiting for her. Suddenly, the grandfather clock went off as if someone had lit fireworks. *Cling, clang, clung.* It was midnight. Karina moved quickly down the hallway, while the clock echoed throughout the house, drowning out her footsteps.

The next obstacle was her brother's room at the end of the hallway, right near the stairs. The door to his room was wide open. Karina inched forward and peered ever so slightly around the doorframe, hoping he wouldn't notice her. Oliver paced back and forth, talking angrily on his phone. Thankfully, his back was to her. Karina leaned her back against the wall, trying to remain hidden. If her brother caught her and told her parents, she would be grounded for well over a month.

"Don't ever call me again! We're so done!" yelled Oliver, slamming the door shut in frustration.

Karina waited a moment. She felt bad for her brother and really wanted to see what was wrong, but Hannah was waiting. Karina took a deep breath and then rushed for the stairs.

This was the last challenge. The stairs creaked worse than her bedroom door, like an old fishing boat croaking in the wind. Some of the steps sounded like they were about to break anytime you stepped on them.

Karina debated what to do. Her eyes immediately became drawn to the railing. All she could think about were the countless movies she'd seen with kids sliding down railings, and she had always wanted to try it. Karina was certainly not the most coordinated girl, which was probably why she was terrible at sports. She positioned herself onto the railing and slowly slid down. Halfway down her shirt got bunched up. Karina's stomach rubbed up against the railing, causing a high-pitched squeaking noise from the friction. As she reached the bottom of the railing, she looked up at Oliver, who stared back at her in complete shock. She was so embarrassed, while he jokingly shook his head. Oliver gave her a comforting smile and motioned for her to go. Karina smiled back at him, dismounting the railing carefully. Her brother was the best! She knew he would never rat her out, given all the secrets she had kept to herself concerning him. Karina waved to him and scurried out the back door.

As she descended the back steps of her house, she scanned the yard for Hannah. But she was nowhere in sight. Did she already go back home?

The stars and moon shone especially brightly tonight. Crickets chirped and buzzed. Karina gazed up at the night sky, lost in thought, when Hannah quietly snuck up behind her and shook her. Hannah slipped her hand over Karina's mouth, silencing her scream.

"Quiet. You're going to get us both caught," whispered Hannah.

"Sorry," replied Karina barely above a whisper.

"Do you have a bike?" asked Hannah.

Karina nodded her head, pointing at her bike lying on the ground next to her garage.

"Okay. Come on," said Hannah.

Karina glanced over her shoulder, making sure her parents hadn't awakened. Thankfully, no lights had blinked on yet. Karina could only imagine how angry they would be at her for sneaking out in the middle of the night. She had never done anything like this before.

Hannah took the lead, pedaling down the long driveway, while Karina jumped on her own bike and followed close behind. The warm summer breeze flowed through the girls' hair, bringing smiles to their faces. The twinkling stars provided some light as they wound their way down the gravel road. Adrenaline coursed through Karina's veins at their exciting adventure. She was still worried that she would be caught, but she was even more excited and anxious to see where they were going.

"So, which way?" asked Hannah as they reached the end of the bumpy road.

"What do you mean? I thought you were leading the way."

"Well, I don't know where anything is."

"Where did you want to go?" replied Karina.

"Remember that lake you were talking about earlier?"

"You want to go there now?"

"Yeah, why not?"

"I don't know. It's kinda late and dark out."

"We'll be fine. I have a flashlight," replied Hannah, jokingly shining the light into Karina's eyes.

"It's not really safe."

"Come on, please, please, please!" pleaded Hannah.

"All right, all right," replied Karina, shielding her eyes from the light.

Hannah shrieked with excitement. "Good. I'll follow you then."

Karina took a deep breath, wishing streetlights would magically appear, illuminating the way. She was petrified of the dark, especially outside, never knowing what might be lurking around, ready to pounce on her. Her paranoia of the dark all started when she had encountered a rabid raccoon in her backyard when she was little. It was frothing at the mouth and was about to attack her when her brother thankfully saved her. Ever since then, she had been petrified of any nocturnal critters and being in the dark with them. She swore she could feel their presence as if they were watching her every time she went outside.

"You good?" asked Hannah, disrupting Karina's thoughts.

"Yeah." Karina glanced to her right and left, making sure no cars were coming from either direction. She propelled her bike onto the road, followed closely by Hannah, who had a flashlight dangling from her bike by a tiny piece of string. The road was lined with endless rows of pine trees, their intoxicating scent filling the night air. It was a peaceful and familiar smell, one that always reminded Karina of home. She couldn't imagine ever living in an area without trees.

"Wahoo!" yelled Hannah.

Karina couldn't help but chuckle at how carefree and wild Hannah was. Even though they were still getting to know each other, it felt like she had known Hannah for years. This was by far the most daring and adventurous thing Karina had ever done, which she never would have even thought of if it weren't for Hannah. Karina was practically afraid of her own shadow and barely did anything that would be even marginally risky.

From out of nowhere, a large deer charged out of the woods, nearly colliding with Karina. She swerved just in time and almost slammed right into Hannah. Her bike came to an abrupt halt, squeezing the brakes hard. A cloud of dust filled the air.

The deer stood in the middle of the road, gazing at the two of them as if nothing had happened, while Karina's heart beat out of control. The girls watched the majestic animal trot across the road, eat a couple of leaves, and then disappear between the pine trees. The deer had nearly died or could have seriously maimed itself, yet it was as carefree and nonchalant as Hannah was.

"That was insane!" yelled Hannah, causing the two of them to burst out into laughter.

"I know, right?" replied Karina, her heart still beating wildly.

"That was probably one of the craziest things I've ever seen," said Hannah.

"Yeah. Me too." Karina took a deep breath, trying to bring her heart rate back down.

"If only we'd recorded that. We could have gone viral."

"You're right. What were we thinking?"

"Ah, well, let's keep going."

The girls got back on their bikes and continued pedaling farther down the road. Several minutes later, they passed the sign for the lake.

"We're here," said Karina.

"Awesome!" replied Hannah.

They turned onto Lakeshore Drive, where a dim streetlight buzzed loudly above them, barely illuminating the dark road. It flickered and sparked like a dying ember in the wind. They continued down the dirt road as pine needles and rocks crunched beneath their tires.

Up ahead were a few cars and a roaring campfire. Rock music blasted from the speakers, while several teenagers partied around the fire.

Hannah grinned from ear to ear. Meanwhile, Karina's stomach was in complete knots. She felt so out of place. Her hands began to tremble. The thought of being judged or bullied by these strangers not only intimidated her but also made her want to vomit. This was one of the main reasons she was not super thrilled about going to high school in a month. Sure, she was excited about more challenging classes and different electives, but she'd barely fit in at her middle school. Soon, she was going to be at the bottom of the food chain as a freshman, and who knew what would happen to her. She had heard so many stories and rumors about high school over the last couple of months, which only compounded her anxiety.

"We should go," Karina said, her body shaking and her insides churning.

"Oh, come on; don't worry about them," Hannah replied, the two of them standing side by side while straddling their bikes. "Have you ever had alcohol before?"

"No," replied Karina, feeling her stomach sink even further. She couldn't give in to peer pressure, no matter what, but she really didn't want to appear childish to Hannah. Her parents would kill her if she even attempted to drink. "You?" asked Karina with apprehension.

"Me neither. And I don't plan on starting today," said Hannah.

"Okay, good," replied Karina, feeling beyond relieved. The knots and tension in her stomach instantly released.

"Do you know anyone over there?" asked Hannah.

"I don't think so," replied Karina, guessing they had to be juniors or seniors.

"I got an idea."

"What?"

Hannah ignored her. She ditched her bike on the edge of the dirt parking lot. Karina did the same, following Hannah along the edge of the parking lot toward the beach.

"Where are we going?" asked Karina.

Hannah ignored her again, motioning with her eyes for Karina to keep following her. They quietly went past the group of teenagers, ducking under a low tree branch. Hannah led Karina onto the moonlit sand, away from the loud party and the harsh glare of the campfire. As they approached a large boulder hanging over the edge of the lake, the music slowly faded. The rhythmic ripples in the lake spread peacefully onto the shore. A sense of tranquility washed over

Karina, as she focused on the serene beauty and calmness of the lake. She took a couple of deep breaths, letting the fresh air fill her lungs.

They carefully balanced themselves, climbing onto the slippery rocks that led to the boulder.

"Help me up," said Hannah.

"How?" asked Karina.

"Grab onto my feet as I try to lift myself."

"I got you," replied Karina, grabbing onto Hannah's feet. Karina pushed as hard as she could. Hannah clutched onto a jagged part of the boulder and pulled herself easily up. She reached down and helped Karina to the top of the boulder, while some of the partying teens curiously watched from a distance.

"Did you bring your swimsuit?" asked Hannah, the two girls teetering on top of the boulder while towering over the lake.

"No," replied Karina curiously. "Were you planning to swim?"

Hannah turned and smiled devilishly back at Karina, kicking her shoes off onto the beach.

"Ummmm, Hannah. What are you doing?" asked Karina.

"Perfect night for a swim, don't you think?" Hannah replied, flashing another devilish grin. She inched out toward the edge of the boulder and leaped into the lake with all her clothes still on.

All the teenagers cheered and hollered with enthusiasm, echoing across the lake. The attention was now on Karina. Everyone stared up at her with great anticipation. She nervously kicked off her shoes, watching Hannah gracefully swim through the lake, illuminated by the moonlight.

"Come on, Karina!" yelled Hannah.

"Jump!" yelled one teenage girl.

"Do it! Do it!" cheered a few of the guys.

"Just jump!" yelled Hannah.

Karina closed her eyes, trying to block out everyone cheering her on. She didn't want people to think of her as a loser anymore, and she certainly didn't want to be an outcast. Feeling some courage, Karina leaped out. She felt a rush of sensation, plunging into the chilly water. When she rose to the surface, everyone cheered with delight. A wide smile spread across Karina's face as she swam out towards Hannah, who splashed her enthusiastically.

The whole night had been amazing and nothing like Karina had ever experienced. She felt liberated from her tightly wound self and felt like she could accomplish anything at that moment. Hannah had awoken her soul. Karina truly felt happy and free for the first time. The girls swam for what seemed like hours, sharing stories and talking about everything they could think of. It was one of the best nights Karina had had in her entire life. She never wanted the moment to end.

Chapter Five

Sunshine filled Karina's room through her white frilly curtains gently blowing back and forth. A box fan in the windowsill hummed and rattled around, causing the pages of her book near it to flutter restlessly. Karina was dead to the world until the roar of a lawnmower jarred her awake. In a daze, she surveyed the room until her foggy eyes settled on her alarm clock. It was already noon. Holy smokes! She couldn't believe she had slept in so late.

Karina tossed her sheets aside and rolled out of bed, almost dropping to her knees. Her body was so sore from swimming and biking last night. She hadn't felt this kind of pain since she had gone to soccer camp a few summers ago. Karina attempted to stretch her body like her cat, Pumpkin, did. She hoped to alleviate some of the pain and loosen up her sore muscles. A couple of loud pops from her back and shoulders brought a smile to Karina's face. She enjoyed the sensation of cracking her knuckles and popping some of her joints to get the air out. At least, she thought it did.

The smell of fresh-cut grass filled the room. Karina took a deep breath, letting the aroma fill her nostrils and lungs. She had always loved the smell and often joked with her family that it would make a great candle scent and probably earn a fortune. "Fresh Cut Grass" or "Summer Vibes" would certainly be a hit.

She lumbered toward the window, letting out an enormous yawn. Heat was already radiating through her window, making the air sticky and stuffy. Her box fan was worthless at this point. It only blew the warm and sticky air throughout her room.

Up on the hill, Noah pushed a lawnmower in waist-high grass and weeds. Sweat dripped down his face, soaking his shirt. The mower repeatedly got jammed. Noah had to keep stopping to pull out the clumps of grass and restart the mower. Karina felt bad for him and wondered if she should offer to help or maybe see if Oliver could.

A faint knocking noise came from her bedroom door. Karina snapped her head around and moved skeptically toward it. She waited anxiously for another knock, wondering if she had maybe heard something from somewhere else in the house. It couldn't be her parents or brother, because they should all be at work, and no one else should be home right now. Was a stranger or robber on the other side of the door? Karina leaned her back against the door, deciding what to do. Should she call the police, or was that too dramatic? Perhaps her mom had swung home in between seeing clients. A second, louder knock made Karina's body tremble. She braced her back against the door, knowing she had to deal with whatever was on the opposite side.

"One second," muttered Karina. She had finally gained enough strength to turn around to see who was there. With shaky hands, she turned the doorknob reluctantly. Hannah peeked through the tiny slit in the doorway.

"Hey neighbor," said Hannah, making a goofy face with her eyes.

"Oh, hey Hannah." Karina relaxed her grip on the doorknob.

"So, we have a problem," replied Hannah.

"What do you mean? What problem?" As soon as Karina could spit out the words, the door swung open and Molly stepped from behind Hannah with a nasty little smirk.

"Hi, Molly." Karina exhaled sharply.

Molly didn't respond. She stood in the doorframe with her arms crossed, giving her a smug little smile.

"She knows," said Hannah.

"She knows what?" Karina replied, trying to pretend that last night hadn't happened.

Molly continued to grin as if she were the biggest brat on the planet. "I know you both snuck out last night and didn't come home until like three in the morning. I know you two were at the lake with older kids who were smoking and drinking," said Molly.

"But we didn't do anything bad," said Hannah.

"So what? Mom and Dad will kill you for hanging out with this weirdo, sneaking out, staying out past curfew, going to a lake at night, and going to a party with alcohol. You will be grounded for the rest of the summer when they find out," replied Molly.

"So what?" Hannah shouted.

"How do you know all this?" asked Karina.

"Hannah told me," replied Molly.

"I had to. I had no other choice," said Hannah.

"Unless you want me to tell your parents, you're going to do anything I want you to. Got it?" said Molly.

"You're blackmailing us!" said Karina.

"I don't know what that means. All I know is, I have about twenty boxes in the moving truck that need to be brought upstairs and unpacked, or I lose my phone. You two are gonna do it for me," said Molly.

"Yup, that's blackmail," said Karina angrily.

"Don't be a little brat," said Hannah.

"I'd watch the words you call me. I can add those to the list," replied Molly.

"You are so annoying!"

"So are you."

Karina and Hannah looked at each other, knowing they had no way out. "Fine!" said Hannah.

"Let's go," demanded Molly.

Karina and Hannah reluctantly followed Molly out of Karina's house. The hot summer sun instantly hit them. Karina could already feel beads of sweat forming on her forehead.

"Go get the rest of my boxes," said Molly.

"We're not going to be your slaves all day," said Hannah.

Molly burst into an evil laugh. "All day? How about the rest of the year!" replied Molly.

"Yeah, I don't think so. Only today, and that's it," argued Hannah.

"Yeah, right, Hannah! I'll just go tell Mom and Dad right now, then. Hey, Mom!" Molly started to yell.

"Molly, stop! We'll do the boxes. Okay?"

"Good," replied Molly with a smirk. "And then what?"

"What else do you want me to do?"

"I want to go to the lake tonight."

"No way! You're way too young," said Hannah.

"Who cares? It's not a school night, and I'll be with you," replied Molly.

"Not gonna happen."

"That's fine. Let me run downstairs and tell Dad something. Wait here."

Molly started to walk toward the house before Hannah blurted out. "Fine. We'll do it. But, after tonight, we're not doing anything else for you. Got it?"

"Yup, got it."

"I really don't think you should, Molly," said Karina.

"Stay out of this, weirdo. It's none of your business," replied Molly.

"Molly, stop calling her names!" demanded Hannah.

Without saying another word, Molly ran off toward her house.

"Hannah, I don't think this is a good idea," said Karina.

"I agree. But there isn't much else we can do," replied Hannah.

"What if something happens to her?"

"We'll wait until it's late. She'll either be asleep, or no one will be at the lake by the time we get there. Cool?"

"I guess," replied Karina.

Karina and Hannah reluctantly each grabbed a box from the back of the moving van. Karina struggled carrying hers as the sun beat down upon them. She barely made it halfway toward the house before she had to put the box down. Karina was out of breath with sweat dripping down her back. It felt so gross!

"Hurry up," Molly demanded, running ahead while playing on her phone.

"I truly hate her sometimes," Hannah said, grinning.

Karina forced a laugh as she picked up her box again.

The two girls spent the rest of the day lugging all the boxes up the hill and being bossed around by Molly. She made them unpack every single item from the boxes and arrange her entire room, while she lay on her bed, playing on her phone the entire time. All Karina wanted to do was yell at Molly for not helping and being so rude to them, but she didn't want to upset Hannah or have Molly tell her parents about them sneaking out. She could tell Hannah was getting as frustrated as she was. She snapped at Molly several times, and you could see that Molly was getting under her skin. The unbearable heat and humidity certainly didn't help. Neither of them had eaten anything all day and were getting hungry.

Hours later, Karina was finally home. Every muscle in her body ached and throbbed with exhaustion. Her legs and back were stiff and sore. She managed to shuffle into the kitchen, her throat dry and raspy. After pouring a tall glass of ice water, she guzzled it down in a matter of seconds. The cool liquid soothed her parched throat. She poured another glass of water and drank that as well.

Karina didn't have the energy to stay up late again. She also didn't know how she would be able to physically ride her bike back and forth to the lake. Maybe a quick power nap would help rejuvenate her. Her soft bed engulfed her aching body and calmed her senses. Within seconds, she drifted off to sleep.

She was no longer in her comfortable bed but back in the place she feared more than anything. Karina was back in the middle of the forbidden woods, surrounded by hundreds of dolls hanging from trees. Subconsciously, Karina knew this was only another nightmare. She wished she knew how to wake herself, but nothing seemed to work.

The dolls swayed back and forth from the ropes around their necks. Karina picked up one of them that appeared to be much newer than the others. It looked eerily similar to Ashley. The doll opened her eyes and blinked, staring directly at Karina. She let go of it, watching it sway back and forth as its eyes remained locked on Karina.

"Karina," cried the doll.

"Huh! Did you just talk to me?" replied Karina.

"I need your help."

Karina awoke in a cold sweat, her room in complete darkness. She glanced over at her clock. It was almost midnight. Karina jumped out of bed and fumbled through her dresser and closet, grabbing the first shirt and pair of shorts she could find. After getting dressed in her mismatching outfit, she snuck out of her house without a sound. This time, she had no problem sliding down the railing or leaving without being caught.

As Karina stepped outside and the door shut behind her, she realized she left her phone in her room. She debated going back upstairs to retrieve it but didn't want to risk waking her parents. Karina was so frustrated with herself. She had no way of texting Hannah to see if they were already at the lake or back home.

The faint sound of children crying whispered down from the forbidden woods. Their voices sent shivers down Karina's spine. She gently cracked her neck from side to side, trying to block out the noise.

Karina hopped on her bike, hoping to catch up with Hannah and Molly before they got too far ahead. As she rode down the gravel road, every muscle in her body tensed up. The darkness was overwhelming. She was completely alone, and no one was there to protect her. Unlike the previous night when she had a fearless friend by her side and a flashlight to guide their way, tonight she was filled with fear. Her mind raced with thoughts of dangerous animals lurking in the woods or strangers chasing after her. There was no light except for a few stars and a crescent moon poking through the overcast night sky.

She turned onto the main road, looking back over her shoulder to ensure there was nothing and no one following her or anything nearby. Karina scanned the dense woods for any signs of movement. A few twigs snapped nearby. Karina began pedaling furiously, determined to reach the lake and avoid anything in the woods that was preying on her. Sweat poured down her back, struggling to catch her breath.

An owl hooted loudly, causing her to almost lose control of her bike and veer into the woods. She stopped to catch her breath and wipe the sweat off her forehead. Right when she was about to continue on her way, a large pickup truck came barreling down towards her from the opposite direction. The driver slammed on the horn and narrowly avoided hitting Karina, swerving sharply to the left. The truck screeched to a stop as Karina's heart beat out of control. She stood frozen, her arms trembling, while she straddled her bike. A rough-looking man in his forties rolled down his window and began yelling every curse word imaginable at her.

Karina backed away, trying to distance herself from the angry man. She could feel the blood drain from her face, realizing that she was all alone with a complete stranger in the middle of nowhere. Karina could not call or text for help. Even if she screamed, no one would hear her or come to her aid.

The man got out of the truck, his boots thumping on the rocky ground. "What are you doing out here all by yourself?" he growled, his voice low and menacing.

Karina didn't know what to say or what she should do. She searched her pockets, hoping to find something she could use as a weapon if the man attempted to attack her. She was absolutely petrified.

"I... I'm just trying to get to the lake," she stammered, trying to sound calm.

The man stared at her suspiciously. "At this time of night?"

"I know, crazy, right?" Karina laughed nervously.

"Maybe I should take you home," replied the man, taking a step closer to Karina.

"No, I'm okay. I don't know you," replied Karina, hopping immediately back on her bike. She peeled out and pedaled away as fast as she could toward the lake. Karina had to get far away from this man and find help right away.

Karina glanced anxiously over her shoulder. The man was already back inside his truck, but he was still stopped in the middle of the road.

The sign for the lake came into view. Karina raced forward, her legs pumping hard. Her heart felt like it was going to explode. The faster she pedaled, the more she felt like the bike chain would obliterate into millions of pieces.

She turned sharply onto the road, almost losing control of her bike on the dry gravel. A cloud of dust and dirt filled the air underneath the old neon streetlamp. It buzzed loudly, while a swarm of mosquitoes surrounded it. Karina stopped briefly to catch her breath before continuing down the road.

As she rolled into the parking lot, she realized she might have already missed Hannah and Molly. Which meant she was all alone. It was a very real possibility. There were no cars, bikes, or any signs of people in the parking lot or on the beach, except for a small fire smoldering away. Karina ditched her bike next to the campfire and collected a few nearby branches. She tossed them into the fire, which brought it back to life. A few embers drifted off into the night sky. Karina slumped down on a large log a few feet from the campfire, hoping to rest her legs before she made her way back home.

Karina stared off into the campfire, lost in thought. Unfortunately, she didn't even notice the pickup truck approaching until it rumbled into the parking lot. In a panic, Karina lay down on the ground, using the campfire log as a shield to hide from the man. She knew it wouldn't offer much protection if he came closer. Glancing around, she spotted a large trash can and quickly crawled to it and hid behind it. Karina pulled on her legs, bringing them close to her chest, making sure no part of her was visible. She peeked out from behind the trash can. The frightening man circled the parking lot in his truck before coming to a stop.

Karina's chest felt heavy watching the man get out of his truck. Gravel crunched beneath his boots the closer he got to Karina. He stopped in front of the log where she was previously sitting. Karina watched in horror as he reached down and picked up her bike. Every instinct in Karina told her to jump out and fight, but she knew better than to give herself away. She couldn't afford to take any chances. Not now.

The man inspected the bike, turning it over in his hands. He tossed it back down onto the ground with a snort of disgust. "Piece of junk," he muttered to himself.

Karina sighed with relief but knew she couldn't stay hidden forever. She closed her eyes, praying he wouldn't find her.

Miraculously, the man's cell phone started to ring from his pocket. He answered it after a couple of seconds. "Yeah. I'll be home in a few," replied the man, letting out a belch.

Karina was so relieved as the man sauntered back to his truck. He cranked up some heavy metal music from his speakers and peeled out of the parking lot. He floored his pickup truck down the dirt road, leaving a cloud of dust. Once he disappeared from sight, Karina stood up from her crouched position, her heart still beating out of control.

Karina felt a tap on her shoulder. She let out a frightful scream as she snapped around. Hannah and Molly stood there dripping wet in their bathing suits.

"What was that all about?" asked Hannah.

"That man almost killed me," replied Karina.

"Seriously?" asked Hannah.

"Yeah. He almost hit me with his truck and then followed me here."

"Are you okay?"

"I'm fine. I'm just glad he's gone, and I'm so happy you two are here."

"Do you want to go home or call the police?"

"No way!" screamed Molly.

"I already told you. I'm fine," replied Karina.

"Okay. I'm sorry we didn't wait for you. But you never responded to any of my messages," said Hannah.

"I know. I fell asleep."

"Well, we had fun without you," Molly said, snickering under her breath.

"Molly, be quiet for once!" snapped Hannah.

"I'm sorry," said Karina.

"It's not your fault. I feel horrible that you almost got attacked by a creep," replied Hannah.

"It's fine. Maybe we should head back home if you both already swam," said Karina.

"Did you want to?"

"I'm good. I didn't remember to put on my bathing suit, so... "

"Can we at least dry off before we leave?" asked Molly.

"That's cool with me," said Karina, feeling the feud between Hannah and Molly heat up.

The crisp scent of burning wood filled the air. The leaves and twigs crunched beneath the girls' feet as they approached the campfire. Molly scowled at Hannah, who was trying to encourage her to apologize to Karina by making a motion with her eyes. The only sound breaking the stillness were muffled whispers between Hannah and Molly. Karina remained quiet, avoiding the growing tension.

The three girls awkwardly sat down around the fire on separate logs. Hannah continued to stare at Molly while Karina pretended not to notice Hannah whispering through her teeth at her sister. Molly shook her head in defiance. Hannah eyed Molly sternly.

"Fine!" said Molly. "I'm sorry for what I said, Karina."

"It's all good," replied Karina, avoiding eye contact. She gazed up at the moon and stars shining brightly above the peaceful lake. The clouds must have cleared during her ordeal with the man in the truck, thought Karina. She searched for familiar star constellations, hoping to lose herself in the vastness of the Milky Way.

Hannah and Molly studied Karina curiously. She could feel their eyes fixated on her, making her feel very uneasy.

"So, Karina, can you tell us more about the forbidden woods?" asked Hannah.

"Huh?" replied Karina, pretending not to have heard Hannah.

"About the forest behind our house," replied Molly sharply.

"What do you want to know?" asked Karina, desperately wanting to avoid the subject yet again.

"Anything," said Hannah.

"You both will just think I'm crazy, like everyone else," said Karina.

"I already do," replied Molly, snickering obnoxiously.

"We won't. We promise," said Hannah, elbowing Molly.

"I know you will, but here goes." Karina took a deep breath before she spilled everything she knew about the forbidden woods. She didn't hold back or skip over any detail, truly wanting Hannah and Molly to believe her and understand the real terror in the woods.

"How many kids do you think have gone missing?" asked Hannah.

"I'm not sure exactly. Probably more than five hundred. Maybe even a thousand."

"That's a lot of kids."

"Well, it's been going on for over two hundred years."

"You are seriously crazy." Molly laughed as she stood up.

"Molly!" yelled Hannah.

"She's either crazy or thinks she can scare us, because we are just so stupid."

"Not at all!" replied Karina.

"I'll prove there is nothing in the woods," said Molly.

"Please don't even think about it," said Karina.

"Tomorrow morning, you'll see," said Molly fearlessly.

"What are you talking about?" asked Hannah.

"I'll go into the woods, and then, I'll come right back out," said Molly.

"No! You both need to trust me, okay? I'm not lying, and I'm not trying to scare you. I know you think I'm this crazy weirdo, but you have to believe me," pleaded Karina.

Molly burst out into laughter. "Yeah, you are a weirdo. That's the best way to describe you. Weirdo, weirdo, weirdo," laughed Molly, hopping onto her bike. "Let's go, Hannah."

"Will you please listen to me! You'll never come back. Horrible things will happen!" screamed Karina.

"Don't worry about her. Nothing is going to happen," said Hannah.

"What? Now you too?" asked Karina, disappointed.

"Honestly, it's a little hard to believe."

"Then why do you keep asking me? I'm not making anything up."

"Tell you what. If Molly goes in and comes back out, then we know your story isn't true. If she doesn't, then I get a bigger room," joked Hannah. She flashed Karina a smile while straddling her bike.

"It's not a joke, Hannah. I'm dead serious. How else do I have to prove it to you?" demanded Karina.

"I just told you. Let her go in," replied Hannah.

"Fine! Then go!" screamed Karina.

Molly and Hannah took off on their bikes.

Karina walked over to her bike and threw it back to the ground, screaming in frustration.

"Weirdo, weirdo, weirdo," chanted Molly in the distance.

"Stop calling me that!" screamed Karina. Her blood was boiling. She was an active volcano ready to erupt. She had finally hit her limit. No one ever listened to her or believed a word she said about the forbidden woods. It always ended in tragedy.

Chapter Six

In a dimly lit room, five teenage girls draped in emerald-green cloaks encircled a young girl lying on her stomach, unmoving. Several candles were scattered across the floor casting eerie shadows onto the walls. The girls' faces were hidden beneath their hoods as they chanted softly. Their hypnotic whispers filled the room with a sense of mystery and magic. A musty and earthy scent filled the air, mixed with a faint hint of burning incense.

Suddenly, the girl in the middle levitated off the floor. The candles also ascended into the air, surrounding her with ambient light. As the chanting continued, the girl fell to the ground and flipped over onto her back without anyone even touching her. There she was. Karina lay unconscious at the center of their circle, clutching tightly onto a porcelain baby doll.

"Come to us, Karina," the girls said in unison. A huge gust of wind whipped through the room, blowing out all the candles simultaneously.

The girls watched Karina's hands begin to twitch. Karina's eyes snapped open. She sat straight up. The porcelain doll fell from her hands in a blur, shattering into thousands of pieces all over the floor.

The five girls gasped, stepping back slightly. Karina staggered to her feet, a wild look in her eyes. She tilted her head to the side and began to speak in their language. Karina waved her hands, causing the candles to relight themselves, making the room brighter and brighter. The intensity of the light made the five girls shield their eyes. It was as if the sun had been summoned, casting a radiant glow around Karina, while she stood imposingly at the center. The porcelain shards from the doll sparkled like glittering stars, bouncing around the room.

Karina seemed lost in a trance, her wild eyes unable to see anything in the physical realm. Her body moved with an unnatural grace, her hands weaving intricate patterns in the air, speaking in a language that sounded ancient and forgotten. Each word uttered seemed to intensify and feed the light until the room was as bright as the sun.

***

Karina jolted awake in her own bed, breathing heavily. She placed her hand across her chest, trying to control her breathing. Her eyes darted around the comforts of her room, reassuring her that she was safe. Karina exhaled sharply and then took a couple of deep breaths.

What just happened? She'd never had that particular nightmare and hoped she never would again. Her mind raced with questions. Who were those girls in cloaks performing spells on her? Were they linked to the forbidden woods and the dolls from her dreams? What language were they speaking, and how could she magically speak their language? There must be a reason she kept having these nightmares. It was no coincidence by any means.

Karina threw off her sheets and stumbled over to her window. It was such a dreary and cloudy day, which didn't help her mental state. Storm clouds were rolling in, and surely rain was coming any minute. Karina gazed out at the forbidden woods, hoping the forest could somehow speak to her and reveal its secrets. She needed to know more than anything where all the kids and teens had disappeared to. Something peculiar was happening, and she knew deep down that she would discover the truth one day. Karina didn't understand why more people did not want answers or get to the root of the evil that was lurking inside the forbidden woods.

Karina stared out at the forest lost in thought. Two ravens flew out of the woods, perching themselves on a tall pine tree on the edge. They shook their dark feathers before flying back into the forbidden woods. Karina suddenly realized she had forgotten entirely about Molly's plans. She needed to stop her and hoped it wasn't too late. Karina changed out of her pj's as fast as humanly possible and rushed over to her door. When she opened it, Oliver appeared in the doorway. Karina shrieked, almost jumping out of her skin.

"Did I scare you again, little sis?" asked Oliver jokingly.

"Maybe," replied Karina.

"Sorry. I wanted to apologize for being an awful brother lately," said Oliver, avoiding the awkward eye contact with his sister.

"It's okay."

"Not just lately. For the last few months."

"Ollie, it's cool. Don't worry about it."

"Sarah and I broke up a couple of days ago."

"I'm sorry. I know you really liked her."

"It's fine. She honestly wasn't the girl I thought she was. If that makes any sense."

"No, I get that. Can we talk about this in a second? I have to go check on something," said Karina, squeezing past her brother and out of the room.

"By the way, we seriously need to practice how to properly slide down the railing," Oliver said with a grin.

They both laughed as Karina hurried down the stairs. She hated that she left her brother so abruptly, but she couldn't waste any more time, knowing what Molly was trying to prove.

Karina dashed outside, scanning the whole area, but Molly and Hannah were nowhere in sight. Karina was at a loss on what to do next. She couldn't go over to Hannah's house without risking her father's wrath, yet she also couldn't keep pacing around her own yard like a crazy person. A terrible thought crept into her mind. Maybe Molly already went into the woods. What if Hannah went in with her, possibly even with Abby?

A loud rumble of thunder interrupted Karina's thoughts. Seconds later, the sky opened up, unleashing a downpour. Muffled barking came from the top of the hill. Karina snapped her head around. Molly stood at the edge of the forest, holding onto the dog's leash, as Hannah snapped pictures of the two of them.

Karina sprinted as fast as she could up the hill toward them. Molly noticed and pointed at Karina, laughing at her lack of athleticism and snail-like speed.

"Wow! You are very slow!" taunted Molly.

Karina was about halfway up the hill when she slipped on the wet grass and fell to the ground. Molly burst out in laughter. Hannah elbowed Molly, trying to get her to stop. Karina struggled to her feet and continued up the hill.

"Zip it, Molly!" yelled Hannah, while Molly continued to snicker.

Karina finally caught up to both girls.

"You need to get more exercise," said Molly, scolding.

"I don't care," said Karina in between loud, deep breaths while the pouring rain continued to soak all of them. "I'm begging you, Molly. Don't go in there. As much as I don't like you, I don't want to see you disappear."

"Look, I've got Bash with me. If anything happens, he'll attack them," replied Molly.

Hannah rolled her eyes. "Why don't we do this another day. It's pouring out," said Hannah.

"It's only a little rain. What am I going to do, melt?" joked Molly.

"Probably," muttered Karina. She hurried to the edge of the woods, blocking the path so Molly couldn't get by. "You're not going anywhere!"

"It's fine. Let her go," pleaded Hannah.

Molly shoved Karina to the side, knocking her to the ground. "Thought so," said Molly, and without any hesitation, Molly and Bash entered the forbidden woods.

"Come back!" screamed Karina, scrambling back up. "Molly, you need to listen!"

Molly ignored her and arrogantly continued walking down the path with Bash. "Please, come back!" yelled Karina again.

Molly picked up her pace and faded away from view behind the curtain of trees. Karina took a few steps toward the path and then restrained herself from charging into the woods.

"She'll be fine," said Hannah. "If she sees anything scary, she'll get spooked and come running home."

"I still don't think you understand," replied Karina, pacing uneasily along the edge of the woods. She strained her eyes, searching for any sign of Molly. Karina was so angry and frustrated. Molly had vanished like all the other girls, and there was nothing she could do about it now.

Karina sank on wet ground in frustration, keeping her back to the woods. She couldn't bear to look at it anymore. She truly wished her family would finally move away from Sturbridge, so she could forget these woods and horrible memories. Then maybe her nightmares would finally stop, and she could move on and be a somewhat normal girl. Her obsession had consumed most of her life and soul. It was so painful to continue to watch kids disappear right before her eyes.

As Karina sat there, feeling numb and hopeless, she thought back to a few years earlier, right after Ashley had vanished. In her desperation, Karina had grabbed her father's gas can and planned to set the whole forest ablaze. She wanted it all to disappear. Unfortunately, (or maybe fortunately, depending on how you looked at it) Oliver had intervened right before she could carry out her plan. He had to practically rip the gas can out of her hands. Since then, every time Karina got a whiff of gasoline, she always thought back to that day. What if he hadn't stopped her? Would she have burnt down the entire forest and ended the curse that had plagued Sturbridge for centuries? Her parents desperately wanted her to see a counselor or psychiatrist, but Karina refused until she was blue in the face, finally able to convince them otherwise.

"Come on, come on, where are you, Molly?" Hannah stood anxiously waiting on the edge of the woods, straining her neck every which way to catch sight of Molly. "Where is she?"

"Gone," replied Karina, with no hope.

"I wish you wouldn't say it like that," said Hannah. She ran along the edge of the woods frantically looking through the dense trees. She rushed back over to the opening of the path. "I'm going in."

"Give her a few more minutes," replied Karina, even though she knew deep down Molly was never coming out of the woods.

"I think I see something," said Hannah as two black ravens emerged from the woods, flying directly toward the girls. Hannah ducked when the ravens soared over her head and flew up to a nearby tree. "What was that?"

"Ravens, I think." Karina got to her feet.

"No. I mean, did you hear that?"

"Hear what?" replied Karina.

Hannah pointed with her finger toward the end of the path, near a cluster of tall pine trees. "See, right there," Hannah said, straining her eyes through the heavy rain. Her face became ghostly white. "Never mind."

Bash sprinted down the path and out of the woods with his leash still attached and a small doll clutched in his teeth.

"Where is Molly, Bash?" asked Hannah.

All the color drained from Karina's face when she grabbed the doll from Bash's tight grasp. As she turned the doll over, she saw a striking resemblance to Molly. Karina began to vomit all over the wet grass.

Hannah tried to comfort Karina while she scanned the woods looking for her sister. "Bash, where is Molly?" asked Hannah as the dog ran off down the hill back toward their house.

"Karina, we have to go in after her," said Hannah.

After Karina wiped her mouth, she walked over to Hannah, clutching the doll close to her chest. She didn't want Hannah to catch a glimpse of its face.

But then, something strange happened. Karina felt a wave of courage wash over her as she gazed deep into the forbidden woods. She was no longer afraid and knew that whatever lurked in the forest, she could overcome. Her destiny was awaiting, and she knew what she must do. "Let's go!" said Karina, full of confidence.

"You sure?" Hannah asked.

Karina nodded her head.

"Okay then," replied Hannah.

The two girls stood shoulder to shoulder, staring down the path that led into the forbidden woods. As the rain subsided to a light mist, Karina's strongly commanded, "Let's go."

Chapter Seven

The forbidden woods were nothing like Karina had ever imagined. A chill in the air sent goosebumps up her arms. Very little light filtered through the canopy of trees. Gnarled branches twisted and reached out like skeletal fingers from the imposing and ominous oak trees. Countless towering pine trees filled the dense forest. To her surprise, there were no signs of any wildlife. It was as though the animals knew to avoid these woods and for good reason. *Why do animals seem to possess such a strong intuition and an ability to avoid danger which humans seem to lack?*

Karina pushed the thoughts aside as she and Hannah cautiously made their way down a winding, narrow path. Neither of them spoke a word or made eye contact for several minutes. Karina tightly clutched the doll in her arms like an innocent child. She tried her best not to show how truly afraid she was.

"Molly, where are you!" yelled Hannah, quickening her pace.

"Molly!" Karina called, knowing deep down there was no chance of finding her.

"Wait!" Hannah put her arm out to stop Karina from moving another step. "Do you hear that?"

"Hear what?" Karina froze in her tracks. Her body instantly became stiff as a board as the faint sound of children's laughter and hysterical crying sent shivers up and down her spine. Her mind went right back to all the nightmares she had been having for the last few months.

"That must be Molly," said Hannah, bolting down the path out of sight.

"It's not her," said Karina under her breath. She couldn't move. Her hands and arms began to tremble. Karina was now living her absolute worst nightmare. Her newfound confidence and courage had vanished. She braced herself against a tree, trying to control her breathing. She knew what was waiting for them deep within the woods. How did she subconsciously know about it all this time?

Hannah re-emerged from behind a large oak tree at the sharp bend in the path. She ran frantically over to Karina and pulled on her arm. "Let's go!" screamed Hannah.

"Just leave me here," replied Karina.

"Stop being such a baby!"

"We have to go back home. Before it's too late."

"It's already too late. Molly is gone. Are you going to help me or not?"

"I don't know if I can."

"I thought you were my friend!"

Hannah's words stung and hit Karina like a ton of bricks. She was Hannah's friend and would do anything to help her, which is why she had already entered the woods that she had avoided her entire life. It was the one place she promised herself she would never go.

Karina took a deep breath, making her chest tremble. She reluctantly let Hannah drag her away from the tree. As Hannah yanked on her arm, the doll dropped to the ground and rolled right below Hannah's feet.

Hannah bent to pick up the doll. Her face became ashen. Hannah brushed the dirt away from the doll's face like a mother tending to a child. Tears filled her eyes and began to stream down her face. "Is this supposed to be Molly?" asked Hannah.

"I don't know. But it sure looks like her," replied Karina.

"We have to find her. We just have to. I don't care how much of a brat she is."

"We will. I promise," replied Karina, even though she had no idea how they were going to do it.

Suddenly, the doll blinked her eyes. Hannah shook in surprise, nearly dropping the doll. A single tear trickled down from the doll's face. Hannah and

Karina looked at each other in horror as the doll turned its head and stared deep into Hannah's eyes.

"Help me, Hannah," cried the doll.

Hannah screamed at the top of her lungs. "We have to go. She must be in trouble. She never asks for help."

Karina nodded in agreement and followed closely behind Hannah, who was running down the path with her Molly look-alike doll in hand. The children's whining grew increasingly louder, eventually reaching an unbearable pitch of ear-piercing screams.

As the girls approached the edge of the hill, Hannah's foot slipped on some loose rocks. She lost her balance and began to lean forward. Karina instinctively reached out to grab her, but Hannah's body jerked awkwardly in the opposite direction, pulling Karina along with her. The two girls tumbled down the hill together. Several feet down, their bodies collided with a sharp tree root and jagged rocks, cutting and bruising their skin.

Moments later, Hannah toppled right into Karina, causing Karina to fly up into the air a few feet. She slammed back down on her elbow, making her grimace in pain. They rolled to the bottom of the hill onto their stomachs. Karina moaned from the bruising she took, while Hannah whimpered in pain, clutching her wrist.

"You okay?" asked Karina.

"Not really. But I'll be fine. You?" replied Hannah.

"Only my elbow. I think I hit my funny bone or something."

Hannah rolled onto her back while clutching her wrist, her eyes fixed on the many porcelain and plastic baby dolls dangling above her head. "Oh, my goodness!" exclaimed Hannah, while the dolls whined above her, swaying in the gentle breeze from the ropes around their necks. "What is this?"

Karina already knew exactly what Hannah was looking at. She wanted to keep lying there, hoping any minute she would wake up from this horrible nightmare. But this was real life, and she was never going to wake up.

Hannah reached out, encouraging Karina to roll over. "You gotta see this," said Hannah. Karina braced herself with her good arm to push herself up off the ground.

The girls slowly turned to confront the eerie sight of hundreds of dolls hanging from almost every large tree branch as far as they could see. In unison, all the dolls fell silent. Hannah grabbed the doll resembling Molly and held it in the air near the other creepy dolls, who seemed to be watching her every move with their glossy and twitching eyes.

"This is insane. Who would do this?" asked Hannah.

"I have no idea," replied Karina.

Every doll suddenly burst into tears and began to loudly whimper and whine. Karina forged her way through the thicket of dolls, their plastic arms and legs reaching out like vines. Hannah trailed closely behind. The dolls seemed to close in on them, brushing against their heads as if they were deep inside a jungle. Karina's skin crawled with unease and frustration with the incessant whine from the dolls. She had to restrain herself from tearing down one of the dolls and tossing it across the woods. The madness reminded her of screaming toddlers and babies who throw a fit inside stores when they don't get what they want from their parents.

"Stop crying!" screamed Karina until she was blue in the face.

The dolls whimpered softly a few times before they began crying out Karina's name. She did her best to tune them out, navigating her way through the grove of dolls. "Karina, Karina... Karina," the dolls mocked and chanted.

Karina spun around, but Hannah was nowhere to be seen. "Hannah! Where did you go?" Karina yelled back, pushing her way forward through the dolls.

"Karina, Karina," the dolls laughed.

"Please stop," Karina muttered under her breath, covering her ears. She bolted through the never-ending sea of dolls pleading, "Please stop, please stop." But, of course, the dolls didn't listen. Her cries for mercy only seemed to fuel their fire, causing them to chant and mock her.

"Hannah, where are you?" Karina called out, pausing to get her bearings beneath a paper birch tree that was white as snow. The tree was unique and majestic looking, especially with only a single doll hanging from one of its branches. Its striking white bark stood out among the disturbing and eerie dolls hanging from other trees.

Karina leaned up against the tree, surveying the collection of dolls before her. A black scorched ring encircled the base of the tree, as if someone had once lit a fire there. She gazed up at the lone doll dangling from the branch and recognized the face. Karina couldn't place it at all. It was certainly not one of her previous neighbors or friends. But she knew the face from somewhere. Perhaps it was from one of the newspaper articles she had read.

"Help me, Karina!" screamed Hannah from somewhere close by.

Karina hurried in the direction she thought the scream came from. She quickly pushed her way through the hundreds of dolls. Hannah shouted her name again, this time with even more urgency.

"I'm coming!" yelled Karina, knowing she was getting closer.

"Please hurry," replied Hannah.

"Where are you?" called out Karina, the dolls brushing up against her face as she ran past.

"Over here!" yelled Hannah.

"I don't see you at all," said Karina between deep breaths. The dolls erupted into laughter, while Karina swatted them away irritatingly. "Stop laughing at me!"

"Help me!" yelled Hannah.

"Weirdo, freak, crazy girl, nut job," taunted the dolls.

"Leave me alone!" screamed Karina.

Karina paused to catch her breath and orient herself. Dolls were suspended all around her, their laughter and taunts ringing in her ears. She frantically searched for Hannah, but her vision blurred as panic set in. Desperate to block out the noise, she covered her ears and took a deep breath. Crouching down low, she noticed a small gap between the dolls with a wide-open space beyond. She propelled forward, crawling underneath the dolls, ignoring their mocking voices, until she reached the open area. "You'll never find her," they sneered, but Karina was determined to keep going.

"You're too late," laughed another doll.

At the edge of the opening was an old, deteriorating water well, its bricks crumbling, hidden beneath layers of leaves. Two ravens were perched on top of the well with their dark, glossy eyes trained on Karina. She crawled toward the well, and the ravens took off, disappearing into the sky above.

Karina then noticed the doll that looked exactly like Molly. Her body trembled as she picked up the doll. "Hannah!" yelled Karina. "Hannah, where are you?" The dolls laughed devilishly. Karina leaned over the edge of the well, bracing herself so she wouldn't fall in. Peering into the depths of the pitch-black abyss, she couldn't see a thing. "Are you okay?" yelled Karina, her voice echoing off the musty brick walls. "Hannah," she called again, pushing herself away from the well. "Where are you?" Her voice was becoming raspy.

Dark red teardrops began to fall from the doll's eyes. Karina gently laid the doll aside, her insides churning and her body trembling. A nearby tree was adorned with a brand-new doll, featuring shimmering brown hair and a nose ring. It resembled Hannah. Karina instantly started to dry heave a few times until she fell to her knees beside the well and let it all out of her stomach. Were Molly and Hannah dead or lost for eternity? Was she next?

As she got to her feet, the dolls stared at her, watching her with suspense. Karina had that eerie feeling that someone or something was behind her. She was petrified to look over her shoulder. The dolls stared at her with blank expressions, anticipating what was to come. Karina reluctantly turned around. The dolls disappeared in a slow blur until not one was left in sight. An ominous silence and stillness fell upon the woods.

Karina rubbed her eyes to make sure she was not dreaming again. As her foggy eyes regained focus, immense rays of light streamed through the trees, illuminating the mysterious birch tree, now adorned with vibrant yellow autumn leaves. At the base of the tree sat a girl a couple of years younger than Karina, dressed in a pristine white dress. She played with an intricately designed porcelain doll, paying no attention to Karina, who cautiously crept towards her.

The girl rose to her feet, jogging behind the tree.

"Wait!" called Karina.

The girl took off even faster toward a small white colonial house, hidden right behind the tree. Karina was beyond confused. Where had the dolls vanished to? Who was this mysterious girl? How could the season have changed so abruptly? And how did this house materialize out of thin air? The girl turned and gestured for Karina to follow her inside.

In a trance, Karina made her way towards the house, feeling like she was under some sort of spell. She followed the girl up the dilapidated steps of the house and right through the weathered door like a zombie. Blinding white light hit her in the face as she moved through the doorway.

Chapter Eight

As Karina passed through the portal from the forbidden woods, a tingling sensation spread throughout her body. Bright and colorful lights consumed her body. She propelled forward, seemingly floating through the air with no control over her limbs. Karina felt numb and disconnected from her surroundings, unable to hear or feel anything. Her mind was blank, having no sense of what was happening to her.

The bright light faded away. Karina's body began to regain feeling, her five senses returning to her. She now stood in a wonderful grove of white birch trees that stretched as far as she could see. The air was filled with the songs and fluttering wings of countless birds, each one displaying its magnificent colors. They were like nothing she had ever seen. The sky above was a clear baby-blue without a cloud in sight. Karina took a deep breath, inhaling the strong scent of fragrant flowers.

Karina was mesmerized with the world she had just stumbled upon. If there were a Heaven, this is what she imagined and hoped it would be like. If only she had a book with her, she could sit in the birch grove for hours, surrounded by all this beauty.

"Karina," called a soft voice from behind one of the birch trees. Karina surveyed the endless rows of trees until she spotted the girl from the woods who had led her there.

The girl blended in well with the trees in her white, lacy dress and golden hair. She motioned with her hand for Karina to come to her. Reluctantly, Karina left her spot and navigated through the trees, weaving in and out in the direction of the girl.

As Karina got closer, she noticed a massive stone wall looming in the distance. The girl signaled for Karina to be quieter and to crouch down low like she was doing. Karina's mind raced with a million questions, but she knew they would have to wait. With darting eyes, the girl scanned the surrounding trees before signaling Karina to follow her. They zigzagged between the trees toward the wall looming above them. The sky started to darken right beyond the grove.

"Where are we?" asked Karina.

"Quiet," whispered the girl.

The stone wall formed a perfect circle around the entire grove of trees. The girl pressed her back against the cool stones and pulled Karina by the hand closer to her. "Climb up the wall and tell me if you can see them," the girl whispered.

"Who is *them*?" asked Karina quietly.

The girl avoided eye contact with Karina, appearing concerned about whatever was behind the wall. Karina began to worry even though she had no idea what she should be afraid of. The girl leaned over, whispering in Karina's ear. "Please, go now."

She nodded in agreement, feeling as though the girl possessed a certain power and unique ability to manipulate her thoughts and actions. Karina looked up at the towering wall, at least three times her height. She found a few protruding rocks within her reach and began to pull herself cautiously upwards. With each stone she grasped, a wave of fear washed over her, but she willed herself to climb higher. Her heart pounded in her chest as the stone wall seemed to grow taller with every inch she ascended. The smooth, cold stones were slippery from the earlier rain, making her task even more difficult. A few patches of moss provided some relief for her fingertips.

After a few minutes of climbing, she had only managed to climb about halfway up the wall. Her grip was weakening, and her arms and legs were already sore and bruised from her earlier fall down the hill.

"I can't hold on much longer," whispered Karina.

Karina struggled to reach for a good rock to grab onto. She was almost able to brace herself until she lost her grip on a crumbling rock and tumbled down to the ground. Karina groaned in pain, while the girl dashed over to help her up.

"Sorry," said Karina, feeling embarrassed.

"It's okay. I have another way," whispered the girl.

With a sense of urgency, the girl quickly led Karina along the wall, covering a few hundred feet in what felt like seconds. Karina struggled to keep up, her body exhausted and sore. Finally, the girl stopped next to a cluster of beautiful birch trees that were growing over the wall in every direction. The girl gestured towards a rope ladder hanging from the trees.

She spoke quietly. "Be careful. It's a bit old."

"What am I looking for?" Karina examined the rope ladder, which had seen better days. Its worn and weathered fibers were frayed in every direction.

"Just go up and tell me what you see."

Karina braced herself tightly on the ladder, eager to discover what was on the other side of the wall and who this mysterious girl was. Without another thought, Karina began to climb the rickety rope ladder as carefully as she could. The wooden steps felt like they were going to snap with every step she took.

"Stop," whispered the girl, surveying the wall and surrounding trees for any signs of potential movement. She approached the wall cautiously, pressing her ear up against it. After what felt like forever, the girl motioned for Karina to continue upwards.

As Karina reached the top of the wall, the wooden step beneath her foot snapped in half. She grabbed onto the wall, while the ladder dangled between her body and the stone wall. Carefully, Karina pressed her back against a nearby birch tree and slowly pulled herself up farther. All she needed was a glimpse over the wall to understand what had caused the other girl's panic. Using her elbows, Karina mustered enough strength to lift her chin above the top of the wall. On the opposite side, the sky was completely dark, in stark contrast to the clear blue sky above the grove of trees. It was as though something went horribly awry on a painter's canvas.

The stone wall must have been over a hundred feet down on the opposite side. The grove of trees was situated on the top of a hill. At the bottom of the wall, a pack of coyotes prowled around, their noses to the ground. Several girls in emerald-green cloaks paced along the wall as if they were security guards. In the distance, enormous willow trees stretched out to the rolling green mountains on the horizon.

"What do you see?" asked the younger girl barely above a whisper.

"Only some girls in green cloaks and a pack of coyotes," said Karina.

"How many girls?"

As Karina began to count the girls, an enormous brown bird with a white chest swooped down from the sky, landing on the wall beside Karina. Its incredibly long talons grasped Karina's hand, making her grimace in pain. With piercing black eyes, the bird stared directly into hers. The bird tightened its grip on Karina's hand, puncturing her skin and causing blood to trickle down her arm. It slightly moved its head and let out a terrible screeching noise inches from Karina's face and placed its other talon on her left hand, drawing even more blood. A blinding flash of light came from behind Karina, hitting the bird in the chest, absolutely enraging the creature. Karina was still in shock at what had just happened.

"Jump!" yelled the girl, while the bird screeched incessantly.

Karina wiggled her hands away from the bird as forcefully as she could, feeling a sharp pain shooting down her arms and into her hands. The massive bird screamed again, and within seconds, several more huge birds descended from the dark sky, swooping down to perch on the rock wall beside the first bird.

Without hesitation, Karina released her grip from the rock wall, crashing to the ground onto her side. Pain radiated throughout her body, but she didn't have time to lie there and complain. The giant birds shrieked simultaneously, sending vibrations down the wall.

"Run!" yelled the girl.

Karina staggered to her feet, and the other girl took off at full speed along the wall. Karina trailed closely behind. The sky was now filled with even more birds, ready to pounce on them.

"What are those things?" asked Karina.

"Hábróks," replied the girl.

"Hábróks? Never heard of them," replied Karina, rather confused. Despite all the bird-watching trips she had taken with her grandfather and all the nature shows they watched together, she couldn't recall ever hearing about a Hábrók.

"Most people haven't," replied the girl as they sprinted along the wall, more Hábróks descending from the sky. It didn't matter how fast they both ran. The girls were surrounded. Hábróks completely encircled the grove atop the wall. "You will only find them here," said the girl, while the creatures screeched relentlessly, sending echoes throughout the grove.

The girls backed up to a section of the wall overgrown with dark green vines. The young girl turned toward the vines, uttering "Offavatibus." The vines instantly curled up, revealing a hidden tunnel within the wall. "Follow me," the girl said.

Karina was in shock, stumbling toward the tunnel in a trance, her feet stumbling over a pile of rocks and roots. The vines instantly grew back along the tunnel until it was completely covered.

Chapter Nine

As the girls made their way through the pitch-black tunnel, the air was cool and crisp. The smell of fresh earth reminded Karina of the freshly tilled soil right before her family planted their vegetable garden in the spring. The screeching of the Hábróks rattled the tunnel walls, causing Karina's hands to tremble.

Karina stood motionless, waiting for this mysterious girl to say or do something. She hated being in the dark, especially in a strange new place and not knowing her surroundings. "Where are you?" whispered Karina.

"Lichalous," said the girl. Right when the words came out, a bright light appeared from the end of the girl's finger, illuminating her face. She reached for a torch that was secured to the wall of the tunnel. "Feuannis," she murmured. With a quick flick of her wrist, the torch ignited. The fire gave the tunnel a fair amount of light, as the light faded away from the girl's fingertip. "Come along," the girl urged.

Karina squinted her eyes, adjusting to the glow that now lit up the narrow tunnel. Her mind was racing with questions, her curosity running on overdrive. She had no idea where she was, where they were going, who this girl was, what language she spoke, or how this girl could do magic. Her curiosity was killing her, and she desperately needed some answers before they went any farther. Impulsively, Karina jumped in front of the girl, attempting to block her way. "Where are we? Where is my friend? Who are you and where are we going?" demanded Karina.

With a snap of her fingers, the girl appeared on the opposite side of Karina. She turned to face Karina and flashed a playful smile. "Try to keep up," she teased.

"Wait. What just happened? How can you do that?" asked Karina.

"You ask too many questions," replied the girl.

"Why can't I ask questions?"

"Because we are running out of time, and questions will slow us down."

"Okay, but... I"

"You may ask one," said the girl, cutting Karina off before she could finish her thought.

"Why only one?"

"Because it is the only one that you will have. I will answer everything else later."

Karina pondered for a minute. She couldn't simply ask one. Her mind was on hyperdrive and felt like it was about to explode any second. She had so many questions racing through her head.

"Well, what will it be?" the girl asked.

Without giving it another thought, Karina blurted out, "Who are you? I don't even know your name."

"My name on Earth was Elizabeth. But in this Realm, I am called something different."

"Realm? Where are we then?"

Elizabeth shook her head, annoyed. "I said only one question."

"Fine. Then tell me, what is your name in this Realm?"

"Rayna."

"Rayna. That's beautiful," replied Karina, noticing a silver and gold tattoo with a series of intricate curls painted on the girl's temple. "Don't you want to know my name?"

"I already do, Karina," said Rayna with a radiant smile.

"What? How do you know who I am?" replied Karina.

"We've been waiting for you," Rayna replied, causing Karina to become even more confused and frustrated. She couldn't understand how someone like

Rayna could possibly know her name or why they had been waiting for her. And who is "they?" The questions swirled in Karina's mind like a tornado.

"*We've been waiting for you?* I don't understand. What do you mean by that?" Karina probed.

Rayna's smile softened, while she placed a gentle hand on Karina's shoulder. "We have to keep moving. I know this is a lot right now, and I get that. But time is really of the essence."

"Okay," replied Karina, sulking.

Rayna turned back around, sending sparks from her torch to the tunnel ceiling, casting a radiant glow onto many strange symbols and graphic pictures carved into the walls in another language. The engravings covered every inch of the tunnel, from floor to ceiling, creating a mesmerizing display.

"What is this all over the walls?" asked Karina. "I know, I know, I know. Only one question."

"It's simply our art, history, and stories," replied Rayna.

Karina studied the wall carvings, trying to make sense of them. She felt like an explorer discovering the caves of ancient cultures. One picture caught her eye. A massive wolf stood on the top of a mountain, looking down at a series of small huts circled around an enormous fire which rose as high as the mountain.

Suddenly, the torch waved inches from Karina's face, blinding her with its fiery light. The intricate engravings were no longer visible, only the flickering orange and yellow flames. As the heat grew more intense, her skin began to burn, making her step backward.

"We're almost there," said Rayna, waving the torch back away from her.

"Sorry," muttered Karina.

The girls continued down the tunnel in silence. They didn't get much farther when a snake poked its shiny black head out of a hole in the ground. It slithered up beside them, displaying its vibrant hues of red, black, and yellow. Rayna walked past the snake without noticing it. Meanwhile, Karina froze in her tracks, her body shaking from head to toe. She had never been comfortable around snakes, and the sight of this one sent shivers down her spine. She instinctively took a step back, almost bumping into Rayna. "Red on black, never make it back. No, that's not it," she muttered, bracing herself against the wall, waiting to be attacked. "Red on yellow, save a fellow. Not that one either." She couldn't move. Then it occurred to her: "Red on yellow, kill a fellow. Red on black, won't hurt Jack," said Karina. When she realized the snake's stripes were red on yellow, she collapsed to the ground, waiting for her demise.

The snake stalked Karina like a predator, showing off its venomous fangs. In a sudden burst of movement, the snake's colors shifted to mesmerizing silver and purple. She wanted to scream for help but was overcome with fear and unable to move. She felt completely paralyzed.

Rayna spun around, pointing her finger at the hissing snake, which sprang towards Karina. "Svehtat zut Steinapis," she commanded. A bolt of lightning struck the snake, turning it to stone when it was only inches from Karina's neck. It landed on top of Karina's back as she curled her body into a ball. She quickly brushed off the stone statue of the snake and stood up, completely shaken by the encounter.

"Oh my goodness! You saved my life!" exclaimed Karina.

"Welcome to Norlandis," replied Rayna.

"Huh? Is that where we are, Norlandis?"

"You got it," replied Rayna as the girls had finally reached the end of the tunnel. A few beams of light filtered through the overgrown vines and the slight cracks in the door to the outside. Rayna lifted her torch near the adjacent wall of the tunnel door which illuminated the elaborate engravings. Her light focused on a picture of an imposing giant with long hair and a bushy beard, who towered menacingly over a crowd of girls.

Rayna explained, "This picture shows the giant Skrýmir, who stands guard right outside this tunnel."

"Oh, great," muttered Karina.

"He protects this entire area and all of the surrounding land."

"The girls look terrified," replied Karina, studying the engravings.

"Wouldn't you be?" replied Rayna, while the ground began to shake beneath them. Dirt fell from the tunnel ceiling as the rumbling intensified.

"What was that?" asked Karina.

"Skrýmir," replied Rayna.

"Seriously?"

"Yes, we're too late."

"Is there another way?"

"Not from here."

"Okay. So, what are we going to do?" asked Karina, staring at the picture of Skrýmir.

"We'll have to wait until he's asleep. We have no other choice. I was hoping we would catch him during his afternoon nap, which he almost always takes."

Karina turned around, surveying the tunnel, hoping there might be another way out that Rayna didn't know about.

"I'm telling you, there is no other way," said Rayna.

"Then what do we do?"

"Please wait and have patience. We will have our chance."

"Okay," replied Karina, exhaling deeply.

"I'm sure you're probably hungry and exhausted."

"I really am," replied Karina, her stomach grumbling. "Can I ask you another question?"

"I guess."

"How old are you? You don't act or talk like other girls your size," said Karina.

"Twelve," said Rayna.

"Only twelve?"

"Well, I've been in Norlandis for a long time. So, you could say I've been twelve for about two hundred years."

"What? You've been here for two hundred years?"

"Yes. That is what I said."

"I don't understand. How are you the same age, then?"

"When you enter Norlandis, you never age as time passes on Earth. The Coven placed an aging spell on these lands, probably so that they could stay young and feel immortal."

Karina stared, and Rayna continued. "What I don't know is what happens when we finally return."

"Return where?"

"Home."

"And where is home?" Karina asked.

"Sturbridge."

Karina stared at Rayna in complete shock, her jaw practically dropping to the floor. "Seriously? Sturbridge?"

"Yes. My home was one of the first houses ever built there. I hear there are many more now."

"Wait! You've been here for two hundred years. Why haven't you gone back?"

"I've tried. Believe me. There is no way back."

Karina gasped, finally putting the pieces together as she recognized Rayna's face from an old newspaper clipping. Of course, it was only a sketch of her, and not an actual photograph. The story was about siblings who had disappeared into the woods with five other girls, who were never seen again. The families were put on trial, and rumors of witchcraft circulated. However, Karina never discovered what happened to them or the outcome of the trial.

"May I ask how you got here?" asked Karina.

"That's a very long story. Let's move away from here. I don't want Skrýmir knowing we're here. I'll explain in a moment," replied Rayna, leading the way back down the tunnel, away from the door.

After walking in silence for a couple of minutes, Rayna stopped Karina with her arm. "Here is fine." Rayna bowed her head slightly, waving her hand at the ground. "Feuannis," said Rayna as a small campfire appeared.

Karina slumped to the ground, leaning her exhausted body against the wall, while Rayna nestled in next to the fire. She wanted to ask Rayna more about Norlandis, but her mind was too foggy. Karina stared into the warm fire, watching the flames dance around. Before she knew it, she had drifted off to sleep.

Chapter Ten

The air was crisp and windy. Harvest season was quickly approaching, which meant there was plenty of work to do. Miles of farmland surrounded a charming little white farmhouse and stretched beyond the horizon. In the far distance was the only other house nearby, looming ominously on the top of a hill. The town of Sturbridge was in the very early stages of being settled by immigrants.

The sun was beginning to set over the farmland with splendid pink and orange colors. A strong gust of wind swept through the cornfields, shaking loose some of the vibrant golden-yellow leaves from the lone birch tree standing in the front yard of the farmhouse.

Karina stood on the edge of the cornfield right beyond the yard, observing Rayna. Lost in her own world, Rayna played happily without a care in the world. She sat by the base of the tree holding a delicate porcelain doll. Leaves floated and fluttered down around her. Rayna paid no attention to Karina as if she didn't even exist. They were far from Norlandis, and Karina didn't have the slightest idea where they were.

Rayna's mother emerged from the house in a frilly white apron, clutching a wooden spoon. The screen door slammed shut behind her. She descended the steps of the porch toward Rayna. "Dinner time, darlings. Please come in and wash up," said the mom, disappearing back inside. Rayna didn't respond to her mother but carried on playing like she hadn't even heard her.

Darlings? Karina pondered. Could Rayna's mother see her, or was someone else there? Karina scanned the yard and the surrounding fields. Her eyes landed on a pair of feet sticking out from behind the tree on the opposite side of Rayna. Curious, Karina strolled along the edge of the cornfield. A boy slightly older than Rayna sat up against the side of the tree, reading a book. He, too, seemed to be lost in another world and didn't notice Karina watching him.

From out of nowhere, the sky darkened. Funnel clouds began to quickly form. Neither Rayna nor the boy seemed to be concerned. Time seemed to be moving in slow motion as if they were stuck in an alternate universe. Karina wanted to warn them to get inside before the storm arrived, but when she tried to say something, no words came out of her mouth. She tried again and again. Karina could barely manage to open her mouth. It was like something took the air out of her lungs every time she started to speak. Maybe she could shake the two of them to get their attention.

Karina was about to approach Rayna, when five teenage girls in emerald-green cloaks appeared from the cornfield. They brushed right past Karina, their faces slightly covered by hoods. The leader of the group had hair as dark as charcoal. The other four girls had striking cobalt blue eyes and wavy blond hair that was almost white. One of the girls passed right through Karina as if she were invisible. Together, they formed a small circle around Rayna, the boy, and the tree.

"Back again?" Rayna asked. She continued playing with her doll, while the boy carried on reading without even lifting his eyes. Neither of them seemed bothered by these girls appearing out of nowhere.

The ominous dark clouds swirled around as the leader of the group bowed her head, motioning with both hands to the ground. When she uttered the words "Kreiulus av Feuannis," a small ring of fire formed around Rayna, the boy, and the birch tree.

The four other girls formed a circle, holding hands. The flames grew higher and higher. Rayna held onto her doll tightly, with her eyes shut, while the boy clutched his book with both arms. Rayna muttered something under her breath, while the girls began to recite a spell in unison.

A blinding light radiated from the girls' hands toward the tree. As their powers combined, a tornado emerged from above them, swirling violently down towards the group. Lightning bolts and rings of fire intertwined within the tornado, creating a cataclysmic effect. The brightness was overwhelming, making Karina shield her eyes with her hands.

In the blink of an eye, Rayna, the boy, and the five girls were all pulled into the vortex of the tornado and vanished into thin air. The ring of fire was extinguished with a powerful blast of frigid wind. The sky above normalized and clouds dissipated. The grass surrounding the tree was burned to a crisp.

Karina stumbled over to the tree as Rayna's mother came rushing down the porch steps. "Elizabeth! Benjamin! Where are you?" she cried out. Their mother scoured the area around the tree and the edge of the cornfield before racing back into the house in a panic. "Thomas! The kids are gone!"

At the base of the tree was the boy's leather-bound book titled *Norlandis*, and a small toy soldier. Out of the corner of Karina's eye, she noticed Rayna's doll dangling from a branch of the birch tree. The doll's once generic face now bore a striking resemblance to Rayna. A single tear rolled down the doll's porcelain cheek. "Karina," cried the doll.

Suddenly, Karina awoke inside the tunnel of Norlandis next to the smoldering fire. Rayna stood over her, gently shaking her. "Karina, we gotta go," said Rayna. Karina rubbed her eyes, realizing she wasn't in her cozy bed but stuck in this new, mysterious world.

"Did you sleep okay?" asked Rayna.

"I guess," replied Karina.

"Did you have any strange dreams?" asked Rayna with a devilish smirk.

"Yeah. Actually, it was about you," said Karina.

"I know," replied Rayna.

"How do you know?" Karina sat straight up.

"I have a way of entering people's dreams."

"It was about you and, I'm guessing, your brother."

"I know; I was there."

"Did that really happen?"

"Yup," replied Rayna, while helping Karina to her feet.

"Is that how you came to Norlandis?" Karina studied Rayna curiously.

"Yes. It was the last time I was home. Over two hundred years ago," said Rayna with sadness in her eyes.

"Then, is your brother here as well?" asked Karina.

"No, he is not. I haven't seen him since that night."

"I'm sorry, Rayna."

"It's fine. We need to get moving before Skrýmir wakes up." Right when Rayna finished speaking, the walls began to shake, and the ground rumbled beneath their feet.

"Oh no, he's awake!" said Karina.

Rayna motioned for Karina to be quiet by placing a finger to her lips. They crept silently toward the end of the dark tunnel. The walls and ground rumbled around them like ocean waves.

The exit of the tunnel was covered by lush green vines. Rayna secured the extinguished torch to the wall with a rusty metal latch. The vines vibrated back and forth. Karina realized that Skrýmir must be sleeping, because his loud snores were causing the whole tunnel to vibrate as if there were an earthquake. She thought of her father's thunderous snoring and how much louder it would be if he were a giant like Skrýmir. The whole tunnel would probably collapse. Karina covered her mouth to stop herself from laughing. Rayna gave her a scolding look, and Karina's smile faded away.

Rayna gestured with both hands, whispering, "Tvako schvarteous Kappelis." In an instant, two black cloaks appeared in her hands. She gave one to Karina and draped the other over her own shoulders.

"Stay as low to the ground as you can and be as quiet as possible. Skrýmir can hear even the slightest sound," whispered Rayna.

"Okay, got it." Karina finished putting on the soft, warm cloak over her head.

"Follow me." Rayna pointed her hand at the vines, muttering, "Offavatibus." The vines curled up, revealing a hole leading outside. Rayna cautiously climbed out of the tunnel with Karina close behind.

Chapter Eleven

Three magnificent moons glowed brightly, casting a purple hue across the night sky. A massive moon, about ten times the size of the one that orbits Earth, was between two smaller moons. Karina gazed up, completely awestruck and unable to move. It was crazy to think that something this amazing existed, yet most people would never experience the moons of Norlandis.

The dry ground crunched beneath Rayna with every careful step she took. She turned back around to see Karina barely a foot out of the tunnel. Enraged, Rayna rushed back, shaking Karina hard. She mouthed the words, "Come on."

They darted across the barren land toward one of the few dead trees on the entire landscape. The girls pressed their backs against the rough bark, attempting to camouflage themselves. Karina lowered her cloak just enough to see through. She glanced several times back up at the moons and then at Rayna to ensure she was not being watched.

Rayna grabbed Karina's chin, bringing her to eye level. She stared deeply into Karina's eyes, attempting to get her to focus on their task at hand. Rayna gestured with her head towards Skrýmir, who was sleeping heavily, his enormous frame slumped against the hillside, covering the entrance to the tunnel. With the giant being the size of a small building, Karina couldn't believe his weight didn't collapse the tunnel.

With each loud snore from the giant, the ground trembled beneath their feet. Rayna scurried to a nearby tree more than a hundred feet away. Karina hurried after her but couldn't resist glancing back in awe at the enormous beast. Completely distracted, she tripped over her own feet, kicking up a cloud of red dust from the dry ground. Rayna gasped in horror, covering her mouth. Karina scrambled to her feet, glancing back at Skrýmir, who was no longer snoring. She was able to reach the base of the tree and tried to blend in among the enlarged tree roots. Karina's heart pounded in her ears. She clutched onto a root, averting her eyes from Rayna. Karina prayed that Skrýmir would begin snoring any second now. But sadly, after a few tense minutes, he did not.

As Karina pulled the cloak's hood down toward her shoulders, dense fog rolled in off the hills. It swiftly covered the entire ground and night sky, blocking the glow from the three moons. Karina felt a jab under her ribs. She moved the soft fabric of the cloak to the side to see Rayna reaching up for her from her crouched position.

Right when Karina reached out for Rayna's hand, the tree roots around them were torn up from the ground. A cloud of dust filled Karina's lungs. Skrýmir towered above the girls, holding onto the dead tree as if he had simply pulled a weed effortlessly from his garden. His fingers alone were longer and wider than both of the girls combined.

Karina dangled from a jagged piece of root with one arm as Skrýmir lifted the tree upward. But she couldn't hold on for much longer. She lost her grip and plummeted to the ground with a loud thud. She rolled over and struggled to rise from the ground.

Rayna helped her to her feet. "Follow me," she exclaimed, sprinting through the thick fog and out of sight. Karina could barely keep up with her, only able to see a short distance in the darkness.

"Rayna!" yelled Karina, swatting at the fog hanging in front of her face like cobwebs. She looked behind to see if she could spot Skrýmir, but the fog made it nearly impossible to see anything. Somehow, it seemed to be getting thicker. Karina turned back around and could finally see the bottom of Rayna's black cloak.

The ground began to reverberate; Skrýmir was getting closer. Rayna ducked behind a small boulder. Karina followed suit. "We have to get to that large tree over there and find a way to get Skrýmir on the ground," said Rayna.

"How are we going to do that?" asked Karina.

"I'm not sure. It's the only way we will have a chance to get out of here."

"Can't you cast a spell or something?"

"No. I cannot use my magic to kill any creature in Norlandis."

Suddenly, the girls fell flat on their backs. Skrýmir was standing inches from their faces. His hairy and dirty toes brushed up against Karina's face. He lifted the boulder above his head as if it were a tiny marble. The towering giant chucked the boulder far into the distance like it were nothing at all. He reached down to grab the girls, but they were able to scurry back to their feet. They instinctively ran in opposite directions. Skrýmir screamed ferociously.

Karina zigzagged every which way, trying to avoid the giant. Skrýmir reached down again, swatting at Karina and missing her by an inch. Frustrated, he screamed again.

"Stay still!" bellowed Skrýmir.

"Rayna! I need your help!" yelled Karina, feeling the giant's cold and scaly fingers close around her neck and legs. Skrýmir held her up by only two fingers.

"Help!" screamed Karina.

Suddenly, two blasts of fireballs struck Skrýmir's fingers, making him drop Karina back to the ground. Skrýmir let out another roar. Rayna helped Karina back to her feet.

Skrýmir lumbered forward after Karina, while she screamed for help. She spotted a tree a few feet away and darted towards it for refuge, hiding underneath her cloak. Karina knew it was no use, but there was nothing else she could do. Hiding against the tree reminded her of when she was younger. When she pulled the covers over her head, hiding from monsters she thought were in her closet and under her bed. Even as a kid, she knew the thin blanket wouldn't provide any real protection, but somehow blocking out the sight of the imaginary monsters made her feel safer.

Rayna rushed over, out of breath. "Not this tree," she gasped. "I meant the one over there," she said, pointing through the thick fog, her finger barely visible in the mist.

"I can't see anything," replied Karina.

"Ventigra Nebuma," said Rayna, swooping her hand in a circular motion. The fog evaporated into the night sky, making way for the three moons to shine down upon them. Rayna pointed at a massive tree at the edge of a cliff, not too far away.

Out of nowhere, Skrýmir appeared right in front of the girls, blocking their path to the tree. He reached out to grab them, but Karina dodged his hand and darted around to the right side. Meanwhile, Rayna dashed in the opposite direction.

Both girls circled back between the giant's long, hairy legs, which were as thick as tree trunks. Skrýmir attempted to catch them, while they zigzagged back and forth in a figure-eight pattern in between his legs. They continued to weave around him, causing him to roar with anger. Skrýmir lost his balance as he tried to reach for both girls, and his arms became crisscrossed. He thumped loudly on the parched ground, causing the earth to ripple like a tidal wave, sending dirt and debris into the air and creating a small dust storm.

Rayna stormed toward Skrýmir with her finger aimed at him. She sputtered "Spinandelnet." Instantly, a thicker spider web-like net formed around Skrýmir, trapping him to the ground. He screamed and thrashed around, trying to break free from his restraints. Even with his impressive strength and size, the giant remained trapped on the ground, which only infuriated him further.

"Let me go!" the giant screamed.

"Quick! This will only hold him for so long," shouted Rayna. She sprinted toward the imposing willow tree with thick vines cascading down like a blanket.

"You will pay for this!" shouted Skrýmir.

The girls crept underneath the hanging branches as Skrýmir roared about. Rayna snuck inside the narrow slit in the tree, followed closely by Karina.

Chapter Twelve

The hollowed-out tree was completely dark inside. Rayna snapped her fingers and muttered, "Lichalous de Kernus." In an instant, the massive tree was illuminated by flickering flames from long wax candles, which were scattered around the smooth roots and spiraled all the way up the stem of the tree. The candles cast dancing shadows of the two girls on the walls, giving the tree a mystical and eerie feel. The earthy and musty scent, mixed with the smoke from the candles, filled the girls' lungs.

Skrýmir bellowed from outside and pounded about on the ground, making the candles flicker around the tree. Karina looked at Rayna, concerned. Rayna's calm face and demeanor reassured her that Skrýmir would not find them in their hiding place.

"Let's rest for a bit," said Rayna. She slumped to the ground, urging Karina to do the same. Rayna chanted "Vassi," and a tall bronze chalice filled with water appeared between them. "Have some water. You must be thirsty," said Rayna.

"Thank you." Karina put the intricately engraved chalice to her lips and guzzled the ice-cold water until it was empty. "Sorry, I didn't mean to finish it."

Rayna snapped her fingers again, and the chalice refilled with water. "Not a problem," laughed Rayna. "Have some more if you wish."

Karina took another long sip of the refreshing water and handed the chalice to Rayna. "How do you keep doing things like that? Are you a witch or something?"

"Yes and no."

"What do you mean?"

"Well, the night when the coven tried to perform their spell on me, it gave me powers as well."

"Interesting."

"I don't have as much power as they do, though."

"What are you able to do?"

"Many things."

"Like what?"

"Well, you must be hungry, right?

Karina nodded. "I'm starving."

"Very well then." Rayna motioned with her hand towards Karina's hands, muttering, "Suppenti unt Brodt." A warm bowl of soup and a piece of bread appeared in Karina's hands. Her mouth watered as she gazed at the savory soup filled with chunks of potatoes and vegetables. The mix of herbs and broth made her stomach growl with anticipation.

"Any way I could get a spoon?" asked Karina.

"Skoffel," said Rayna with the flick of her hand and a devilish grin. A spoon magically appeared in Karina's bowl.

Karina grabbed it and devoured the food as if she hadn't eaten in weeks.

"Anything else I can get you? A pie, some lemonade, or perhaps a pony?" asked Rayna playfully.

Karina started to laugh while trying to swallow her spoonful of soup. It caused a piece of food to get stuck. She coughed a couple of times, struggling to dislodge the food in her throat, until she finally coughed up a piece of potato onto the ground.

"Ewww, gross!" laughed Rayna.

"You made me do it," Karina replied, bursting out into laughter. "Don't make me do it again."

Rayna continued to laugh, while Karina gorged herself on the food. For some reason, the food brought back memories of home. Eating soup was one of the few things she enjoyed about winter back home. Growing up in New England was always challenging in the winter. The frigid temperatures and vast amount of snow made each day go by very slowly. Karina's mom made the most delicious and hearty soups that would warm your soul with every bite and always hit the spot.

Karina coughed up another small piece of potato, pulled it out of her mouth with her fingers, and flicked it to the ground.

"Well, when you are done being a disgusting little troll, we need to get out of this tree," said Rayna. She took another sip of water.

"How?"

"The ladder."

"What ladder?"

Rayna pointed at the wall of the tree behind Karina, which had a wooden ladder that was secured to the stem of the tree and stretched the entire way up, as far as she could see.

"I don't know how I missed that."

"Most girls do."

"Before we go, can I ask you another question?"

"Okay," replied Rayna. She then drank the rest of the water.

"Do you have any idea where my friend Hannah or her sister Molly went?" Karina finished the rest of her soup, anxiously waiting for Rayna's response.

"I haven't seen or heard anyone by either of those names. But we can check with the others when we get to the caverns."

"What others?"

"Our group. We call ourselves the Shadow Embers."

"Shadow Embers? I don't understand."

"You will meet them soon enough."

"So, you are part of the Shadow Embers?"

"Yes."

"And what does your group do?"

"We are part of the resistance, against... "

"Against who?" asked Karina.

"The Coven of Norlandis."

"Were those the girls on the other side of the wall near the birch grove?"

"Yes. And we're all stuck here from their curse."

"Curse?"

"The one they created the night they performed their incantation on me."

"I don't understand," replied Karina.

"All of Norlandis is cursed. When the Coven created this Realm, they cursed the entire land so that no one could ever leave. They control everything. The trees, the animals, the creatures, and everyone in the Coven are controlled by Amelia and her sisters. No one is safe from her evil clutches." Rayna's eyes seemed to get lost in the flickering candle between the two of them.

"Who is in the Shadow Embers then?"

"Everyone who has a sincere heart and opposes the Coven."

"So, am I now part of the Shadow Embers?"

"Yes. Assuming you want to be. There is a reason I came for you."

"How did you know to come for me?"

"Destiny."

Karina didn't understand how Rayna knew to find her in the forbidden woods. What was her destiny? All she wanted to do was find Hannah and Molly. That was her destiny, right? She never imagined she would be caught up in an entire world of madness.

"And are you telling me there is no way back home?" asked Karina.

Rayna strained her neck uncomfortably. "There must be. It won't be easy, though."

"What do you mean? I don't want to be stuck here forever."

"Then we will have to break the curse, won't we?"

"And how do we do that?" asked Karina, shifting uncomfortably.

"I really don't know. I've tried many different things over the years, but nothing has worked. Perhaps you can find the way. I believe that is part of your destiny."

"How many kids are here on Norlandis?"

"I wish I knew. You've seen the dolls, right? How many are there now?"

Karina stared at Rayna in shock as it hit her like a ton of bricks. Every doll in the forbidden woods represented a lost girl trapped in Norlandis. She always knew the woods were haunted or cursed, and she felt deep down that the kids were somewhere. She never would have imagined that they would be stuck in another Realm.

"There are hundreds. Maybe even a thousand," said Karina, disappointed.

"That sounds about right," replied Rayna as she stood up.

Karina looked down at the ground, tears forming in her eyes. "We're never going home again, are we?"

Rayna turned her back on Karina, fighting her own emotions of longing for home. "We certainly can't ever get back by just sitting inside this tree worrying about it."

"Yeah, I know," muttered Karina under her breath.

"Listen, I know it's tough to accept. But we need you. We all need you." Rayna put a comforting hand on Karina's back.

Karina's mind began to wander, thinking of all the people she knew who had disappeared over the years. She couldn't bear to lose anyone else and was determined to break the curse for herself and everyone on Norlandis. They needed her. No one had ever needed or counted on her before, but they did for some reason. She would do whatever it took to find Hannah and Molly and help the Shadow Embers. If this was her true destiny, then she needed to embrace it. Beaming with confidence, Karina rose to her feet. "Show me the way."

"All right. We need to go slowly up the ladder. It's a long way up. So, if you fall... well, it wouldn't be good," replied Rayna.

"I understand," said Karina, feeling a sense of urgency.

Rayna led the way up the wooden ladder built into the wall of the tree. Karina stretched out her arms and back, releasing a satisfying pop from her joints. She braced herself on the bottom of the ladder, staring directly upwards. It was a mesmerizing sight, with all the flickering candles casting shadows up the hollow trunk of the tree.

"You coming, or what?" called Rayna from above.

"Yeah, sorry. This is all so incredible." Karina began to climb. She took it one step at a time, making sure not to look down, and keeping her eyes focused only on the ladder.

The long wax candles cast a dim light on the tree's walls, making Karina wonder how the tree hadn't caught fire yet. Or why weren't there any burned or charred marks anywhere? As she continued to climb upwards, loud screeching noises erupted from outside the tree.

"Ignore them," said Rayna calmly.

"Are those Hábróks?" asked Karina.

"By the sounds of it, I'd say so. Skrýmir is probably free and has beaconed the Hábróks for help."

"Great."

"Don't worry about them right now. We are completely safe inside here."

"And what about when we have to go outside?"

"Focus. Okay?"

Karina nodded in agreement. Her hands began to sweat profusely, making the wooden steps even more difficult to hold onto. The Hábrók screeches grew louder and louder. She dreaded what awaited them at the top of the tree. She imagined the creatures were ready to ambush the two of them as soon as they made their way outside. But perhaps there was another secret passage like the tunnel.

About halfway up the ladder was a small nook nestled into the tree. Rayna waited for Karina, motioning for her to join her. With one hand gripping the ladder, Karina used her other arm to steady herself while shifting onto the wooden platform. She carefully maneuvered her body over and crawled next to Rayna.

Karina strained her neck, peering through a tiny opening in the trunk of the tree. As the rising sun peeked over the hills, gentle rays of light illuminated the land. Beams of sunshine filtered through the gap in the tree, providing some warmth. Giant Hábróks flew gracefully through the burnt orange morning sky. Their enormous wings flapped effortlessly, while they searched the area for their prey. Sadly, the girls were their targets. Karina leaned in closer, hoping to catch a glimpse of Skrýmir somewhere in the distance, but was unable to spot him anywhere. Instead, she tried to count how many menacing Hábróks were out there. But there wasn't enough space to see through the cracks, so she could only spot a few.

Rayna pulled Karina back by the shoulder. "I told you not to worry about them."

"What are we going to do? They're going to attack us the moment we go outside."

"Please trust me, Karina. If we are going to survive, you'll have to believe in me."

Karina let out a deep sigh and shook her head. "I don't really have any other options, do I?" She wondered if she had trusted Rayna too much already. For all she knew, Rayna was leading her to the Coven for her own gain.

"You're right. I'm all you've got right now," replied Rayna.

Rayna inched past Karina, making sure not to knock her off the platform, clutching onto the ladder to pull herself up. Karina gave one last glance at the Hábróks before grabbing onto the ladder.

They swiftly made it to the top of the tree, where a hollowed-out section formed the shape of a fluorescent lightbulb. Across from the ladder on the opposite side was a narrow slit in the tree, where a few thick vines hung, running down the trunk of the tree. Without hesitation, Rayna reached for one of the vines, grasping it with both hands and feet and then skillfully swinging herself across to the opening. She carefully balanced herself onto the ledge before squeezing through the opening in the tree.

"Wait!" yelled Karina.

Karina's hand trembled as she reached out for the vine. She attempted to swing herself towards the opening, but missed the ledge, slamming against the wall of the tree, before being flung back out towards the ladder. Desperately clinging onto the ladder with one hand and the vine with the other, Karina propelled herself towards the opening again, this time successfully landing on the ledge. Right when she felt herself start to fall backwards, Rayna's hand appeared through the opening. With a swift motion, Rayna pulled her through the gap in the tree trunk.

Chapter Thirteen

The intensity of the bright orange sky hit Karina like a shock wave as she emerged from the hollowed-out tree. A wooden platform encircled the entire stem of the tree, similar to a tree house Karina played at when she was a little girl. On the other side of the platform, a weathered rope bridge stretched across a deep ravine. The bridge creaked from the straining and stretching of the old ropes.

Rayna approached the bridge casually, stepping onto the bridge. "Come on," said Rayna.

Karina inched forward, her gaze fixated on the roaring river flowing through the ravine. The rushing sound of the river filled Karina's ears, drowning out all other noises. The air was crisp and clean, with a hint of dampness. Mist surrounded Karina. The hairs on her arm stood up, and the cool mist landed on her skin.

The bridge began to sway slightly. "Be careful!" yelled Karina.

Rayna turned around and smirked at Karina before confidently making her way across without ever looking back. She swirled around with an enormous smile. "Now, your turn!"

Karina's chest tightened as fear gripped her. She had always been terrified of heights, which is why she could never finish the ropes obstacle course in her gym class. She always took an "F" on those days and sat out, preferring to watch her classmates courageously risk their lives. However, Karina knew she had no other option but to overcome her fears right now. She would have to find strength within herself.

Her feet felt like they were weighted down by cement. She took short and hesitant steps forward. Karina clung tightly to the ropes on both sides, her hands trembling. She glanced down at the turbulent river again and could not take her eyes off it. Her anxiety and phobia were unbearable, making her unable to take another step forward. She glanced up at Rayna, who was encouraging her to keep going. Karina hadn't even taken her first step onto the bridge, yet her body trembled out of control.

"I can't do this!" she yelled.

"You have to Karina! There is no other choice at this point."

"Why can't you use your magic to get me across?"

"I can't do that. Otherwise, I would have by now."

"I really can't do this."

"You need to hurry. They're coming for us."

"Who?" asked Karina worriedly, bracing herself with both hands and stepping onto the makeshift bridge.

Rayna ignored her question, making her way back towards Karina. "You know who. Karina's knees buckled beneath her, causing the bridge to sway back and forth.

"Calm yourself. Focus on looking ahead and nothing else. The more you move side to side, the harder it will be," said Rayna.

"Easy for you to say," Karina muttered under her breath as she slowly made her way, step by step, toward Rayna.

Karina knew she couldn't look down, according to every book and movie she had ever read or watched. But she needed to know what danger lurked beneath her. It was almost impossible not to look down when she knew how dangerous the task ahead was. She tried to fight every compulsion she had. Unfortunately, curiosity got the best of her. She couldn't resist looking down over the edge of the bridge. Her body instantly became as stiff as a board.

The roaring river below may have sounded close, but it looked like it was thousands of miles away. Karina's eyes widened to the size of golf balls as paranoia took over. She closed them briefly, trying to regain control of her breathing and calm her anxiety. When she opened her eyes again, she could feel the blood returning to her veins. Her limbs started shaking, causing the bridge to sway back and forth like a pendulum.

Suddenly, ear-piercing screeches echoed from above. The Hábróks had tracked them down.

"Karina! Hurry!" yelled Rayna, while a flock of Hábróks shot through the sky like lightning. In a matter of seconds, they swooped down one by one, toward Karina.

With trembling legs, Karina shuffled along the wobbling rope bridge, desperately attempting to reach the other side before the Hábróks attacked her. But they were too quick, and she was far too slow. The Hábróks surrounded Karina, perching on the rope railing on both sides of her. Their shattering screeches sent pulsating pain through her ears, causing her eardrums to vibrate. Karina crouched and covered her head with both hands in a feeble attempt to protect herself.

A Hábrók landed on her back. Its sharp talon dug into her shoulder blades, causing horrific pain. Karina screamed, trying her best to shake the creature off her back.

Suddenly, a powerful stream of water shot out from Rayna's hands, soaking the Hábróks. They shrieked, shaking the water from their feathers. The Hábrók on Karina flew up the rope bridge, while it continuously got sprayed with water.

However, they were not deterred and continued their assault on Karina, swooping down with their sharp talons outstretched. Two of them managed to grab hold of Karina, wrapping their wide and dirty talons around each of her arms.

"Help me!" she cried.

Rayna retaliated with bursts of fire towards the Hábróks, only fueling their anger. They further tightened their grip, making Karina's arms burn in pain.

"Get away from her!" yelled Rayna as she sent shock waves in the direction of the Hábróks. A few of them were struck in the chest, thrusting them backward, causing them to fall from the bridge. But they quickly recovered, swooping back upward.

Karina struggled against the grip of the two Hábróks, who had their disgusting talons still wrapped around her arms. They had her pinned down hard against the wooden planks, making the bridge sway violently back and forth. With brute force, the Hábróks caused the wooden planks beneath Karina's back to snap in half. As Karina plummeted through the gaping hole in the bridge, the Hábróks flew upwards towards the top of the railing. She grabbed onto the bottom rope with her left hand and swung her right arm over to grab onto the other rope.

Rayna unleashed fireball after fireball at the Hábróks, while they tried to attack her. They shrieked at her, even more deafening. They decided she was not worth the trouble, returning their attention to Karina. The largest Hábrók of the flock landed on the rope that Karina was holding onto for dear life. Immediately, it began pecking at her fingers as if it hadn't eaten in weeks. Pain shot up Karina's arms, while her fingers bled. The other massive birds swooped down and followed suit. The pain was unbearable. Karina was losing all her strength very quickly. She couldn't hold on any longer.

"I'm sorry," said Karina, letting go of the rope.

"Karina!" yelled Rayna.

As she fell through the chilly air, Rayna and the Hábróks grew smaller and smaller, her stomach sinking with every passing second. Her vision began to blur, while her body became numb. The shrieks of the Hábróks became distant the farther she fell. She could feel her blood coursing through her veins. Images of her home and family flashed before her eyes. She always thought she would have died from a horrible disease or old age. But this was it. This was the end. No one would ever know what happened to her. Oliver and her parents would always be left wondering.

"Goodbye world," muttered Karina. Her back radiated with pain the moment she struck the frigid river, as if she had smashed into a sidewalk. Darkness swallowed her, and she plummeted to the bottom of the rocky riverbed. Somehow, she wasn't dead yet. This wasn't the end. She still had a chance.

Karina kicked off from the rocks at the bottom of the riverbed with both legs and propelled herself toward the top. When she lifted her head above water to catch a quick breath, the rapids pulled her back down toward the bottom. She kicked up even harder this time, thrusting her head above the choppy water. She gasped for air as she bobbed up and down. On the side of the riverbank was an enormous tree that had fallen and was partially submerged in the water. Karina attempted to grab it, but the bark was way too slippery, and she couldn't hold on. The rapids thrust her farther downstream.

Karina struggled to lift her head above the turbulent water. It pushed and pulled her around, smashing into her face. She was able to get a quick breath of air before being pulled back down by the strong current. As she swam hard towards the surface again, a huge log nearly smashed her head. The current pulled her back under, and the rapids throttled her forward out of control. She bobbed her head in and out of the water, gasping for air each time. She couldn't see any break in the rapids or calm water farther downstream. She didn't want to drown and had no idea how she was going to get out of the river alive. It would be a horrible way to die, and she refused to let it happen to her.

Gasping for air, Karina surfaced and spotted a group of teenage girls along the riverbank. She tried to make sense of what she was seeing. She suddenly slammed into a pile of rocks and was swept back into the churning rapids. The intensity of the current pushed her farther down the river. She bobbed her head slightly above the water. Up ahead, the river split into two directions like a fork in the road.

Karina tried her best to swim towards the rocky shore, when a dark shadow appeared in the water. A branch extended down from the bank only a few feet away. She stretched her arm out as far as possible but was unable to grab onto it. Another branch sank toward her and almost smashed her in the face. Reacting quickly, she grasped it tightly with both hands and pulled herself upwards.

Karina lifted her head above the water, breathing heavily. A group of girls on the riverbank were extending branches out towards her, desperately trying to save her. She pulled tightly on the stick, while the girls lined up behind each other like it was a tug-of-war game. They pulled her up just enough for Karina to grab onto the shore with both hands. As she got to her feet, three teenage girls wearing matching navy-blue cloaks studied her, intrigued with her struggles and determination.

Chapter Fourteen

Karina shivered uncontrollably in her soaking wet clothes as she stood on the rocky shore, unsure of what to do. The three girls who had rescued her from the water scrutinized her with caution. The tallest one had long, wavy red hair and a face covered in freckles. She looked slightly older than Karina by a couple of years. She stepped in front of the other girls and circled slowly around Karina, examining her like she was some sort of sculpture at an art exhibit. Karina couldn't help feeling uneasy under the redhead's piercing, clear blue gaze, causing her to stare nervously at the ground while shaking with the icy chill.

The redhead removed her blue cloak and delicately draped it around Karina. "You must be freezing," she said as she circled back toward the other two girls who were still staring at Karina.

"Thank you," said Karina softly.

"Are you okay?" the redhead asked.

"Yeah, I think so. I'm a little bruised, but I'll be all right." Karina rubbed her ribcage, feeling the bruises that sent radiating pain throughout her body. "Thanks for saving my life."

Without reacting to the comment, the redhead tilted her head, studying Karina as if she were a newly discovered species. "You must be the new girl Rayna went after."

Karina felt a small sense of relief. If they knew Rayna, she assumed they were trustworthy. Maybe they were part of the Shadow Embers. However, she couldn't shake the question of how Rayna knew she was coming. "I think so," replied Karina, nudging a rock with her foot. "I was just with her before I fell from the bridge."

"Then you must be Karina," said the redhead.

"Wait! How do you know who I am?

"Rayna told us she was coming for you."

"I don't understand. How did she know I was coming?" asked Karina.

"I know it's confusing. I honestly don't know how she knows what she knows. No one has ever been able to get a straight answer from her."

"Strange."

"You'll find that about Norlandis. Everything is that way."

"Yeah, I've noticed," Karina said with a laugh.

"Then, welcome to the Shadow Embers. We're all so glad you're finally here," said the redhead.

Karina suddenly realized who this mysterious girl was. She had seen her face before on countless missing poster signs all over Sturbridge. She distinctly remembered riding her bike with her brother several years ago when she saw one of the posters on a telephone pole. It was the first time she had learned about the kids who had been disappearing all over her hometown. Now, she was also one of those kids. Tears started to well up in Karina's eyes as she imagined her picture plastered all over town and her family desperately searching for her. The pain her parents and brother were feeling must be unbearable. If only there were a way she could let them know she was okay and would be back as soon as she possibly could.

"What's wrong? What did I say?" asked the redhead, clutching Karina's shoulders for support.

Karina wiped the tears from her eyes. "Are you Jenny?"

Her jaw dropped in utter shock. The other two girls, silent thus far, also looked stunned. The redhead pulled Karina closer, so that they were only inches apart. "How do you know who I am?" she asked sternly.

Karina wondered why Jenny had turned so aggressive, even though she already knew who Karina was. "I remember seeing your posters all over Sturbridge when I was little. You look almost the same as you did in your picture."

Jenny became visibly shaken but tried to remain strong. She cleared her throat, forcing back her emotions. "Yeah, I've been gone for several years."

Karina stood there awkwardly, not knowing what to do or say. She averted her eyes and tried to focus her attention on the other two girls, who seemed equally as uncomfortable, avoiding eye contact with each other.

"Do you know if my family is still around?" asked Jenny, breaking the awkward silence.

"I'm not sure," replied Karina.

Jenny turned away to wipe tears from her eyes. Karina glanced back at the other two girls with their cloak hoods hiding most of their faces. She wondered if they were also from Sturbridge, or perhaps a neighboring town.

"Hi, I'm Karina." Her voice was barely audible, and she gently waved her hand at them. She felt awkward introducing herself when they clearly already knew her name. But, for some reason, it felt necessary.

Without saying a word, the two girls smiled back at Karina and pulled back their cloaks, revealing their long black hair and pretty, almond-shaped eyes.

"You're twins!" exclaimed Karina.

The identical twins smiled from ear to ear. Karina studied them curiously wondering why neither of them had spoken yet. "I don't know how I didn't notice earlier," she continued.

Jenny noticed Karina eyeing the twins. "They cannot speak, if that's what you're wondering," Jenny said sharply.

"I'm sorry. I shouldn't have stared at them like that."

"It's okay. This is Dana on my left and Diana on my right. Yes, I know. Very confusing."

"Yeah, a little."

"Their parents must be crazy," Jenny added.

Karina and Jenny both laughed, while the twins continued to smile.

"Don't worry if you get them confused. We all do. They're used to it by now," said Jenny.

"If you don't mind me asking, why can't they talk? Were they born that way?" asked Karina.

"No. Not at all. The Coven took away their ability to speak in our last encounter with them."

"I see," mumbled Karina, trying to remember an article she had read about the twins. About fifty years ago, two twin Chinese sisters vanished one winter day after going out sledding with some friends and never returned home. Their parents assumed they had been kidnapped and launched a massive search for them, but no trace of them was ever found. When they never found either of their bodies, they moved back to China because the pain was too unbearable.

"By any chance, are you the Zhao Twins?" asked Karina.

Dana and Diana's eyes bulged as their chins dropped. They both looked at each other in astonishment. After a few moments, they nodded.

"I read about you girls. Your parents thought you were abducted the day you went sledding. I think it was a long time ago, though."

The twins gently nodded again, looking down at the ground trying to hide the tears starting to well in their eyes.

"I'm surprised you know so much about us already," Jenny said, her eyes wandering skeptically.

"Yeah, I'm kind of a nerd, obsessed about the forbidden woods and all the kids who've disappeared." Karina forced a smile, wondering if all the missing kids were here in Norlandis or perhaps elsewhere.

"Well, we should all get moving. The Coven will surely be looking for you by now," said Jenny. She led the way up the rocky river embankment, followed closely by the twins.

Karina glanced back at the roaring river that had almost taken her life. From the corner of her eye, she noticed a fierce-looking beast, covered in blood, emerge from behind the thick brush on the riverbank. The menacing, wolf-like creature approached Karina, lips quivering, revealing its enormous fangs and razor-sharp teeth.

"Girls––please––help me," Karina said, taking short, exasperated breaths in between her words. The beast stalked Karina as if it were ready to pounce on her any second. "You don't want me. I'm only skin and bones," she said.

"Quite the contrary," snarled the beast, spitting out gobs of drool between its fangs. He moved closer, his eyes fixated on Karina.

"You can talk," said Karina, backing away from the steep riverbank.

"Of course I can."

"I promise you, I won't be that tasty. I've barely eaten anything for days."

"I'll be the judge of that," snarled the beast, exposing its fangs even further.

From out of nowhere, a jagged wall of ice shot out at the ferocious beast, stopping his advance. He growled at Jenny, Dana, and Diana, who stood at the top of the riverbank ready to strike again.

"Stay away from her, Garmr!" yelled Jenny.

"Or what? What could you possibly do to me?" snarled Garmr.

"You know very well what I can do to you. Don't make me do it again."

Garmr let out a menacing growl and gnashed his terrible teeth. He lowered his head, pretending to retreat, but then swiftly lunged toward Karina's throat. Jenny shot bolts of electricity from her fingertips, striking Garmr in the chest. The beast whimpered as he slid down the riverbank.

"You have no business here in Norlandis. Go back to your own Realm!"

Garmr stared Jenny down before howling in her direction. "One day I will get my revenge on you." He then darted back toward the brush and vanished before their eyes.

Chapter Fifteen

Karina was still in shock from her unexpected encounter with the blood-hungry beast. Her body trembled as she tried to slow her breathing. If not for Jenny's swift actions, she wouldn't be alive right now. Jenny and the twins had saved her life twice now. Karina knew somehow she would have to make it up to all of them.

Jenny broke the silence. "Are you okay?"

"Yeah, I'm fine."

"You sure?"

"Yeah. I guess I'm a little shaken up," replied Karina, her thoughts racing. She wondered who Garmr was, which Realm he belonged to, and how many more Realms there were. "Thank you for saving my life... again. If it wasn't for you, I would be––"

"You're welcome. We all need to watch each other's backs, right?" interjected Jenny.

"Of course."

"He shouldn't have been here anyway. But it was certainly a warning."

"What do you mean?"

"Danger is coming," replied Jenny. Dana and Diana nervously nodded their heads. "Stay close."

Karina nodded and followed along. Jenny and the twins navigated the steep embankment and slippery rocks. Beyond the riverbank was a beautiful meadow filled with vibrant wildflowers and waist-high weeds. Towering sunflowers swayed high above their heads in the cloudless sky as the warm sun beat down upon the girls.

Jenny and the twins seemed to be guiding Karina toward a forest in the near distance. The sight of the trees reminded Karina of the forbidden woods and the last time she had seen Hannah. "Have any of you seen my friend Hannah by any chance? She was with me when I came to Norlandis."

"Hannah?" replied Jenny.

"Yeah, do you know her?" asked Karina eagerly.

"No. The name doesn't ring a bell. I know a girl named Savannah, but not a Hannah."

The twins shook their heads.

"Sorry," said Jenny.

Karina sighed deeply. "Rayna didn't know who she was either."

"She might be with the Coven or on the islands."

"What islands?" asked Karina.

A chilly breeze swept through the meadow scattering dandelion seeds high into the air. The delicate, puffy seeds danced about, floating every which way. One particular seed lingered around Karina's head before gently landing on her cheek. She pulled it off and blew it back out into the meadow.

Jenny and the twins stopped in their tracks and turned to face Karina. "The Islands of Runa," replied Jenny.

"I don't understand. Why wouldn't she be here on Norlandis?" asked Karina.

"When you enter this Realm, there are three places fate will send you. It has something to do with the curse that Amelia and the Coven put on the forbidden woods."

"Okay," replied Karina, listening eagerly.

"You might come to Norlandis through the Birch Grove, as you have done. Which, of course, is only for those who are pure in heart. When that happens, fate has decided that you will become one of us, part of the Shadow Embers. Or you enter Vallaborg and are forced to join the Coven of Norlandis, which is for those who have a wicked and very troubled spirit. Their souls are bound to the Coven until they leave Norlandis or until the curse is broken. Lastly, some have lost souls and are neither pure in heart nor evil. Fate sends them to dwell on the Islands of Runa."

"So, you think Hannah could be there?"

"Maybe, or with the Coven. We have no way of knowing."

"I need to find her and her sister Molly," replied Karina.

Another gust of wind whipped past the girls, shooting more dandelion seeds up into the air. The seeds twirled about as the clear sky darkened rapidly, and within seconds, it was almost pitch black. Frigid and powerful winds came from every direction.

"Run!" yelled Jenny.

Jenny and the twins sprinted as fast as they could toward the woods. Karina's eyes darted around, panic rising in her chest. She sky grew darker. Flashes of lightning illuminated the sky. Karina stood motionless when a flash of lightning struck the ground only a few feet away from her. Smoke billowed up from the scorched earth, making it impossible to see. "Jenny! Dana, Diana! Where are you?" yelled Karina, cautiously creeping through the smoke.

Suddenly, several girls in emerald-green cloaks appeared, ready to fight. Karina immediately recognized them from her dream about Rayna. The Coven had found them. She didn't know whether to scream or run. Karina was trapped.

The Coven approached her, led by Amelia, who had penetrating hazel eyes and hair as black as night. She stared into Karina's eyes, and the rest of the Coven formed a circle around her. Amelia chanted words barely above a whisper, the rest of the Coven joining in. Their voices grew louder when, suddenly, Karina began to spin uncontrollably. As she spun faster and faster, her vision became blurred, and she lost all sense of control.

"Stop it!" yelled Karina. Her body twisted and turned wildly, causing the Coven to erupt in laughter. Amelia flicked both of her hands down, causing Karina to gradually come to a stop.

Karina was so dizzy that she felt like she was going to vomit. She stumbled around in a circle, staggering every which way like a fool, before finally collapsing onto the ground in a heap. The Coven again burst into laughter.

"Had enough yet?" teased Amelia.

Karina clenched her fists, struggling to stand. Stars bounced around inside her head until her vision returned to normal. She wanted to attack Amelia and the entire Coven with every fiber of her being. But she was completely outnumbered, ten to one. Jenny and the twins were nowhere in sight. But Karina refused to let these girls torture her to death. She had no other choice but to fight them alone.

Amelia flicked her wrist again, causing Karina to immediately fall to her knees. Tears welled up in Karina's eyes, and she begged, "Please, just leave me alone. I've done nothing to any of you to deserve this."

The shortest girl from the Coven's circle stepped forward, appearing oddly out of place among the towering girls around her. "Good morning, freak. Did you miss me?"

Karina gasped as Molly removed the cloak from her head. With the most devilish grin, Molly approached her. Karina hated that evil smile and wanted to smack some sense into her.

Molly leaned in close and gently wiped away the tear from Karina's cheek. "Aw, are you crying? Do you need your mommy?" said Molly as she circled and mocked Karina.

Karina ignored the girl, keeping her head bowed, while Molly continued circling. "You were right about the woods after all. Did you ever think it would be this amazing? Now, I'm thankful that we moved. I would have never found Norlandis if it weren't for you and your craziness. Well, I guess you're not all that crazy, come to think of it. Aw, well, it will all be over soon."

Karina avoided eye contact with Molly, wondering why this girl was filled with so much hate and anger.

Molly stopped circling and moved closer to Karina. She attempted to force-fully lift Karina's chin, but Karina resisted, keeping her eyes fixed on the ground. "Look at me when I am talking to you! Didn't anyone ever tell you it's rude not to make eye contact! Look at me!" screamed Molly.

Karina shook her head. "Where is Hannah?" she asked, breaking her silence while still avoiding eye contact.

"I don't know, and I do not care."

"She's your sister!"

"And I care, why?"

"Because Hannah would care about you," replied Karina, locking eyes with Molly and wishing she could burn a hole right through her tiny little head. Karina's body trembled from the rage building inside her. She grabbed Molly's leg and slammed her to the ground. Karina rose quickly, pressing her foot firmly on Molly's stomach, pinning her down. "Why don't you care about your own sister?" screamed Karina in a rage.

"I wouldn't do that if I were you," cautioned Molly. The Coven's circle closed in on her, chanting words in a language similar to Rayna's.

The Coven surrounded Karina like a swarm of bees as she pressed her foot harder into Molly's stomach, making her moan in pain. "Where is Hannah? I don't care if you don't give a crap about her, but I do," screamed Karina.

"I already told you, I don't know," replied Molly. The Coven's chanting got louder.

Incredible pain shot up Karina's legs, causing her to drop to the ground. She rolled next to Molly, who crawled away in a hurry, taking her place in the circle.

Amelia stepped out, placing her hand on Karina's shoulder. "Sweet little Karina, what are we to do with you?"

"Leave me alone!" yelled Karina.

"You've chosen the wrong side. So, you can either join us now and have more power than you've ever dreamed of, or you will die here all alone."

Despite the pain shooting through her legs, Karina bravely faced Amelia. She was tired of being bullied her entire life and refused to give up without a fight, even if she had zero chance of winning. No one could force her into something she didn't believe in or want to be part of. "Go ahead, kill me now," she declared defiantly. "I will never join you. Not in a million years. This world has no place for people like you."

"This world? This is not Sturbridge or your cute little community!" replied Amelia, jabbing her finger into Karina's forehead and turning her fingernail like a screwdriver. A drop of blood trickled down onto Amelia's finger as she continued, "WE are Norlandis. This is my world. Don't think for a second you can tell me what to do." Amelia backed away and pulled her cloak back over her head. She simmered with rage, joining the rest of the Coven. "She's made her decision, girls."

The Coven began to chant in unison, "Taccipere de Luftilma fran," under their breaths, gradually getting louder and louder. Karina stood in the center of their circle, hoping for a miracle as she looked up at the sky. There was nothing else she could do at this point but pray.

Seconds later, arrows arced through the air, raining down upon the Coven, who scattered instantly in different directions. Karina crouched down, covering her head. She glanced back over her shoulder. At the edge of the woods stood Jenny, Dana, and Diana, surrounded by a group of girls with their bows aimed towards the sky. The Coven tried desperately to find cover as chaos ensued.

Amelia stood fearlessly in the middle of the field, while multiple arrows soared through the sky toward her. "Descrusota!" shouted Amelia, causing the arrows to disintegrate into a cloud of dust. Four other blond-haired girls from the Coven joined Amelia, all of whom Karina recognized from her dream about Rayna. They quickly turned their heads towards Karina, focusing their attention on her once again. Amelia's smile widened as the Coven began to whisper a chant.

Karina slammed down onto her back, feeling an immense force weighing on her. Before she knew it, she was being dragged through the field by her hair. But no one was near her. She reached out to grab hold of some nearby weeds in a desperate attempt to stop herself, but the force was too strong. The weeds held firm, slicing into the palms of her hands.

Karina came to an abrupt stop and was soon surrounded by Amelia and the four blond girls.

"Stand up!" yelled Amelia.

"No way," replied Karina.

"Then I will make you," shouted Amelia, motioning with her hand in a swooping upward motion.

Karina's knees locked, causing her legs to go rigid. Her body was thrust upwards, lifting her off the ground momentarily. As her feet hit the ground, she staggered around the circle, having no control of her legs. The power of Amelia and the Coven controlled every movement of her body as if she were a marionette.

Several arrows flew through the air, striking the field around Karina, but it didn't deter the Coven one bit. Karina tried to control her movements but couldn't stop herself from being manipulated by the girls.

An arrow whizzed past Karina's face, striking the ground. "They almost hit you," laughed one of the blond girls from the Coven. They continued to enjoy the spectacle of Karina skipping around in a circle.

"Leave me alone, before I--"

"Before you what?" Amelia said, laughing in Karina's face.

From out of nowhere, an arrow came whistling through the air right over Karina's shoulder. Amelia's eyes widened at the sight of the arrow. She jerked her hand quickly to the side, causing the arrow to snap in half. Amelia let out an evil laugh as the arrow fell to the ground.

"Who tried to take me down?" Amelia roared.

Jenny sprinted toward them with a recurve bow in her hands, her face etched with determination. The coven froze, and for a second, even Amelia looked shocked.

Karina's heart leaped in joy at the sight of Jenny charging at the Coven. Jenny wasted no time, pulling another arrow from her quiver. She aimed again at Amelia.

Miraculously, a fire roared to life, almost engulfing the Coven. It crackled across the field, consuming everything in its path like a raging inferno. Smoke filled the air, making it nearly impossible to see. Amelia motioned with her hands, extinguishing some of the fire by creating a smoke-filled path for the Coven. They all vanished within seconds.

Meanwhile, Jenny and several other girls from the Shadow Embers ran toward Karina. "Come on!" yelled Jenny.

Right when Karina was about to follow the girls, she noticed Molly lying motionless in the field. An arrow was lodged in her back, pinning her to the ground. Jenny and the other girls urged Karina to follow them.

"Forget her," whispered one of the girls.

"I can't," replied Karina, knowing there was no way she could leave Molly behind. She had to help her in any way she could, no matter how much she disliked her. Otherwise, she would never forgive herself.

Chapter Sixteen

Karina sprinted through the smoldering field toward Molly, who still lay motionless. Jenny and the other girls from the Shadow Embers had put out the wildfire. The rest of the Coven were nowhere in sight. They had abandoned Molly and clearly didn't care whether she lived or not. Otherwise, they would have tried to save her, thought Karina as she rushed to Molly's side. She fell to her knees in the tall weeds and placed her hands gently around the arrow protruding from Molly's back.

"I wouldn't worry about her!" said Jenny, while Molly moaned loudly, kicking her feet on the ground.

Karina shook her head in defiance. "This is going to hurt," said Karina, placing one hand on Molly's back and the other on the arrow shaft close to Molly's skin.

"Don't touch it," Molly pleaded.

"I have to get it out."

"Please don't. It'll hurt too much," groaned Molly.

"I'm sure it already does," said Karina with a wry smile.

Molly kicked her feet and pounded her fists into the ground, writhing in pain. "I wanna go home," she cried squirming every which way.

"I need you to be still and try to relax," said Karina in a soothing and calm voice.

"Okay, okay, okay. Just do it," said Molly.

"Okay, ready? One, two, three!"

With a swift and forceful movement, Karina pulled the arrow from Molly's back, causing her to cry out in agony. Karina placed her hands on Molly's back to put pressure on the wound. She closed her eyes tightly, trying to avoid any sight of blood.

Molly screamed and thrashed about on the ground, while Karina pressed down harder. She had to get Molly to relax, or she would go into shock. Karina didn't know what else to do, so she made a soft shushing noise like her mom had done to her to help her fall asleep.

A warm and tingling sensation started to radiate down Karina's arms and into her hands, and finally into her fingers. The energy was transferred from Karina's fingertips into Molly's flesh. Her back instantly became warmer to the touch, as if she had been sitting by the fire for hours. Molly gradually stopped thrashing. Her screaming ceased and her back began to cool. Within seconds, she was calm and no longer in pain. Her skin temperature had normalized, and the tingling sensation was gone from Karina's hands and fingers.

Jenny and the group of girls from the Shadow Embers surrounded Karina and Molly in amazement. Karina cautiously lifted her hands to see how bad the bleeding was. No one could believe their eyes. There was not a single drop of blood. Even Karina's hands were as dry as Molly's cloak. There wasn't a single blemish or scar on her back. No one would have ever known that an arrow had even scratched her skin, never mind being lodged in her body.

Karina stared down at her hands. "What just happened?"

Molly turned over onto her back, staring at Karina. Her eyes went from shock to apologetic, clearly unsure of what to say. Molly tried to grasp what had happened. She sat up without saying a word, but her eyes and expression gave it away like she wanted to speak. Molly slowly rose to her feet, giving Karina an encouraging and thankful smile, but still could not find the words to say. She took off through the field, glancing back over her shoulder at Karina.

"Come back!" yelled Karina as Molly disappeared into the meadow.

The crowd of girls continued to stare at Karina in amazement. Jenny leaned forward to help Karina to her feet.

"Are you THE Karina?" asked Jenny.

"I'm not sure what that means. You already know my name."

"What I mean is, are you her?"

"I'm still confused," Karina replied, scratching her head.

"Quick! Put your hand on my arm," said Jenny as she lifted her arm covered with several jagged and deep cuts.

Karina cautiously did what she was told, placing her arm over a large cut that ran almost the whole length of Jenny's forearm. Once again, Karina felt the warm sensation rush throughout her body, radiating from her fingertips and into Jenny's arm. The cuts and scars began to disappear before their eyes until Jenny's skin was perfectly smooth and healthy.

Jenny covered her mouth in shock, then removed her hand and grinned like there was no tomorrow. "You are her!" exclaimed Jenny, proudly displaying her arm to the group of girls. They gasped in astonishment. They swarmed Jenny, excitedly examining her arm one by one. In awe and disbelief, they turned to stare at Karina.

"I don't understand what's happening," she said.

"You see, the prophecy says that a girl would appear one day with the powers of healing, who is named Karina," replied Jenny.

"What prophecy?" asked Karina.

"The one as old as Norlandis," replied Jenny.

"But I am no one special," said Karina.

"Oh, but you are! You truly are. You healed that girl from the Coven and instantly healed my wound better than any doctor would have. You can help so many other girls on Norlandis. Karina, you are the ONE!"

The crowd of girls all got to one knee with Jenny, bowing their heads.

"Please get up. There is no need for any of that. I'm not a queen or anything," said Karina.

"But Karina, you are equally as important as a queen," said Jenny.

Karina didn't know what to say or do. She was still in shock herself. So much had happened since she had arrived in Norlandis. And now this! How amazing this journey was turning out to be.

"Can you fix my broken finger?" a shorter girl with a slight lisp asked.

"No! Fix my infected leg," said a tall and lanky girl, pushing her way closer to Karina.

"No way! Me first," exclaimed another girl.

The girls pushed and shoved each other, eager to be next in line. One of them thrust her elbow in front of Karina. "I'm next, girls," exclaimed a girl with broad shoulders, trying to cut in front of the group.

"I don't think so. I'm first," said a girl with broken glasses.

Karina lifted her hands in the air, trying to move away from the group that followed her around like a herd of sheep.

Suddenly, a loud whistling noise came from the edge of the forest. Everyone snapped around to see Rayna watching them. The group of girls took off running toward Rayna in excitement.

Jenny and Karina walked behind the enthusiastic group of girls, followed by the twins.

"I told you, you are special," said Jenny. The twins nodded their heads.

"I guess," replied Karina, forcing back a grin. "So where are we headed?"

"The Caverns," replied Jenny with a smile. "Glad to have you here, Karina. Welcome to Norlandis. We've been waiting a long time for you, if you couldn't tell already. We truly need your help. Your destiny awaits," said Jenny as she patted Karina on the back. She and the twins took off toward the woods, joining Rayna and the group of girls who greeted Rayna like they hadn't seen her in ages.

Karina looked down at her hands, smiling. "I have powers. Incredible powers," she muttered to herself.

Chapter Seventeen

Karina approached the group of girls from the Shadow Embers who were gathered on the edge of the forest. Behind them, tall bamboo trees swayed gently back and forth. Light speckled through the forest, casting an ethereal green glow. Bizarre noises of creatures Karina had never heard before shrieked, buzzed, and bellowed from the forest. Maybe this was what a rainforest would sound like.

Rayna waited for Karina on the outskirts of the forest, while the other girls from the Shadow Embers lingered behind her. She stepped forward and hugged Karina. "I was so worried about you. I honestly thought that fall would have killed you," said Rayna.

"Me too," replied Karina.

"And I heard from the girls that you learned about your unique and special power."

"Yeah! It's amazing, isn't it?

"Well, enjoy it. You possess an incredible ability that no one else in Norlandis has. Not even me or Amelia, for that matter," said Rayna with a smile.

"Wow!" replied Karina, gazing down at her hands.

"Now, let's get you to your new home." Rayna moved through the crowd of girls, leading them onto the pathway.

Everyone but Karina filed behind Rayna like soldiers following their General into battle. They marched onto the narrow path that was only wide enough for one person. Karina watched the girls wind their way down the path as she took a deep breath. She was starting to feel uneasy and suspicious about

Rayna. Karina couldn't quite put her finger on it, though. Rayna had made no attempt whatsoever to come find Karina and was nowhere to be found when the Coven almost killed her. Karina couldn't comprehend why Rayna hadn't tried to save her from falling from the bridge. She had a feeling in her gut that Rayna's powers were much stronger than she had been led to believe. Perhaps she was overreacting, but Karina felt like she was betrayed. She tried to shake these thoughts, now running wildly through her head. "Wait for me," called Karina, stepping onto the dirt path that wound through the bamboo forest.

As she entered deeper into the woods, the sounds of unfamiliar animals and creatures seemed to close in around her like a dense jungle. The other girls were nowhere in sight. She had been so caught up in her thoughts about Rayna that she didn't realize how much time had passed. Karina ran along the path which appeared to be getting narrower. "Where are you?" Karina called out nervously.

The strange noises grew louder. On both sides of her, hundreds of little eyes glared directly at Karina. She stopped dead in her tracks to see what was watching her. In a nearby tree, a few feet from the path, sat a small, reddish animal similar to a squirrel. But it had unusually long ears and a tiny horn in the middle of its head. Noticing Karina staring back, it scurried down the tree. "Hello," squeaked the little animal.

Karina's jaw dropped. "Did you just say hello to me?"

The animal's beady eyes studied her curiously, and it made a squeaking noise. Seconds later, several other squirrel-like animals ran down the tree, watching Karina's every movement. The group of creatures squeaked back and forth at each other as if they were having a full-on conversation about Karina.

"What are you saying about me?" asked Karina, stepping off the path, eager to pick up one of the furry animals to pet. She felt like Charles Darwin on the Galapagos Islands, wanting to learn all about this new creature and why it could talk. Karina reached out to touch one of the animals when someone grabbed her from behind and yanked her back onto the path. She swirled back around to see Jenny standing there, breathing heavily.

"Don't ever touch them," said Jenny sternly.

Movement caught her eye, and Karina noticed the tiny creatures scurry away. She craned her neck, watching their bushy little tails bounce up the bamboo trees. At the top were a few huge, rounded nests the size of a tree house. A terrifying Hábrók poked its head out, while the creatures scurried up and over the nest. One of them stopped inches from the Hábrók, standing on its back legs. It looked down at Karina and Jenny and then back at the Hábrók as if it were reporting what it had seen. The Hábrók stood up on its massive legs and took off into the sky, letting out a vicious squawk.

Karina turned back around. Jenny stood in the same spot with her arms crossed, her eyes bulging in annoyance.

"I'm sorry," muttered Karina.

"You need to stay with us at all times until we're out of this forest."

"I understand."

"It's fine. Let's get going. We still have much farther to go."

"What are those things?"

"They're called Ratatoskr. But we call them Ratis for short."

"Ratis; very interesting," mumbled Karina.

Suddenly, the rest of the girls from the Shadow Embers appeared out of thin air. Rayna continued to lead them down the path in silence. Some of the girls glanced towards Karina and Jenny.

"I need you to promise me that you won't leave this path again," said Jenny.

"May I ask why?" muttered Karina.

"There are hundreds of different kinds of creatures all over this forest who are controlled by the Coven. If you step an inch off the path, they will attack you."

"Okay."

"The Ratis you saw may look cute. But they can become quite aggressive if they sense any danger."

"They looked harmless to me."

"Believe me. They are far from it. And what's worse is that they serve as messengers to the Hábróks, who then report back to Amelia and the Coven."

The rest of the girls were much farther up the path than Karina and Jenny. "Come on. We have to catch up," said Jenny. They both jogged down the path toward their group.

"I guess I don't understand completely. Why do I need to stay only on the path? What difference does it make?" asked Karina.

"The path protects us from them. Rayna put a spell on the pathway to keep everyone out of harm's way. As long as you stay with us and keep to the path, you will be safe."

"Got it."

They had finally caught up to the group. A few leaves rustled across the path, drifting gently across to the other side. Nearby, a powerful and menacing brown bear dug its claws into the bamboo, tearing off pieces to chomp on. The bear had a musky odor, and Karina's eyes widened in fear when it stood up on its hind legs, revealing its imposing and enormous size. Unleashing a viscous roar, it watched the group of girls move farther down the path.

Karina got closer to Jenny, so she was only inches away. "Do you see him? He's huge!"

"Ignore him and you will be fine," replied Jenny.

Karina swallowed hard and stayed closely behind Jenny. She tried her best not to let her eyes wander and kept them straight ahead. The tunnel of bamboo trees never seemed to end. Karina glanced back over her shoulder to make sure nothing was approaching. On her side were two fierce-looking goats with sharp and jagged horns, munching on leaves as she passed. They lowered their heads, their horns pointed at Karina, attempting to intimidate her. Then, the two goats charged at each other, playfully butting their heads.

"Just breathe and ignore them, too," whispered Jenny.

Karina looked once more at the goats, who were ready to charge at them any moment. Once the girls were farther down the path, the two goats playfully continued ramming into each other. This brought a smile to Karina's face, reminding her of her childhood trips to the farm where she would pet and feed all the adorable baby goats and lambs.

The bamboo forest seemed to stretch on forever. Every time Karina thought they were getting close to the forest's outskirts, it led to even more twists and turns. It felt like they were walking through an endless maze.

Karina stopped to catch her breath for a moment. Her throat was getting dry and raspy. As she took in a few deep breaths, she noticed something in the bushes several feet away shaking violently. The leaves rustled and crunched beneath the animal's feet. Karina braced herself when a wild boar came charging out of the brush toward her. It stopped close to the path, squealing at her, inches from her face. At first, she was startled but then found herself laughing at the boar's attempt to intimidate her.

Karina made a loud squealing noise back at the boar, mocking it. "Keep squealing, little pig, and I might be having some bacon later."

"You're too funny," said Jenny.

"I try." Karina laughed, her eyes darting around to make sure they were all safe. She knew the path was supposed to protect her, but she had a feeling she still needed to be on her guard.

Karina's smile faded, and she froze in fear. Several black and yellow-striped spiders, the size of cars, descended from their webs in the nearby trees. Their webs were as thick as the rope Karina used in her gym class. The hairy and terrifying spiders gnashed their enormous fangs while weaving their intricate webs.

Karina flinched when she heard a loud, scraping sound above her. A spider shot its web directly toward her. She instinctively covered her head with her arms, crouching down to the ground. The spider's massive, hairy legs carefully avoided touching the pathway, straddling it with all eight of its legs around the path. The hairy legs loomed over Karina, creating a dark, jail-like cage around her. A little sunlight filtered through the legs, casting terrifying shadows. She was trapped unless she could squeeze herself through the gaps in between the spider's disgusting and jagged legs. Karina's eardrums began to hurt from the noise of the spider's legs scraping against the ground mixed with her frantic breathing.

"Help me!" yelled Karina. She crawled along the ground, hoping Jenny or any of the other girls would notice her. Karina thought maybe she could dig underneath the legs before the spider devoured her like a bite-sized piece of candy.

The spider emitted another high-pitched screech, causing Karina to cover her ears in excruciating pain. The vibrations were so intense that her eardrums felt like they might burst. She rolled on the ground in agony until she was entirely off the pathway.

The spider scurried over to her, and before she knew it, the spider was spinning a web around her. Karina attempted to shake free, but the spiderwebs were too thick and strong to break through. Within seconds, her entire body was enveloped in the webs, like a cocoon.

Chapter Eighteen

There was total darkness. Karina's body was stiff as a board. She could no longer see or hear anything. Karina's nose burned, and she was nauseous from the dank and putrid odors. She wanted to yell for help, but even her jaw couldn't move. Instead, she grunted and groaned, hoping someone would hear her.

Before she knew it, Karina was lifted off the ground and rolled upward, making it next to impossible to breathe. She felt like she was going to suffocate any second. The webs were rough and sticky, like a cocoon made of tape. Every inch of her skin felt tightly constricted like she was being crushed by an invisible force. Her body was completely numb. Karina attempted to scream again, but the webbing was wrapped too tightly across her face. She managed another muffled plea for help, which was practically inaudible.

The spider tightened its grasp on her, and in that moment, a blinding light illuminated the cocoon, followed by a muffled scream. Karina felt a burning sensation all over her body as she dropped to the ground. She was no longer engulfed in the webbing and finally able to breathe. The spiderwebs had burnt right off of her, turning to ash and reeking of burnt hair.

Rayna stared fiercely at the spider as she hissed at it. Suddenly, four more spiders appeared and morphed into the blond girls from the Coven. The spider that had almost taken Karina's life had transformed into Amelia.

"I almost had her like the others," said Amelia, smirking at her victim.

"Yeah, well, not this time," replied Jenny.

"You need to leave this forest right now," said Rayna.

"Don't tell me what to do, little girl!" demanded Amelia as she approached. "These are my woods and my creatures."

"We outnumber you and could easily destroy you," said Jenny.

"Perhaps, or perhaps not," replied one of the blond girls from the Coven.

"I'm going to give you three seconds to leave before I do something I really don't want to do," said Rayna.

"Very well," replied Amelia. She and the other girls from the Coven transformed back into spiders, hissing and gnashing their sharp teeth.

"Now!" yelled Jenny.

The spiders scattered and climbed the bamboo tree, disappearing in a matter of seconds.

Rayna kneeled beside Karina. "Are you okay?"

"I think so," muttered Karina, snapping out of her trance.

Rayna helped Karina to her feet and onto the pathway. "Good," said Rayna as she patted Karina's shoulder, squeezing past the girls to the front of the line.

Jenny leaned over her with her arms crossed. "What did I tell you?" she asked angrily.

"I'm sorry. I am so afraid of spiders, it's not even funny."

"I know. We all hate them. They're very hard to ignore."

"Especially when they're the size of my bedroom," said Karina, grinning.

"You're too funny." Jenny laughed and continued, "Why don't you go in front of me. That way, this won't happen again."

"Okay, sounds good."

"We can't afford to lose you."

It was a strange feeling to be needed by so many of the girls. Karina wasn't sure if they truly liked her for herself, or if it was simply because of her healing abilities. It made her wonder why they didn't keep a closer eye on her, considering the dangers lurking in the forest. But regardless, she was happy to finally be needed and to feel a sense of belonging.

The group of girls walked in silence, their heads bowed and eyes averted as they made their way through the dense bamboo forest. Karina couldn't resist stealing glances at the fascinating array of creatures. All kinds, sizes, shapes, and colors. Jenny tapped Karina's shoulder and cautioned her to keep her head down. She motioned for her to stay focused on the trail ahead and avoid attracting unwanted attention.

Karina knew her eyes would wander. She pulled her cloak over her head so she could sneak a few peeks here and there without drawing the wrath of Jenny or Rayna.

As the sun sank behind the bamboo trees, its eerie green glow faded away. It was now only a small sliver of light, barely visible, like a flickering tealight candle. There was an autumn-like chill to the air, and a slight breeze rustled the fallen leaves around the girls.

Karina's stomach gurgled and rumbled. She placed her hand across the top of her abdomen, hoping none of the girls had heard how hungry she was. It didn't matter too much, though. Karina was beyond exhausted. Her entire body ached in pain. She would kill for a nice, comfortable mattress and blanket right now. A disturbing thought crept into her mind. What if she were now stuck in Norlandis for eternity, like all the other girls, and never made it home? What if she never saw her parents or brother again? Karina was incredibly intrigued by Norlandis and could not wait to see what adventures might unfold, but the depressing thought of being stuck here without ever returning home was more unsettling than she could bear.

"We're almost there," whispered Jenny, disrupting Karina's thoughts.

"Cool," replied Karina. She nodded her head, having absolutely no idea what Jenny was talking about. Perhaps she was referring to the caverns, like Jenny had mentioned earlier.

The Shadow Embers had almost made it to the opposite end of the bamboo forest. Rayna and the other girls slowed their pace, eventually coming to a full stop close to the edge of the forest. There were no animals around this part, and everything was eerily quiet.

Karina felt a gentle tap on her shoulder. Jenny motioned upward, drawing her attention to a cluster of bamboo trees. A spiral staircase made entirely of bamboo with rope railings ascended to the top of the trees. Nestled within the branches were two rounded tree houses shaped like spheres. Several of the trees were roped together to support each of the sphere homes. Karina had never seen anything like this before. It looked like something out of a science fiction movie.

Rayna looked around to make sure no one else was there, except for their group of girls. At the bottom of the spiral staircase was a wooden door covered with vines and several different elaborate locking mechanisms. "Offavatibus," said Rayna.

The vines curled up instantly as the different locks clicked and sprang open. Rayna swung the door wide, allowing the girls to pass through and make their way up the stairs. She stood at the entrance, waiting for all of them to file through. "Wait here," said Rayna to Karina.

Jenny snuck past Rayna and Karina, following the girls up the spiral staircase. A dim light flickered inside each of the homes as the girls hurried inside, laughing and chattering. Jenny glanced down at Rayna and Karina curiously before walking into one of the spheres. "All right, settle down, girls," said Jenny.

Karina waited anxiously for Rayna to say or do something. Rayna stared up at the homes, smiling ever so slightly. After what seemed like hours to Karina, Rayna finally turned her attention to her. "Come with me for a second."

"Okay, are we not going up?" replied Karina.

"We will. Just not now." Rayna led Karina toward the end of the forest. As they strolled, Karina had to wonder what she had done or said to upset Rayna.

Beyond the bamboo forest, an open field was illuminated by the three mesmerizing moons above. Without exchanging any words, Rayna sat on a slight hill along the path that led to the forest. "Any idea why I brought you out here?"

Karina sat down next to Rayna. "Not a clue."

"I wanted to talk to you alone."

"Okay."

"The other girls don't need to hear this. They've been here long enough and have a handle on what's going on here."

"Okay," replied Karina, knowing she was about to be berated.

"I really need you to start listening to all of us in the Shadow Embers. Especially to me and Jenny. There are dangers in every part of Norlandis. If you value your life and if you ever want to return home, you need to listen carefully to everything we are saying. You have only been here a few days, and you've almost killed yourself several times. Some of us have been here many years and know what to expect. You haven't. We will no longer be your babysitter. We can't always be around to protect you whenever evil comes your way. I have to lead all the girls in our group. All you need to do is take care of yourself. Do you understand?"

Karina took a deep breath, trying to stop herself from screaming. It took all her willpower not to punch Rayna right in the face. Her body was pulsating with adrenaline and rage. Before Karina could respond, Rayna stood and marched away in anger. Karina picked up a small rock beside her and threw it into the empty field, letting out a scream in frustration. She had never been this angry in her life.

Chapter Nineteen

Not many things got under Karina's skin. She had endured plenty of bullying and teasing over the years without letting it affect her too much. Her mom had taught her to be emotionally and mentally tough and to learn how to block out the bullies. But somehow, Rayna had pinched a serious nerve.

After pacing around in the dark for a while, Karina had still not been able to calm herself down. Her blood was boiling. All she wanted to do was storm up the stairs and give Rayna a piece of her mind. Let her know she couldn't talk to her like that. Rayna wasn't her mother or teacher. She was only a little girl. And she was even younger than Karina was. What right did she have? But Karina knew deep down that it wouldn't solve anything. The other girls looked up to Rayna. She was their leader and had been in Norlandis the longest. Who knows how the girls would respond if Karina started yelling and making accusations toward their leader?

Karina was finally able to calm herself down after a few deep breaths, taking the crisp air into her lungs. She knew this was not the time or place to confront Rayna and voice her frustrations. Karina would simply have to swallow her pride and apologize. There would be another opportunity to talk to Rayna in the future. After all, she was stuck in Norlandis and had nowhere else to go. She had no idea where anything was. She had to rely on the Shadow Embers to survive.

Giggling and laughter filtered down from the spherical homes, causing the rest of Karina's anger to dissipate. She exhaled sharply and made her way back toward the stairs. Karina looked back over each shoulder to make sure no person or creature was around before entering through the gate. As she climbed the spiral staircase, Karina wondered if they were truly safe from the Coven in this secluded part of the woods. Judging by the girls' carefree laughter, they didn't seem to be worried in the slightest. Maybe she could let her guard down as well. Or perhaps, they had learned to enjoy life no matter the circumstance.

A smile spread across Karina's face when she reached the top of the staircase. She was surprisingly winded after climbing close to a hundred steps. If she ever made it out of Norlandis, she would surely be in shape for the first time in her life.

Karina marveled at the intricate and unique spherical homes, unlike anything she'd ever seen. Each home was surprisingly spacious, with multiple small circular windows and one large, rounded window facing each other. The doors were made of vertical pieces of dried-out bamboo. A tiny lantern hung outside each home, while several tiki torches surrounded the landing.

Unsure which home she should enter, she was about to knock but paused. Laughter spilled out of each room. Karina didn't know if she should call for someone, or if she should poke her head inside. She felt very much like an outsider, as if she were trying to crash someone else's party. She stood there awkwardly and indecisively, when Jenny appeared in the doorway of the home on the left side.

"What are you waiting for, an invitation?" asked Jenny.

"I, uh... " mumbled Karina.

"Come on in."

Jenny led the way inside, and the other girls watched as the two of them entered. Several lanterns hung from the walls, casting a warm glow throughout the room and making it feel cozy. There were two bunk beds next to a large window overlooking the bamboo forest. A small loft with a bed was located directly above the window on the opposite wall, facing the neighboring home.

Dana and Diana were sitting on the floor with one other girl, to whom Karina had not yet been introduced. The girl had short brown hair right below her chin line and bulging eyes that studied Karina moving around the room.

"Karina, I don't think we've introduced you to Sophia yet," said Jenny.

"Hi, nice to meet you," said Karina.

"You too," replied Sophia.

"Grab a seat," said Jenny. She motioned to the floor for Karina, while she settled on one of the comfortable bunk beds.

Karina sat next to Sophia, who was a couple of years older than her, like the rest of the girls in the home. It almost made her feel like she was a little sister tagging along at a sleepover.

"So, are there no boys in Norlandis? I haven't seen a single one yet," said Karina, trying to sound older and somewhat cool.

"Gosh, no," laughed Sophia.

"Unfortunately not," replied Jenny.

"Believe me, I wish there were," said Sophia smiling, showing off her dimples.

"Why not?" asked Karina.

"Amelia placed a curse on boys entering Norlandis," said Jenny.

"Why would she do that?" asked Karina.

"Because they are a distraction," replied Sophia.

"I don't understand. Many boys have also disappeared in the forbidden woods," said Karina.

"I know, hundreds. A lot of cute ones, too," said Sophia as the twins nodded in agreement.

"Strange. I wonder where they went," said Karina.

"They must be in another Realm. Either way, you won't find any here," said Jenny.

"What about adults? I haven't seen any of them either. Unless you count that hideous giant."

"You won't find them here either," said Sophia.

"Really. Why is that?" asked Karina.

"Just another curse by the Coven. No adults are allowed in Norlandis or any of the other Realms," replied Jenny.

"Strange," muttered Karina.

"And from what I understand, adults cannot see the dolls or the house in the forbidden woods," said Jenny.

"Probably can't hear the voices either," said Karina.

"That would make sense," said Sophia.

"Which is why none of them have ever found Norlandis," said Karina.

"Exactly," replied Jenny.

"I kind of like it that way. I hate my parents," said Sophia as she stood and walked over to the bunk bed where Jenny sat.

"We know you do. Or at least you pretend you do," said Jenny.

"I seriously do. You know what they did to me," snapped Sophia. She shoved Jenny to the side and climbed up the ladder to the top bunk.

"I'm sorry," mumbled Karina.

"Don't be. I'm not. I'm going to enjoy every day that I'm here on Norlandis. I have no desire to go back," said Sophia.

"Why is that?" asked Karina.

"No parents. No annoying siblings. No school or homework. No chores or getting yelled at," replied Sophia.

"I see. How long have you been here?"

"I don't know. Maybe twenty years or so."

"And you really don't want to go home?"

"Not at all. I mean, there are some things I miss."

"Like what?"

"Stupid stuff. Junk food, ice cream, music, TV, my bed, boys--you know."

"I get it. And how are we supposed to go back? We can't be stuck here forever," said Karina with some hesitation.

"That's the million-dollar question, isn't it?" laughed Sophia.

"None of us knows," said Jenny.

"If no one knows, then what are we going to do?"

"Maybe Karina the Healer can figure it out," joked Sophia.

"Yeah, thanks," replied Karina.

Awkward silence filled the room as each girl was lost in their own thoughts. Jenny cleared her throat uncomfortably. "Well, we should probably all hit the hay now," she said.

The twins both yawned almost simultaneously. They lumbered over to their bunk bed.

"You can sleep in the loft," said Jenny.

"Okay. I'm going to go outside for a second for some fresh air."

"Don't wander," said Jenny.

"I won't," replied Karina as she went outside. The lights instantly dimmed when the door closed.

Karina took a deep breath, filling her lungs with the cool air. It reminded her of autumn, which she had always loved more than any other season. She took in another deep breath, trying to process everything she'd just heard and learned about Norlandis.

Suddenly, a faint voice in the distance called out her name. Karina scanned the ominous bamboo forest below but saw nothing. The lights in the other home were already turned off. She wondered if it was Rayna or someone from the Shadow Embers trying to get her attention.

"Karina," whispered the voice.

"Hello," whispered Karina as she left the platform. She hurried, winding herself down the stairs, following the voice. Right beyond the edge of the bamboo forest was a field that stretched out into the darkness. The voice called her name again. Karina scanned the area but couldn't see anything unusual. Whatever the voice was, it sounded much closer this time. Karina looked back at the Shadow Ember homes and then back at the field.

Once again, the voice called out her name. This time, much louder, and it sounded exactly like Hannah. Could she be dreaming? Was it really her? Without hesitation, Karina moved in the direction of the mysterious voice.

Chapter Twenty

Karina rushed through the overgrown field using the moonlight as her only source of light. Insects of all sorts chirped and buzzed. "Hannah!" yelled Karina, stopping in the middle of the field. She looked all around, hoping to hear her voice again. In a panic, she spun around, looking every which way until she became dizzy. Karina finally stopped spinning and gazed up at the three mysterious moons, wondering if she should turn back and go to sleep. Her mind was probably just playing tricks on her yet again, anyway.

In the distance, Karina saw a dark figure shift behind the only tree in the entire field, which seemed oddly out of place. She approached it cautiously as the voice called out her name again. "Hannah," Karina whispered back in a shaky voice.

Karina reached the tree with branches that stretched out like long, jagged fingers. She crept around the wide tree searching for Hannah, but she wasn't there. "Hannah," she whispered, circling back around the tree again and again. Karina burst into tears and leaned her head up against the tree. Where was she, and where did the dark figure go that kept calling out her name?

A chill ran up Karina's spine to the base of her skull as a voice whispered her name inches from her ear. The warm breath of the whisper made her tremble with fear. She could feel the individual hairs on her arms stand up as goosebumps now covered them. The voice sounded very much like Hannah, but something didn't feel quite right about it. Not one bit.

Karina's heart raced, while she slowly turned around. Pure joy swept across her face at the sight of Hannah, standing only a few feet away. They both smiled, as if they were seeing a reflection in the mirror.

"Hannah!" Karina yelled, running forward to give her friend an enormous hug. Right when she went to wrap her arms around Hannah, her friend dissolved into a cloudy mist.

Loud cackling and laughter erupted. Karina spun around, confused. Hannah had vanished into thin air. She was only a hallucination. Karina's mind and curiosity had deceived her again.

The laughter continued, while Karina spun around, trying to locate its source. She finally realized it came from above. Several girls from the Coven were sitting on branches, laughing and pointing at her.

Karina immediately sprinted back in the direction of the bamboo forest. "Help me!" yelled Karina. But she couldn't get more than a few feet away before Amelia and the rest of the Coven stood, blocking her way. Karina scanned each of the girls' faces, and none of them were Molly or Hannah. She tried to run back toward the tree, but the Coven once again blocked her way. She was no match for these girls and their powers. Karina was trapped.

Amelia and the other girls closed in around her.

"Where is Hannah?" Karina tried to sound tough.

The Coven snickered at her question. With a devilish grin, Amelia replied, "Oh, her. Was that your friend?"

"Yes! Where is she?"

"Do you truly want to know?"

"Of course. That's why I'm asking you!"

"Then come with us and we'll show you."

"No way!"

"Why not? I thought you wanted to see Hannah."

"I do. I really do."

"Then come with us. She's waiting for you. I know exactly where she is."

"Promise?"

Amelia smiled evilly again, reminding Karina of the way Molly would smirk at her.

"I promise you this. You will not find Hannah here," replied Amelia.

"So, she is in Vallaborg then?"

"Yes, of course she is."

Karina suspected it was just another trap, but she had to take the risk. She was running out of time and needed to find Hannah.

"So, what's it going to be?" asked Amelia.

"Fine. Show me where she is," replied Karina.

Amelia nodded her head, forcing back a smile. She motioned with her hand for the rest of the Coven to surround Karina in a circle.

"Then sit down and close your eyes," said Amelia.

"Why?" asked Karina.

"Do what you are told if you ever want to see your friend again," replied Amelia.

"Yeah, right. So you can kill me when I'm not looking."

"Why would we want to do a thing like that?" replied Amelia as she put her hand on the back of Karina's head. "That's not at all what we're about. I don't know what those little girls from the Shadow Embers have been saying about us. They are only nasty little rumors. I can promise you that. Now, stay still," commanded Amelia.

Karina's knees buckled underneath her as if trying to hold up a thousand pounds. She collapsed to the ground, no longer having the ability to control her own body. Karina soon felt her arms and legs forcing themselves in directions she didn't want them to go, and she could not stop her limbs from moving.

"What are you doing to me?" asked Karina.

"Helping you," Amelia replied, controlling Karina's body as if she were a puppet, until she was sitting on the ground with her legs crossed underneath her.

"Now close your eyes, or I will force them closed," said Amelia.

Karina shut her eyes but kept one of them barely open so she could see through a small slit.

Amelia took her hand away from Karina's skull and motioned with her hand to one of the girls in the Coven to step out. She had striking blond hair, almost white as snow, and cobalt blue eyes.

"I said close your eyes!" demanded Amelia.

Karina tightly closed her eyelids as a piece of black cloth was tied around her eyes.

"What is happening?" asked Karina.

"It's for your own good," replied the girl with blond hair, backing away from Karina.

Amelia and the Coven stepped away from Karina, forming a circle around the tree. Amelia pointed at the trunk of the old tree and then waved her hand back and forth in the air from side to side like she was conducting an orchestra.

"Taccipere noboss zut de Landra av Salightus," chanted Amelia.

Instantly, the branches of the tree twisted around and stretched out wide and up toward the sky. An incredibly bright light emitted from the tree in every direction as if it were the sun shining down on a hot summer day. An intense light split right down the center of the tree and grew larger and larger to reveal an opening.

Karina wanted to rip the dark cloth right off. The bright light had almost blinded her, even with the blindfold on. She wanted to see what was happening but feared the consequences wouldn't make it worth it. But she couldn't resist any longer. A little peek couldn't hurt, right? Karina tugged at the dark cloth so she could catch a quick glimpse.

The trunk of the tree was completely split open, with bright light shining in every possible direction. Amelia stood in front of the tree, waving her hand around like a lunatic, while the other four girls looked over their shoulders at Karina.

She jerked the cloth back over her eyes. Did the Coven see her peeking? Was the tree going to take them to another magical world or another part of Norlandis? Was she going to Vallaborg? Would she ever see the Shadow Embers again? Was she going to find Hannah? The thoughts and questions swirled through her mind as the bright light continued to radiate through the dark cloth.

"Stand up," said two of the girls, and Karina felt a hand on each of her shoulders. She struggled to get back to her feet. It was awkward trying to get from a sitting position without using her arms to brace herself. The two girls helped pull Karina to her feet and guided her toward the tree.

"What are you doing with me?" asked Karina.

Her question fell on deaf ears, and the blond girl tugged hard at Karina's arm to get her to move faster. Startled, Karina lurched forward, almost losing her balance. The other girl grabbed Karina's side, preventing her from falling. The radiating light from the tree grew even brighter the closer they got to it.

Amelia stood before the tree, while the other two girls waited by its trunk, as if they were guards at Buckingham Palace.

Anxiety started to consume Karina the closer she got to the tree. Wherever they were taking her, she desperately hoped she would find Hannah. But she knew they were taking advantage of her vulnerability and preying on her weakness. She felt her stomach sink.

"Can someone please tell me where we're going?" asked Karina, the bright light engulfing her.

Once again, no one responded to her question. Now she was beyond angry. She dug her feet into the ground and used all her strength to resist being moved. Despite their efforts, the other two girls could not budge Karina any farther. The remaining two girls, who were on guard, left their post by the tree and came up behind Karina, shoving her from behind, while the other two pulled at her arms.

"Leave me alone!" screamed Karina.

Amelia smiled, standing imposingly while Karina was pushed and pulled past her.

"Where are we going?" screamed Karina, trying to shake free.

Karina was only inches from the tree when Amelia got right behind her and whispered in her ear, "To Vallaborg." Amelia gave Karina a slight shove with her hand. Suddenly, they all disappeared through the opening in the tree. The light from the tree blew out like a candle as the opening in the tree sealed shut.

Chapter Twenty-One

Karina shivered in the cold, misty air. She rubbed her goosebump-covered arms, trying to get warm. With a black cloth still covering her eyes, the Coven guided Karina forward through the darkness.

"Stop here," ordered Amelia.

With a quick motion, one of the blond girls in the Coven removed Karina's blindfold. The light faded in and out in a blurred motion as if the whole world were spinning out of control. Trying to focus, Karina felt a shooting pain in her stomach like she'd had the wind knocked right out of her. It was like someone had just sucker-punched her, but no one had even laid a finger on her. Karina clutched her stomach and dropped to her knees, gasping for air. She moaned loudly as a small, cold hand clutched her chin and lifted her head gently. Karina looked up to see Molly standing in front of her.

"Bet you didn't think you would see me again," said Molly.

Karina continued to wheeze until she was finally able to breathe normally. She took a few slow, deep breaths, gathering the strength and courage to stand up to Molly and the entire Coven.

"You're right. I didn't," replied Karina, trying to push herself off the ground. "Is your back okay?" asked Karina. As the words came out of her mouth, Molly forcefully motioned with her hand at Karina's stomach.

Karina collapsed back to the ground in agony. She gasped again for air. Molly bent down and grabbed Karina by her hair and jerked Karina toward her, whispering in her ear, "I'm sorry I just did that. They are watching." Molly released her grip on Karina's hair and then helped her to her feet.

"Welcome to Vallaborg," said Molly, trying to keep a stern face.

The four blond girls walked away and disappeared into the darkness as Amelia approached Molly and Karina. "Molly, take her with you into your hut. We'll come for you two in the morning," said Amelia.

"Yes, my queen," replied Molly.

"Do not let her out of your sight," demanded Amelia.

"I won't."

"Good. That's what I like to hear. She is your responsibility," replied Amelia. She eyed Karina before storming away.

Molly anxiously waited for Amelia to disappear before returning her attention to Karina. "Follow me," said Molly.

Karina nodded her head and wondered what Molly might do to her. Would she try to hurt her again? Did she hate her enough to want to kill her, or was it only an act to impress Amelia and the rest of the Coven? She sure hoped it was the latter.

Molly led Karina beside a tall wooden fence with sharp spears pointed up toward the sky. It reminded her of fortresses she had read about from centuries ago in Viking and Medieval times. The fence seemed to encircle the entire village, stretching as far as she could see into the dark abyss.

"Faster," said Molly, picking up her pace. Her hair swayed behind as they zigzagged between a maze of huts made of sticks and hay. Each of the huts was small and rustic, with thatched roofs and narrow entrances. Karina stayed closely behind her as they approached a newer-looking hut. Molly slowed her pace. The strong scent of hay and campfires filled the cool night air.

"Come inside," said Molly.

Karina glanced at all the other huts, surprised to see that no one else was around outside. She took one last look around before following Molly inside, pushing aside a heavy animal skin that hung in front of the entrance as a makeshift door.

Inside the hut, a few small candles were scattered on the dirt floor, giving off a faint amount of light. A book and a couple of candles sat on a small wooden chair beside Molly's bed. A few sheepskin blankets lay across the bed, which was made of hay.

"Welcome to my new home," said Molly with a forced smile, walking over to her chair.

"It's kinda nice," replied Karina as Molly tossed the book onto her bed.

"Sure is," said Molly through clenched teeth. She set the candles on the floor. "I stayed in a cabin on vacation once that was kinda similar. Except, there were normal mattresses, of course." Molly settled onto the chair by her bed. "Well, I couldn't be happier. Make yourself at home." Molly gestured for Karina to take the other chair in the far corner. She shifted her chair toward the center of the room, near the flickering candles.

"Bring your chair closer to mine," said Molly.

Karina scooted her chair across the dirt floor toward Molly, realizing the girl had no intentions of hurting her.

"I'm sorry about earlier," whispered Molly.

"It's okay," replied Karina, somewhat surprised to hear her apologize.

Molly leaned in closer to Karina and whispered, "The Coven doesn't trust me yet. I had to prove I was one of them."

"I understand. I probably would have done the same."

Molly motioned for Karina to lean in closer until they were inches away from each other's faces. "Hannah is not here. She is nowhere in Vallaborg, as far as I know."

"What! Are you serious!"

Molly held a forefinger to her lips. "You can't talk above a whisper."

"Where is she then?"

"I have no clue. All I know is, she is not here."

"They lied to me, then."

"Of course they did. What else did you expect? They are not good people."

"They promised me."

"That means nothing to them. Do you think they actually care if they lie? They will do or say whatever they have to, to get what they want. Amelia needs you as much as the Shadow Embers do. You have powers that no other girl has anywhere, which makes you that important. Amelia will go to war to keep you here."

Three Ratatoskr scurried into the hut and began to search around, while the girls watched them snoop about. These once adorable-looking creatures Karina had seen in the bamboo forest were no longer cute to her, but disgusting, sneaky little spies. Karina and Molly remained quiet and motionless. The Ratis darted underneath the bed and inspected every nook and cranny before emitting a high-pitched squeak to signal their findings to each other. "Carry on," squeaked one of the Ratis, bringing a smile to Karina's face.

The three Ratis scurried back out of the hut. The flickering candlelight cast dancing shadows on the walls, reflecting silhouettes of the three Ratis lurking right outside. Both Molly and Karina were aware of their presence. Karina knew she had to give them something; otherwise, they wouldn't leave them alone.

"Well, Molly, I can't wait to see Hannah tomorrow. I wish I could go see her right now," said Karina.

"I don't care. You will have to wait for Amelia. You cannot leave this hut until she comes for you. Otherwise, there will be consequences," replied Molly, trying to keep a straight face.

"Please, even for just a second. I've missed her terribly," replied Karina as she dramatically placed the back of her hand over her forehead like she had seen actresses do in old movies.

"No way! Go to sleep. I promise you can see her in the morning when the Queen comes for you."

"Fine, I guess," replied Karina, glancing to the side.

Their conversation pleased the Ratis, as the three of them scattered away from the hut.

Karina and Molly waited for a few minutes in awkward silence. "See what I mean," whispered Molly.

"Yeah, I do. What should I do then? I can't stay here," replied Karina.

"I'm not sure. Let me think about it."

Lost in thought, Karina stared off at one of the wax candles that had almost melted down to nothing. She had been so gullible, believing Amelia. She was always so foolish and too trusting of others. It was a serious fault of hers. People always seemed to let her down.

A loud grumble came from Karina's stomach, disrupting her self-loathing thoughts. She couldn't remember the last meal she had eaten. This was the worst possible time to be thinking about food, but she couldn't help it. Karina would give anything for a pizza or some tacos right now.

Molly suddenly burst into tears.

"What's wrong?" asked Karina.

"I don't want to be here anymore. I just want to go home."

Karina got up from her seat and put her arms around Molly. "Then help us both get out of here," said Karina.

"It's not going to be that easy."

"I know. But we have to try."

Molly wiped the tears from her face as Karina let go of her. "If I can find a way, will you take me with you?" asked Molly.

"Of course. I assume there are no adults here we can ask to help us?" asked Karina.

"No. There aren't any here."

"Strange. That's what the Shadow Embers said as well."

"I think I know why," whispered Molly.

"You do? Why?" asked Karina barely above a whisper.

"Amelia's mom died during childbirth when she had her sisters. Her dad was horrible to all the kids. He used to hit them and yell constantly. Then, one day, he simply left without even saying goodbye. Then, Amelia and her sisters had to move in with the only other family in town. But they were all kicked out of the house for practicing witchcraft."

"I wonder if that's what caused her to put a curse on the woods and Norlandis. She didn't want any adults entering because she couldn't trust them," Karina said.

"Probably."

"Who was the family that took them in?"

"Rayna's."

"Very interesting," replied Karina, her stomach growling, which made both girls chuckle.

Molly reached under her pillow and pulled out a half-eaten loaf of bread. She ripped it in half and handed a piece to Karina.

"Thank you so much," said Karina.

"You're welcome. I'll get more tomorrow," replied Molly.

Karina devoured her bread as Molly slowly ate hers, deep in thought.

"So where did you all live before you moved to Sturbridge?" asked Karina, trying desperately to get Molly to open up to her.

"We were in West Virginia for a couple of years," replied Molly.

"Wow! Very cool. I've never been down that way."

"It was so pretty in the mountains. Everyone was nice and I had so many friends."

"What did your dad do for work?"

"He was a professor at the university."

"Very cool."

"Yeah, I guess."

"I know you hate that you had to move, but I honestly think you'll like Sturbridge."

Molly nodded, fighting back more tears. "If we ever make it back," she said.

"Right," muttered Karina. She had hoped their conversation would distract Molly enough and give her something to fight for. But, she might have pinched a nerve, doing the opposite of what she had intended.

"I need to get some sleep before I pass out," said Karina.

Molly reached over to her bed and threw Karina a sheepskin blanket.

"Thanks," said Karina.

"Good night," replied Molly.

"Listen, Molly. I know we'll find a way out of here and get back home. You have to believe."

"I know."

"And when we get back home, you should tell your dad how much you miss West Virginia. Maybe he'll try to get his job back at the university."

"Then I won't be able to see your weirdo face anymore," joked Molly.

"Hey, it's not that weird. Well, maybe a little," laughed Karina.

Molly burst out laughing.

"Shhh," whispered Karina.

"You're right. My bad," said Molly.

"Good night," said Karina as she snuggled in the corner of the hut with the sheepskin.

"I never got to thank you for saving my life. I can't believe you did it, especially after all the mean things I said and did to you," said Molly.

"And I would do it again."

"I'll make it up to you. I promise."

"I look forward to it."

"Night."

"Good night," said Karina as she wrapped the blanket tightly around herself and drifted off to sleep.

Chapter Twenty-Two

A sudden noise jolted Karina awake. Molly was still sound asleep, not fazed one bit. Karina's blurry and tired eyes took in the dark room. All the candles had melted into pools of wax on the dirt floor. She had hoped that being in Vallaborg was only a horrible dream, but that hope had quickly vanished.

Vallaborg intrigued Karina, but more importantly, she needed to find a way back to Norlandis, no matter what. She knew she should probably go back to sleep or stay inside the hut, but another loud noise off in the distance piqued her curiosity. Karina tossed her blanket aside and rose quietly, trying not to disturb Molly. As she tiptoed through the hut, her lower back began to ache from sleeping on the ground. She pushed the makeshift animal skin door to the side, squeezing her way through the doorway. Radiant beams of sunlight filtered down as the sun rose above the rolling hills.

Outside the hut, the area was much different from what Karina had remembered from the night before. In the distance were luscious green rolling hills with scattered rock walls that stretched across the horizon. A tall wooden fence surrounded hundreds of huts made of sticks and hay clustered together in several different circles. A massive stone castle loomed above the village, where two Hábróks guarded the gate, while the rest of the flock circled the sky above. Off to the side of the castle was an enormous ornamental garden separated by a moat of water.

Karina was surprised again to see that no one else was outside and wondered why she hadn't seen anyone else from the Coven yet. She wondered if they were only allowed out of their huts at certain times. But none of them had watches, undoubtedly, so that wouldn't make sense. Clearly, Amelia was very strict with every girl there, so there had to be specific rules they had to follow.

Behind Karina, a campfire smoldered away. A stick with some kind of charred meat was wedged up against two rocks leaning over the fire pit. The smell was intoxicating, and she didn't think twice. Karina rushed over to the stick near the fire and ripped apart the meat as she imagined a wolf would devour its prey. It was a little more burnt than her dad would have cooked it, but she needed protein badly.

As Karina finished up the scraps, a strange mechanical noise came from beyond the fence. She whipped back around as the wooden gate to the castle cranked slowly down and extended across the moat. Karina took a few cautious steps forward, while the gate lowered all the way to the ground.

Amelia emerged on the back of a horse, galloping toward Karina through the gates. Karina had to do a double take. The horse appeared to have six or eight legs. She was mesmerized by the gorgeous black horse with its ivory white mane. It galloped faster than any horse she had ever seen or ridden. Karina felt no fear as it approached her. She stood her ground, her eyes transfixed on the horse's beauty and power.

Amelia pulled up on her reins, bringing the horse to a stop when she approached Karina. Leaning over, she gently caressed the horse's mane before removing her cloak's hood. With a graceful leap, Amelia dismounted the horse and patted its chest affectionately. "Good boy, Sleipnir. Good boy," said Amelia.

Karina inched closer to the magical creature with not just four, but eight incredibly strong and beautiful legs.

"If you stare at him long enough, he'll grow another leg," said Amelia.

"What? That can happen?" replied Karina.

Amelia snickered. "Of course not. Come over here and give him some love."

Karina went around to the other side of the horse, which towered majestically above her. As she stroked his muscular legs, Amelia circled Sleipnir, watching Karina's every movement.

"Have you ever ridden a horse before?" asked Amelia.

"Only once, when I was about seven or eight," replied Karina. Which was a complete lie. She had always been fascinated by horses and, almost every day after school, she would purposely go by the horse stable up the road from her house. She begged her parents to let her take riding lessons, but they always complained about how expensive it was. So, she decided to volunteer her time and help out around the stable as often as she could. Her reward was that she got to ride the horses for free.

"I can see you itching to ride," said Amelia.

Karina blushed. "Of course. He's beautiful."

"Let's go then."

"I don't know if we should. Molly will be up soon," replied Karina.

"Don't worry about her."

"Okay," replied Karina, hesitating for a moment. She glanced back toward the hut where Molly still slept. But the allure of riding this magnificent creature was too strong.

Amelia started to help Karina mount the horse, but quickly realized Karina knew exactly what she was doing. Karina steadied herself on top of Sleipnir, while Amelia mounted the horse effortlessly. Karina shifted herself back, so Amelia had more space to take control of the reins.

"Are you sure you've only ridden once before?" asked Amelia.

"Maybe," replied Karina with a smirk.

"Yeah, that's what I thought."

Amelia gently tapped her heels into Sleipnir, who let out a thunderous roar and took off like a bolt of lightning.

Amelia grasped tightly onto the reins as they galloped throughout the village and past the imposing castle. Amelia leaned forward and gently guided Sleipnir to the side, jumping over a small hut and landing gracefully next to a fence. They picked up speed as they approached a stone archway made of stones that led out of the village.

Amelia tugged hard on the reins, causing Sleipnir to gradually slow his pace as they approached the archway. Once they were safely through, Sleipnir let out another roar and took off up the hill with incredible speed. He was easily the fastest and most powerful horse Karina had ever ridden.

Karina marveled at the majestic mountains stretching across the horizon. Vallaborg was a hidden gem that only the Coven could appreciate and enjoy. She wished she could capture this to rub it in her classmates' faces and everyone else who had bullied and harassed her over the years. If only she had her phone right now.

Sleipnir trotted down the grassy hill and then picked up speed. He leaped gracefully over a tiny brook flowing between the hills. As soon as he landed, he raced up the next hill which was covered in wildflowers of all colors. Karina tried to hold back her smile, not wanting to show Amelia she was enjoying this, but she couldn't help it. Riding on Sleipnir up and down the hills was the most fun she'd had in a long while. Karina knew she should be wary of Amelia and everything she and the Coven stood for but, for right now, she didn't care at all. She was going to enjoy this and savor it for as long as she could. If only Amelia would let her ride the horse by herself. But she knew that would never happen.

Straight ahead stood a rock wall slightly taller than Karina. Amelia kicked her heels into the side of the horse as they barreled toward it. Karina glanced nervously at Amelia, who was grinning from ear to ear. Amelia pulled up on the reins. Sleipnir easily cleared the rock wall, landing gracefully on his eight feet.

Amelia pulled on the reins to slow Sleipnir's pace down to a slow trot. "What do you think?" asked Amelia.

"He's incredible!" replied Karina.

"He truly is. I'm lucky to have him."

"How high can he jump?"

"I'm not sure exactly. Want to see if he can jump over you?"

"No, no, no. I'm good."

Amelia burst out in laughter. "I'm only joking."

"Right. You got me... Can I ask... where are we going?"

"I thought I would show you around a little bit so you could see how amazing Vallaborg is."

"It's so beautiful here! Everyone back home would be so jealous of me."

"Of course they would be. Which is why you should stay here."

Karina uneasily cleared her throat. She did not know how to respond. She needed to say something, though. As amazing as Vallaborg was and the ride had been, Karina knew she couldn't truly stay. She would never make it back home or find Hannah. Plus, who knew what kind of things Amelia would force her to do? "Can I think about it?" Karina finally blurted out.

"I will give you until tonight," Amelia replied, her brows furrowed and lips clenched together.

"Okay."

They made it up a steep hill in silence. The view overlooking Vallaborg was breathtaking. Across the horizon, there were only trees and open meadows, except for the village of huts and the castle below. There were no homes, buildings, or roads to be seen anywhere. Karina imagined this was how America must have looked when it was first discovered, before it was destroyed by cities and humans.

Karina's mind was still racing. She had so many unanswered questions about Norlandis and Vallaborg. She hated not knowing everything and wondered if she could gather enough strength to ask Amelia. But could she really trust Amelia to answer her truthfully? Especially after she lied to her to get her to come here.

"Hang on!" Amelia shouted as she dug her heels into Sleipnir's sides. The horse galloped down the hill at an exhilarating speed. Karina clung to Amelia tightly, afraid that even the slightest movement could send her tumbling off the horse, and she would probably break every bone in her body.

As they reached the bottom of the hill, Karina felt a pit in her stomach. Her smile faded, and worry now started to consume her. She knew her thrill ride was going to end at some point, but she had no idea what was coming next. Amelia had led her to this private part of Vallaborg for a reason.

Chapter Twenty-Three

S leipnir came to an abrupt stop when Amelia pulled down on the reins. She swiftly dismounted the horse and landed hard on the ground. Without saying a word, she attempted to help Karina get down off the horse, but Karina waved her off. Amelia stroked Sleipnir as Karina dismounted smoothly and scanned the area for any signs of others from the Coven. But it was completely quiet except for occasional sighs and nickers from the horse.

"Where are we?" Karina whirled around, trying to get her bearings and study her surroundings. It was something her grandfather taught her whenever they went on hikes together. Karina and Amelia were in the middle of a valley where the rolling hills converged, making this area well hidden from everyone else. Karina observed a fire pit at the exact center of the valley, surrounded by five distinct hills with five perfectly symmetrical standing rocks at the base of each hill.

"Did you hear my question?" she asked again.

Amelia ignored her. The fire pit erupted in a blaze of red and orange flames, shooting up toward the sky as though it had been doused with gasoline. Amelia marched over to the fire pit with the palms of her hands out and closed her eyes, muttering words under her breath. Six tree stumps materialized around the fire.

"Please have a seat," said Amelia.

Karina obeyed and timidly sat down next to Amelia.

Amelia stared Karina down. "Sorry, I was not clear. Please sit across from me on the other side of the fire."

Karina eyed Amelia, wondering why she had to move and why there were four other tree stumps. As soon as the thoughts entered her mind, she dismissed them. She knew exactly who was coming. It was only a matter of when.

"Now, please move, before I move you myself," said Amelia.

Karina circled to the opposite side of the fire pit. Meanwhile, the sky darkened and a chill filled the air. She settled on a stump and leaned in towards the fire and its warmth. She closed her eyes for a moment, bracing herself for what was about to happen. When she opened her eyes, she saw the other four blond girls from the Coven sitting around the fire with smirks on their faces.

"Did you have fun today?" asked Amelia.

"Yeah. Sleipnir is seriously amazing," replied Karina, shifting around on the uneven stump.

"Good, good, good. He is a magnificent creature. Isn't he?"

Karina nodded, swallowing the lump in her throat.

"I'm sure you must be wondering why he has eight legs."

"Of course. Was he born that way?"

"Well. That is an interesting question. An obvious one, of course. But I would like to answer your question with another question."

"Okay." Karina stared at the ground, avoiding Amelia's piercing eyes.

"Are you familiar with Norse mythology?" asked Amelia.

"Not really," replied Karina, even though she did have a basic understanding. She looked back up at Amelia, who was sitting on the edge of her stump, leaning forward.

"Well, I certainly didn't bring you here to tell you campfire stories or to give you a history lesson. But, seeing as your parents and teachers have obviously failed you and not taught you anything, I'll tell you about Sleipnir and some of the other creatures here in Norlandis and Vallaborg."

Amelia reached inside her robe and pulled out a small cloth coin purse. She untied the twine holding it together and took out a pinch of metallic dust. She tossed it into the flames and muttered a few words under her breath.

Instantly, the flames of the fire danced and formed into the shape of Sleipnir. He galloped around in circles, his hooves sending sparks flying as the flames crackled. He stopped prancing when he caught sight of his master, an older man who towered above him and appeared to be missing an eye. He approached Sleipnir, using his long spear as a walking stick, gently stroking the horse's face before mounting him with ease. The old man let out a ferocious scream. Sleipnir took off and then two ravens appeared out of nowhere and followed the old man and Sleipnir into the darkness.

The fire made a loud popping sound before returning to its normal form. Karina stared at the fire, anxiously awaiting what might happen next. However, the fire remained unchanged, crackling and letting off fire embers into the chilly air.

Amelia waved her hand at the fire, and it took the shape of Sleipnir again. The horse stood there as if he were waiting for Amelia to do or say something.

"Sleipnir was the horse of Odin," said Amelia.

"Odin? I've heard of him. Wait, remind me again, who is Odin?" Karina knew more about Odin than she wanted these girls to know.

"Who is Odin?" yelled the girl sitting closest to Karina, rising to her feet.

"Rowan, sit down, please. Our guest is simply uneducated. We must teach her, instead of screaming at her," said Amelia.

"I am sorry. You're right," replied Rowan.

"Karina, please excuse my sister," said Amelia.

"It's okay. The only thing I know about Odin is that he was Thor's father," replied Karina. She had to give them something, so she didn't look too foolish.

"Very good. Odin is the highest, oldest, and one of the most powerful gods in Norse mythology. He is the God of wisdom, healing, and the one who brought war to our worlds."

"And... Sleipnir was his horse."

"You got it."

"Then how is Sleipnir here in Vallaborg if he was Odin's horse?"

Amelia grinned and glanced at the smug faces of the other four girls who were also smiling as Karina waited for Amelia's answer, even though her smile and silence spoke for themselves.

"He is mine now. I am his master. He belongs to me and only to me," replied Amelia.

"Okay, but you didn't answer my question. How did he get here?"

"I summoned him and all the other creatures you have probably already encountered."

"And how did you do that?" As soon as the words left Karina's mouth, she knew it was a stupid question.

"You know I cannot tell you that," replied Amelia.

"Are there many other creatures?"

Amelia and the four other girls burst into laughter, embarrassing Karina.

"What is so funny?" she asked.

"Of course, there are more," hollered Rowan. She and the other three girls snickered.

"Sorry, I didn't know."

"Which Realm are you referring to?" asked Amelia with a devilish grin.

"Wait! How many Realms are there?"

"Wouldn't you like to know?"

"Of course I do. That's why I'm asking."

"Why do you want to know so badly?"

"I really do. I'm not just saying it."

"Well, I guess you could say there are nine Realms," replied Amelia.

"Nine! How is that possible? Are they all here?"

"Of course not *here*, you idiot!" yelled the blond girl closest to Amelia.

"There will be no such language or name-calling, Olga! You know better than that! Treat our guests with some sort of respect," yelled Amelia.

Olga pulled the hood of her cloak down over her eyes in frustration, so that her eyes were no longer visible. "Whatever," replied Olga.

"I am sorry about my sister. Sadly, she does not know how to behave sometimes," said Amelia.

"She is your sister, too?" replied Karina.

"They all are. They're quadruplets. Can you not tell?"

Karina knew they all looked alike, but it was difficult to tell with their cloaks covering most of their faces. Her eyes wandered around the fire, studying the different sisters with their stunning blond hair. "Wow! I don't know how I missed it."

"I suppose now is as good a time as any to introduce you to all of them," said Amelia. She stood up, motioning with her hand to Olga. "You have already had the rather unfortunate reaction from my sister Olga. Next to her is Runa. She is the quietest of the four, but easily the smartest of all of us."

Runa bowed her head gracefully in response to Karina without saying a word.

The name Runa struck a chord with Karina. She wondered if the Islands of Runa were named after her or if she ruled over them. Karina wanted to ask but feared this was not the right time to do so.

"Next to Runa is Torhild. She is the best fighter and swordstress of anyone here," said Amelia.

Torhild removed the cloak from her head and leaned toward Karina. "Do not do anything that might make me want to kill you."

Rowan burst into laughter. "Torhild, you are too much sometimes, honestly!"

Amelia grinned and motioned to Rowan. "And this, of course, is Rowan."

"And I am the funny one," said Rowan, while making a monkey face at Karina.

Karina giggled at Rowan's face, which made everyone else laugh, except for Olga. "Stop being a goofball for a minute, okay! We barely even know this girl, and you all are pretending like she's one of us," screamed Olga as she rose to her feet.

"Who said anything about that? We're just having a little fun," said Amelia.

Olga stormed off from the campfire and disappeared into the nearby forest.

"Should I go?" asked Karina. She hated awkward moments like this.

"No, of course not. Let my sister cool off. She will come back. She always does," replied Amelia.

"Okay. I'm sorry. I didn't want to cause any trouble between you and your sisters."

"She is fine. We are all fine. Let's eat, and we can talk more about the nine realms and your friend Hannah. That's right, I have not forgotten about her and the real reason you are here."

Karina felt like such a bad friend. She had completely forgotten about Hannah again. She knew there was no possible way she was in Vallaborg. Otherwise, Molly would have taken her to see her the night before. But maybe she was in the castle or locked away somewhere.

Amelia noticed Karina was lost in thought, staring deep into the flames. "So, what would you like to eat?" asked Amelia, trying to break the silence.

Karina was taken aback. She was hungry, of course, but food didn't seem important right now.

"I don't care. You choose," said Karina.

"There must be something you want. Something you have been craving. Maybe something your parents won't let you have. I promise, you can have whatever you would like," replied Amelia.

"Okay. Then, how about some fried chicken and mashed potatoes?"

"And gravy, of course," said Rowan.

"Absolutely! Can't ever forget the gravy," replied Karina.

"Then fried chicken and mashed potatoes it is," said Amelia as she closed her eyes, motioning back and forth with both hands. "Fritaten Kahnullum unt mosattu Karteter," she muttered barely above a whisper. A big bowl of mashed potatoes and a bowl of fried chicken appeared beside the fire.

"And where's the gravy?" joked Rowan.

Amelia shot Rowan a nasty glance. "Brunea Sosas," she said with a smirk directed at her sister. "Are you happy?"

Rowan stuck out her tongue. A small saucer of brown gravy appeared in her lap, and she screamed with delight. "Yummy! You are the best!" she yelled at her sister, then turned to Karina. "Good call!"

Amelia motioned and said, "Secks Tetter unt Skoffel."

A stack of plates and spoons appeared by the two bowls of food as Olga stormed back over to her stump and sat down.

"Olga, will you kindly serve everyone dinner?" said Amelia.

"Why don't you do it or someone else?" snapped Olga.

Tension was building as Amelia and Olga stared each other down. "Because I asked you to," replied Amelia through clenched teeth.

After what seemed like forever, Olga rolled her eyes. "Fine! I'll do it," she said with a deep sigh. Olga grudgingly passed the food around the table while Amelia cast another spell. Golden chalices, with intricate engravings and filled with water, appeared before all six girls.

Karina was salivating at the plate of food in front of her. She couldn't resist any longer. Usually, she said grace with her family, but she was starving, and she doubted a Coven of witches wanted to see her pray. She gobbled up the mashed potatoes within seconds and then ripped apart the chicken like a savage animal, barely breathing between bites. She grabbed the chalice and chugged her water as Amelia anxiously watched her.

Karina's arms became stiff and weak, causing the chalice to slip from her grasp. Her eyes grew heavy. Exhaustion overcame her in an enormous wave. Everything became fuzzy, and the girls around the fire blurred into a hazy mass. Karina collapsed onto the ground, her whole world spinning, as muffled laughter erupted around her.

Chapter Twenty-Four

Karina awoke feeling completely disoriented. Her mind was foggy, and her thoughts and emotions felt disconnected. Her body was numb all over. Amelia, her sisters, the firepit, and Sleipnir had vanished. A familiar smell of pine trees in the hot summer sun filled the air. She was no longer in Vallaborg or Norlandis. Karina found herself sitting alone on the porch of an old, white, decrepit house. She was having a horrible case of déjà vu, causing her breathing to become erratic.

Somehow, she had been transported back to the house where she met and followed Rayna to Norlandis. Karina couldn't bear to see what was in front of her, knowing she was back in the one place she feared most. The one place that kept her awake at night and had given her so much anxiety her whole childhood. She was back in the forbidden woods.

Was this all merely a horrible dream? Were Norlandis and Vallaborg even real? Did Amelia and the Coven exist, or were they simply a figment of her imagination? Where were Hannah and Molly then? Were they in the woods with her? Could she even get back to Norlandis and find everyone if it was all real? She could make it back home and get the help she needed. She would be a hometown hero if she could show her whole community what had been causing all the children's disappearances.

Karina's mind became fuzzier and even more distorted. None of this made any sense. She felt like Dorothy waking up after thinking she had visited Oz. Her vision became extremely blurry, making it impossible to see straight. It reminded her of when she wore the vision impairment goggles when the police had visited her school to teach children the dangers of drinking and driving.

She felt like she was going to vomit, so she closed her eyes to see if that would help. But it only made everything worse. Her mind continued to spin out of control. Karina wanted to scream, but nothing came out. She tried to move her legs, but could barely move them an inch, almost paralyzed. Her body began to tremble as paranoia and fear consumed her. It was like another being or outside force had entered her mind and body. She was determined to fight whatever it was and gain control over it.

A powerful force from deep within Karina's soul surged through her, overcoming every thought, emotion, and feeling she'd ever had. She was no longer a timid, anxiety-ridden, and lonely teenage girl trying to find herself. Instead, she possessed more courage and physical and mental strength than she'd ever had. Her newfound ability to heal others was something truly magical and unique to her alone. She had friends and strangers who needed her help and depended on her. Their very survival rested in her hands. Karina finally understood her purpose and what she needed to do.

She no longer resisted or feared where she was. The forbidden woods would not be her demise and would no longer consume her thoughts or emotions. She took a few deep breaths while closing her eyes. A wave of calmness washed over her body and mind. Her vision normalized as her body and mind relaxed. The tension was gone.

Karina looked out at the thousands of bizarre and deranged dolls swaying back and forth in the wind, and they stared right back at her as if they were waiting for her to do or say something. It was insane to think that every single one of those dolls was a girl lost in Norlandis or one of the other Realms.

Karina got to her feet, stumbling forward awkwardly. A warm sensation tingled throughout her body as her senses returned to normal and her legs no longer felt like rubber. She clutched a wooden post to support herself. She staggered down the rickety steps.

The dolls watched Karina's every move as she approached them, studying their faces. They bore a resemblance to many of the girls from the Shadow Embers. Teardrops flowed down their porcelain faces, while they blinked their eyes. "Karina," the dolls whispered. At that moment, Karina could feel their genuine pain and sadness. They truly needed her more than anything, and she needed them.

At the base of the birch tree lay hundreds of small navy-blue, red, and forest-green tin soldiers. Karina picked up one of the toy soldiers and wondered if these were for all the boys who had disappeared. Interestingly, she hadn't noticed any of these toys the last time she was in the woods. Karina wondered where all the boys had gone. There were piles and piles of soldiers at the bases of several trees surrounding the old house. The boys had clearly gone somewhere, and Karina needed to solve that mystery once she found Hannah.

In the distance, a couple of dolls began to shout Karina's name. The voices sounded very familiar. Karina ran in the direction of the dolls, swatting at the ones in her way as if she were running through a jungle.

"Karina, Karina, help me!" yelled a doll. "Karina! Karina!" yelled another. She continued in their direction as other dolls started laughing at her. Karina tried her best to block out the noise. The laughter and taunts grew louder. They drowned out the sounds of the dolls who were calling for her.

Karina stopped to catch her breath in a small opening in the sea of dolls. She covered her ears to help muffle the noise, trying to collect her thoughts. "You can do this," she muttered to herself. As she relaxed her body and mind, she was able to drown out the dolls' laughter.

"Help me, Karina," cried a doll several feet away.

"Where are you, Karina?" called another doll.

Karina hurried toward the dolls that were near the old water well. A doll resembling Molly lay on the ground next to it. Karina picked it up, and it seemed as if the doll were peering into her soul. "Where are you?" asked the Molly look-alike doll.

"I don't know what happened, Molly. I will find my way back to you," said Karina, trying to think of any possible way she could get back to Vallaborg or

Norlandis. Could she simply go through the same door that Rayna had taken her through before? Was there another portal or way in?

"Karina, be strong," said a doll hanging from a nearby tree overshadowing the well. Karina looked up and saw a doll resembling her neighbor, Ashley, gazing down upon her.

"Ashley? Where are you?" asked Karina.

"In Vallaborg," replied the doll.

"I will find you."

"No, we will find you."

Karina was confused. She didn't understand how she could be having a conversation with these dolls who were trapped in Vallaborg. She wondered what Ashley meant. Either way, she needed to find a way back.

"Karina!" screamed a doll in the distance, sounding like Hannah. Karina bolted in the direction of the voice.

"Hannah!" Karina called back.

"Save me, Karina!" called the doll.

Karina sprinted through the woods filled with dolls until she reached the back of the old house, where she saw a tiny pond. Several willow trees hung over the edge of the pond, their branches cascading inches from the water. Their limbs were littered with dolls hanging from every possible branch.

"Hannah!" yelled Karina.

"I'm over here," called a doll resembling Hannah.

Karina made her way towards the pond, carefully stepping through the over-grown weeds. The dampness from the swampy land seeped into her shoes. The closer she got to the tree holding the Hannah doll, the deeper the water became underneath the weeds. "This is a marsh," muttered Karina, as she realized she should not move any farther.

"Be patient, Hannah. I'm coming for you," called out Karina.

"Please hurry!" replied the doll from the tree.

Suddenly, a loud and eerie voice called out from the front of the house. "Karina, it's me." She snapped back around, her stomach churning, trudging out of the marsh.

"Don't you know who I am?" said the voice playfully. Karina's body began to tremble. The voice was one she had never expected to hear. Not in these woods. Not from the dolls. From no one. "Come here, Karina, it's me."

The voice was hers.

Immediately, Karina's heart began to pound. She didn't want to move in the direction of the voice, her voice, but she had to. Karina sprinted through the sea of dolls all the way around to the front of the house. She felt as though she were moving in slow motion. Time seemed to crawl by. The front of the house was only a little farther. The voice, her own voice, beckoned her, calling her name out, laughing.

Finally, Karina reached the steps of the old house, realizing that these were the same steps she had seen Rayna's mother run down. This was undoubtedly the house where Rayna grew up. Karina wondered where the farmland had gone. Perhaps the forest had taken over the farm over the years, with the land no longer being used after her parents had left or possibly died.

As Karina crept up the porch steps, she noticed a doll sitting on an antique rocking chair, which rocked ever so slightly. She didn't know how she had missed this one before. The doll was identical to her in every possible way. Karina didn't know whether she should laugh or cry. It was eerie to look at an exact clone of herself, staring back at her.

Suddenly, the rocking chair started to rock vigorously back and forth, and the doll smiled ever so slightly. It seemed to be enjoying itself in the chair, its eyes moving from side to side. The doll turned its neck very mechanically to look out at the other dolls before returning its attention to Karina. It blinked its glossy little eyes and then frowned at Karina, who stood there transfixed and mesmerized by her look-alike doll.

"Don't you know who I am?" the doll asked, pouting.

"Of course I do. You're... you're... me," replied Karina.

"You got it," replied the doll with a devilish little laugh.

"I don't know why I'm talking to you, I mean myself," muttered Karina, shaking her head. Suddenly she heard whispering inside her head, and she shook it violently until she was extremely dizzy. The whispering subsided, thoughts running through her head like a never-ending marathon.

The doll smiled up at Karina. "Play with me."

Karina picked up the doll and examined it carefully, curious to see if any markings or signs on the doll would help her figure out the mystery revolving around the dolls and Norlandis. But sadly, it was just an ordinary doll, which of course looked exactly like her and could somehow talk. She knew there had to be a reason her doll was here on the porch, while all the other dolls were in the woods. Karina also wondered if someone randomly placed the dolls, or if magic or another mystical force had placed them there.

As Karina bent down to put the doll back on the rocking chair, the doll's face turned red. "I thought you wanted to play with me!" screamed the doll, becoming hysterical.

Karina picked it up instantly, half expecting someone or something to emerge from the woods to make sure everything was all right.

"I do, I do, I'm sorry," said Karina.

"Good." The doll laughed as the redness flushed from its face.

Karina felt strange holding a doll that looked exactly like herself, alone in the middle of the woods on the porch of an abandoned house. If someone were filming her right now, she would be humiliated and a laughingstock for the rest of her life. Karina did a quick scan of the woods just to make sure no one was around watching her. It didn't seem possible that would happen, but then again, every bit of logic or sense of reality had been thrown out the window since entering the woods.

Karina sat on the rocking chair with the doll, pondering what to do next. She had no idea how she was going to get back to Norlandis or Vallaborg and hoped, more than anything, this doll was the answer. She stared deeply into the doll's eyes and caught a glimpse of something she had not noticed in any of the other dolls. It was as if a tiny video played inside its pupils. Amelia and the Coven were sitting around the campfire with Karina's body lying on the ground. They all seemed to be enjoying themselves at her expense, while the girls danced around her body, holding candles high into the sky.

"What are they doing to me?" muttered Karina.

Suddenly, the doll began to get extremely warm. Karina nearly dropped the doll. It continued to get hotter until she could no longer hold onto it. She had to avert her own eyes away from the doll's eyes as its face began to melt. Before Karina could get rid of the doll, it turned completely black, and within seconds, it burst into ashes.

Karina held a pile of ashes, while the rest of the dolls' remains floated away in the wind. Laughter erupted from inside the house and echoed throughout the forbidden woods. Without hesitation, Karina stormed through the front door, the white light completely blinding her.

Chapter Twenty-Five

Darkness consumed Karina. She tried to make sense of her surroundings but was unable to move either her arms or legs. Karina strained to see what was going on, but the darkness around her made it impossible. This reminded her of the time when she visited a cavern with her older brother a few years earlier. Inside, when all the flashlights were shut off, you could not see a single speck of light. Karina thought it was the most incredible thing at the time. But now she felt extremely uneasy and wished she could see even the smallest bit of light.

Sadness overcame Karina. The thought of her brother crept into her mind. She wondered if he missed her or if he was out searching for her. If he were there right now, she knew he would somehow find a way to protect her and get her out of this mess. But unfortunately, he was not here, and Karina was all alone. She would have to figure it out on her own.

Karina strained to lift her arms but couldn't move them a single inch. Ropes bound her arms and legs tightly. Her body bounced back and forth like a pinball machine. The ropes around her wrists and legs burned her skin from all the jostling around.

Panic set in as she realized she was completely trapped and had no idea where she was. Her body jostled back and forth. It felt like she was being transported in some sort of black carriage or box. The only sound she could hear was the rhythmic clip-clop of a horse's hooves, which was probably Sleipnir, Karina guessed, unless Amelia had found another horse to transport her. She wondered if she was a prisoner, which was something she never thought she would be in her entire lifetime. Karina hated any thought of going to jail, which is why she made sure to stay out of trouble. She had always obeyed the rules at school, home, and, of course, all the laws in society. But none of that mattered now. She had to play and abide by Amelia's rules. Amelia was the most powerful person in all of Norlandis and Vallaborg.

Karina knew, without a shadow of doubt, that Amelia and the Coven had tricked her into coming to Vallaborg and then must have poisoned her. But why would they do this? Did they want her to join them, or did they only need her healing powers? She wondered if they were using her as some sort of bait or ransom against Rayna and the Shadow Embers. Or perhaps they were going to imprison her and only use her when she was needed. Whatever the reason was, it didn't matter right now. She was their captive, and she had to find a way to get back to Norlandis before it was too late.

The rocking back and forth subsided when they came to a stop. Karina could no longer feel every little bump in the road against her back or the rope burning against her limbs. Sleipnir neighed loudly. Karina tried to listen carefully. Amelia and her sisters were whispering outside her carriage. It sounded like they were coming for her. She did not know whether she should pretend to be asleep or keep her eyes open to find out where she was. The rocks crunched beneath the girls' feet as they approached. Karina didn't have much longer to make a decision. Loud whispering was right below her feet. It was now or never.

As a door creaked open at the base of her feet, Karina closed her eyes and pretended to be asleep. She was a terrible actor, and she knew Amelia would know she was faking it. Amelia would expose her and embarrass her for being a phony.

Karina remained calm and kept her eyes closed while Amelia's sisters pulled her out of the carriage by the rope that tied her ankles together. She fought back every possible urge to groan from the pain of the ropes scraping her skin. The four sisters helped Karina to her bound feet. They steadied her, while she wobbled around.

Amelia approached Karina with a knife drawn. "You can cut the act. No one believes that you're still asleep," said Amelia, hiding her knife from view.

Karina opened her eyes to see Amelia standing several feet away beside Sleipnir and the black carriage. She appeared as a silhouette as the three moons cast a glow from behind her. Off to her side, the mysterious castle loomed nearby.

Amelia moved closer to Karina, who stood there awaiting her fate. Amelia drew a knife from her cloak and waved it around in the air like it was only a toy.

"You're going to kill me, aren't you?" said Karina.

Amelia's four siblings burst into laughter. Karina struggled to turn around with her feet tightly bound, nearly losing her balance, only to find all four of them snickering at her, making comments under their breath.

Laughter erupted from behind Amelia's sisters. Karina was astonished to see hundreds of girls laughing and pointing at her beyond the castle's gates. Her heart sank. She wanted to crawl into a hole and die. She hated being ridiculed, embarrassed, and bullied. This brought back the horrible memory of the time someone tripped her at lunch, and she spilled her entire tray of spaghetti and meatballs all over herself in the school cafeteria. Everyone had laughed at her, including some of the teachers. Then the kids made fun of her the rest of her seventh-grade year.

After scanning the crowd, Karina noticed Molly standing off to the side with two other girls. They had hoods on, concealing their identities. Karina was relieved to see that none of them were pointing at her and didn't appear to be laughing. Molly even gave Karina an apologetic expression of sympathy, which instantly boosted her spirit. Karina smiled back at Molly and turned back around.

Amelia circled Karina slowly, waving her knife playfully about. Karina tried her best to remain calm and block out everyone else. She needed to be strong and dare to stand up to Amelia, or at the very least, play Amelia's mind game so she could survive another day and escape from this dreadful place. Amelia stopped in front of Karina and stared intently into her eyes. Then, without saying a word, she whirled around and stepped a few feet away from Karina.

Amelia turned back around and raised the knife high into the air. She threw the knife directly at Karina, who uttered a silent prayer. Her heart beat out of control like it was going to burst through her chest. There was nothing else Karina could do. Within seconds, she would be dead. No one could save her or help her. Everyone back home would look for her for a while and never find a trace of her. She would never find Hannah or save Molly from the Coven. Her life would be over, and her story would be written.

The knife soared through the air toward Karina, while Amelia said a few words under her breath. Karina had no time to react to the knife. Any second and it would be all over.

Miraculously, the knife burst into flames and vanished. Amelia grinned at Karina as she stood there in shock. Her life was not over. Her story was not finished. It had just begun.

"Do you truly think I need a knife to kill you?" asked Amelia, giving Karina a taunting grin. "I have more power than you or anyone else could ever dream of."

Amelia's four sisters joined behind her, while she paced in front of Karina, who had still found no words to say.

Karina shook internally with fear, hoping she wasn't visibly shaking; otherwise, Amelia would prey on her weakness. She had to stay strong and hold her ground. There was a reason she had come to Vallaborg. Fate had brought her here.

"Of course not," replied Karina, scanning the crowd of girls and hoping to recognize someone. The rest of the Coven eagerly waited with anticipation. It was as if they were on the edge of their seats at the movie theater, eating popcorn. "You are the most powerful person I have ever met," said Karina, trying to butter Amelia up. "None of us could ever be as strong as you."

Amelia approached Karina, followed by her sisters. "You have two options right now. You can either join us and be part of something amazing, or we will lock you away with the others for eternity."

Karina hated both options. She had to return to Norlandis and find Hannah. She could not stay here and be manipulated and controlled by the likes of

Amelia and her sisters, and she really didn't want to rot away in some prison. Karina shook her head as Amelia and her sisters circled her with their penetrating eyes.

"What will it be!" yelled Amelia.

"Any other options?" asked Karina.

"Of course, of course. If you would like, I'll help you find your way home, so you won't be late for dinner," snickered Amelia.

Amelia's four sisters chuckled, moving in closer to Karina, making her nervously shift her body around.

Karina wanted to rip the ropes right off and make a run for it. She had to escape, whatever the cost. Karina tried to wiggle her bony arms out of the rope, but it was no use. They would not budge.

"You do have *one* other option," said Amelia, her face becoming more intense.

"And what is that?"

"Death!"

Karina swallowed the lump building in her throat. Her chest rose high before sinking back down. The word stung. She certainly didn't want to lose her life here, of all places. Karina avoided Amelia's piercing eyes, choosing to look over at Molly, who was mouthing something to her. But Karina couldn't tell what she was trying to say. She had always struggled with reading lips. If she ever went deaf, she would be done for.

"You have five seconds to decide before I make one for you," said Amelia.

Karina returned her attention to Amelia, knowing what she had to do.

"Three, two, one," said Amelia.

"Fine! I'll stay here and join you." Karina knew there were no other options.

Amelia strolled closer, until she was only inches away, and leaned in. "Are you sure?"

"Yes, of course," replied Karina.

"I don't believe you. Not a single word."

"I'm not lying. I swear."

Amelia circled behind Karina and whispered in her ear, "How do I know you won't betray me?"

"To prove it, I will do whatever you ask of me."

Amelia circled back around in front of Karina. "Very well then. Fix my scar." Amelia rotated her arm to reveal a long, jagged scar that went from her wrist all the way up her forearm.

"How do you know that I can heal people?"

"I know much more than you think."

"Okay. But I cannot use my hands if they are tied together."

"Not a problem. Lossna de Koyle," replied Amelia, motioning with one hand toward Karina's wrists and the other hand toward her ankles. "Any funny business and the rope will go around your neck."

"I understand," replied Karina as the ropes around her loosened and slid right off her arms and legs. Karina rubbed the rope burns on her wrists, feeling like she was one step closer to freedom.

Karina approached Amelia with her arms slightly to the side, palms facing upward. She wanted to make sure Amelia knew she was not a threat and wasn't going to try to hurt her in any way. Karina gently placed her hands on top of Amelia's scar. She closed her eyes. Karina could instantly feel a warm tingling sensation radiating from her fingertips and into Amelia's skin. Her forearm radiated and almost became a translucent red. This had never happened before. Amelia smirked as she watched with curiosity. "Burns a little, huh?" joked Amelia.

"Sorry. I'm still new to this," replied Karina. Amelia's arm returned to its normal color. The radiating light and warmth had subsided. Karina removed her hands gingerly, praying that her powers would work on Amelia and Vallaborg. Thankfully, the arm was healed, and the scar had completely vanished. "See, you are healed," said Karina.

Amelia examined her arm with delight, twisting it in every direction. Her four sisters rushed towards her excitedly. Once they each confirmed her scar was no longer visible, they looked at Karina differently than they had previously. They must have had their skepticism if they had known about her healing powers. But now it was confirmed, and they knew Karina would be of great use to them.

Without saying a word, Karina looked back at the four sisters. It was an awkward yet very surreal experience for Karina. "Did I pass the test?"

"For your loyalty, I will allow you to stay. But, I have one more task for you before I can fully trust you," said Amelia.

"What task?" asked Karina.

"It will have to wait until morning."

"Tell me, please," begged Karina.

"Sisters, you know what to do with her," said Amelia as she walked away from Karina, looking at her newly healed arm.

Torhild and Runa closed in behind Karina. Olga approached with a black hood, and she slipped it out from beneath her cloak. Before Karina could react, Olga yanked it down over her head, the rough fabric scratching her cheeks and plunging her into darkness. Karina screamed, but the heavy cloth muffled her voice. She kicked wildly, her boots scraping against the stone. The girls forcefully dragged her backward away from the castle.

Chapter Twenty-Six

Karina jolted awake inside a tall metal gazebo surrounded by gardens. A foul odor lingered in the air, making it difficult for her to breathe. Extremely dense fog covered the bushes like a blanket, allowing very little morning sunlight to penetrate. Above the fog towered the castle right beyond the gardens.

Karina got to her feet and realized where the horrible smell was coming from. An enormous wolf, nearly as tall as the gazebo, emerged from the fog, sniffing every bush it passed. Gobs of drool fell between its large fangs, while it approached her. Karina crouched low and pressed her back against one of the columns supporting the gazebo. She tried to remain as still and quiet as possible, hoping the wolf hadn't spotted her yet. Karina imagined she would surely look tasty compared to the little critters it was undoubtedly hunting. She debated making a run for it before the wolf spotted her, but she knew that any sudden movement would only draw its attention to her. Karina was practically defenseless against the beast. If only she could cast a spell to turn invisible or get some kind of weapon to defend herself with. Unfortunately, her abilities as a healer were useless in this situation.

Karina poked her head out slightly to catch a glimpse of the wolf. The fog hovered around the large beast, creating a mystical wall between them. Karina pulled her head back inside the gazebo right when the wolf made eye contact with her. Its fearsome black eyes stared her down with burning fury. Karina stood up and backed up to the edge of the gazebo. The wolf stalked her every step, drawing closer. Karina turned to run, but the wolf growled and blocked her movement.

"I wouldn't take another step if I were you," the wolf said.

"You too can talk?" Karina replied, shaking.

"Of course I can. Just as you can."

"Are you going to eat me?"

"Oh, how I would love to. But Queen Amelia would most certainly not be pleased with me."

"Are you my guard then?"

"You're a smart little girl, aren't you?" The wolf laughed and licked his lips.

"And what is your name?"

"Fenrir, son of Loki."

"Don't you want to know mine?"

"But I already do, Karina."

"Right. Wouldn't you rather be feasting on some delicious animal right now with plenty of meat? Instead of guarding a skinny little girl who wouldn't hurt a fly?"

"Yes, I would. But that can wait. You should make yourself comfortable. It's going to be a while."

"What does she want with me?"

"Patience, little girl. You will know soon enough."

"Yeah, sure. Patience, patience, patience. All I ever do is wait," replied Karina, sinking to the cold metal floor.

The wolf circled the gazebo, disappearing into the thick fog. His stench still lingered, though. Karina scanned the fog-filled garden, racking her brain to get out of this mess. She had no idea what she was going to do. Either way, she had to get out of this gloomy place and back to Norlandis as soon as possible. If she didn't leave now, she would be trapped like Molly and the rest of the Coven. There was no way she would be forced to be under Amelia's control like her obedient little sheep among the girls here. Karina had no idea what task Amelia was going to have her do to prove herself, and she really did not want to wait another minute to find out.

Soft whispers nearby made the hairs on Karina's arms stand up. She couldn't tell where they were coming from. Karina spun around, her eyes darting in every direction.

"Karina," someone whispered from not too far away.

She tried to see through the fog, but it was nearly impossible. It dissipated a little when she waved her arms around.

"Karina," whispered Molly.

Karina suddenly spotted Molly and two other girls crouched low behind a large, round bush, its damp leaves glistening with dew. The two girls beside her wore heavy cloaks that draped over their faces, the shadows concealing their identities. Only Molly's wide, urgent eyes were visible in the morning sunlight. She gave a sharp glance toward the path, silently pleading with Karina for her to leave.

"I can't," said Karina barely above a whisper.

"What did you say, little girl?" replied Fenrir as he turned around.

"Nothing. I was just talking to myself. I do it quite often, actually. Don't mind me."

"Well, don't be talking to yourself, or you will drive yourself insane."

"Yeah, I know."

"Vallaborg has no place for crazy people."

"Then maybe you should send me back to Norlandis."

"Nice try," laughed Fenrir as he turned and lumbered farther into the fog.

Molly peeked out from her hiding spot, motioning for Karina to come toward them.

Karina shook her head. It was way too risky. If she were caught, she would be dead within seconds or tortured by Amelia and her minion sisters.

Molly nodded back at Karina, motioning for Karina to crawl away. It was then that Karina realized Molly, a girl who had hated and mocked her beyond belief, was taking extreme measures and risking her own life to help Karina escape. Molly had been mean since the moment Karina met her, but there was no way she could ignore someone who risked their life for her. Karina needed to seize this moment and take a chance, and she couldn't continue to be scared of possible repercussions or danger. She would never make it back home if she didn't find some courage.

Fenrir stopped pacing around and sat down in the middle of the garden to scout out the area. He jerked his head back to the side. His eyes were transfixed on a majestic buck with an enormous set of antlers. The large deer leapt over a flowering shrub toward the end of the garden, not too far from Fenrir. Normally, Karina would have tried to save the deer's life from this ferocious animal, but this was not the time. It would have to defend itself without her help.

As the deer stopped between two flowering hedge bushes to munch on some leaves, Fenrir left his post and quietly stalked his prey like Karina had seen her cat do many times to catch mice. She wondered how the buck couldn't see Fenrir or at least sense that it was being hunted by a predator. His instincts should have kicked in by now.

Karina crouched down until she was flat on her stomach. She propelled herself forward, stealthily crawling away in the opposite direction from Fenrir. Out of the corner of her eye, she noticed Molly and the other two girls moving between the fog and bushes in the direction she was heading. Karina glanced back over her shoulder at Fenrir, who was lying down several feet away from the buck, ready to pounce any second. Karina's breathing became heavy, waiting for Fenrir to make his move. She knew even the slightest noise would alert the buck and make Fenrir's morning hunt even more challenging. But it might be the exact distraction Karina needed right now and could perhaps spare the buck's life, allowing her enough time to scramble away.

As Karina crawled off the metal gazebo floor and into the garden, she grabbed a small stick and snapped it in half on purpose. The buck instantly cocked its head and noticed Fenrir stalking its every movement. The buck sprinted away, zigzagging between the bushes. Fenrir chased after it.

Karina crawled as fast as she could on the rocky soil between two rows of hedges without looking back. Molly and the other two girls were hiding behind a row of tall and bushy evergreen trees. Molly poked her head out and motioned with her hand for Karina to move faster. Karina noticed the worried expression and sense of urgency in Molly's eyes, which were focused on Fenrir. Karina tried to pick up her speed, army crawling toward the row of trees. She did her best to ignore her sore and scraped-up elbows from all the rocks. She held back every compulsion to groan from the pain.

"Hurry," whispered Molly, motioning repeatedly with her hand for Karina to speed up.

Karina glanced over her shoulder at Fenrir, who was no longer hunting and was now heading back toward the empty gazebo.

"Where have you gone, little girl?" roared Fenrir.

Karina was only a few feet away from Molly and the row of trees. She ducked her head down, trying her best not to be discovered by the massive wolf who leapt through the air right before the gazebo.

"I told you to wait patiently, child!" Fenrir said, its large, jagged teeth exposed. He paced inside the gazebo, sniffing the ground and scanning the garden. Unfortunately, the fog began to dissipate. Fenrir plodded out of the gazebo, its snout scouring the garden path as it headed in the girls' direction.

Karina slithered her way under the row of trees, staying flat on her stomach. She finally reached Molly and the other girls. Her heart was beating wildly against the cool, damp grass. Fenrir's pungent odor became stronger with every passing second. Karina debated whether she should sacrifice herself so the other three could live.

Karina had worked up enough courage to offer herself up, when she felt a warm hand on her back. Karina rolled to her side and stared into the familiar eyes of someone she never thought she would see again. They were eyes she had so badly missed seeing. Eyes that gave her hope and courage. Ashley was here in Vallaborg. She was not kidnapped or murdered as everyone in Sturbridge had thought. She was here and was trying to rescue her. Karina beamed with delight. She wanted to wrap her arms around the girl and scream with happiness.

Ashley gave Karina a comforting smile and stood quickly. She ran down the row of evergreen trees until she disappeared out of sight.

Karina put her head back down. Ashley had vanished just as quickly as she had appeared. Karina rolled to the other side to see Molly lying next to her with her finger to her lips, urging her to be quiet.

Fenrir was getting closer. Karina could feel his warm breath right beyond the hedge of trees. He would certainly pick up her scent or spot her on the ground.

Suddenly, Ashley ran into the garden in a panic. Fenrir snapped back around, expecting to see Karina.

"Oh, it is only you. What do you need from me?" snarled Fenrir.

"Come quickly! Karina was spotted in the village. She's getting away," said Ashley, sounding exasperated.

"Impossible! I can smell that nasty little girl all over this garden."

"I don't know what to tell you, but she is not here."

"Are you sure?"

"Yes, I am sure of it. Amelia wants you now!"

"If the queen insists."

Fenrir rushed away from Ashley in a blaze of flames. The ground gently shook as his paws pierced the ground.

Ashley waited until Fenrir was no longer visible before rushing over to the hedge of evergreen trees. "Let's go," she whispered, her voice fading through the trees.

Karina, Molly, and the other girl jumped to their feet and squeezed themselves between the trees.

"Exactly as we planned," said Ashley to the girls.

"What are we doing?" asked Karina.

"Getting out of here," replied Molly.

"Follow me and stay within the shadows," said Ashley, crouching low and surveying the area to make sure no one was watching them. Karina kneeled right next to her with the other two. Ashley motioned with her fingers to everyone and mouthed, "One, two, three." Then she bolted in the direction of a tall, bushy tree on the edge of the garden. Karina took off, following her lead. Molly and the other girl trailed closely behind.

An old wooden archway, covered in vines, was adjacent to the tree where they were hiding. Ashley cautiously poked her head around the tree to observe everything and then ducked out of view. She nodded to everyone, signaling that everything was okay. Once again, Ashley motioned with her fingers and mouthed, "One, two, three."

Ashley sprinted through the archway, exiting the garden. Karina and the other two stayed right on her heels. They ran over a wooden bridge that crossed a moat surrounding the garden. Two trees stood parallel to each other just beyond the bridge. As they reached one of the trees to hide behind, a teenage girl appeared from behind the other tree.

"What are you doing?" the girl inquired.

"Afriera!" said Ashley, motioning with her hand at the girl, who instantly became frozen.

Karina was stunned. "You know magic?" whispered Karina.

Ashley smiled and winked back at her. "That I do."

Molly and the other girl took the frozen girl and hid her body as best as they could inside the tree. When they turned around, another girl from the Coven approached them, catching them off guard.

"She's––" the girl started to yell. But when she tried to speak, Ashley motioned with her hand at the girl's throat and sharply said, "Stillnadus." The girl from the Coven clutched her throat, unable to speak.

Ashley motioned with her hand again at the girl and said, "Afriera," and she too became frozen. The three girls quickly hid her in the nearby tree next to the other girl, who lay frozen and motionless.

"We need to move," said Ashley to Karina.

"How much farther do we have to go?" asked Karina.

"It's not that far."

"The bigger problem is trying to escape without being seen," said Molly.

"How are we going to do that?" asked Karina.

"Don't worry," said Ashley.

Beyond the dirt path that ran in front of the trees was the castle courtyard and village. In the distance, utter chaos was erupting. Girls frantically searched every possible hut, yelling and scurrying every which way.

Ashley faced the other girl, whom Karina did not know yet. Tears were running down the girl's cheeks. "Are you sure about this, Kayla?" asked Ashley

"Yes, I owe you," replied Kayla.

"Okay. We will wait for you."

"And if they kill me, what then?"

"They will not. I promise you. Do everything I told you to do, and you should be fine."

Kayla nodded her head, wiping the tears from her face.

"Svehtat henner in isi Karina," said Ashley as she waved her hand around Kayla's face. Right when she finished the spell, Kayla turned into an exact clone of Karina. She was identical in every possible way.

"Remember, you only have ten minutes before the spell wears off," said Ashley.

"I know," replied Kayla, pulling the cloak down over her eyes.

"Good luck," said Ashley.

Kayla bolted toward the castle but slowed her pace once she approached the cobblestone courtyard. She hid her face but occasionally looked up, hoping the other girls would catch sight of her.

Karina, Ashley, and Molly waited anxiously for her to be discovered.

As Kayla stepped onto the courtyard, screaming erupted. Kayla pretended to conceal her face and run through the courtyard.

"There she is! There she is!" shouted several girls, while they swarmed in on Kayla like an angry mob, blocking her way. "We found her! We found her!"

"Come on!" said Ashley, taking off down the dirt road, followed by Karina and Molly, rushing past the chaotic scene.

Karina glanced back over her shoulder. Fenrir was standing guard over Kayla as Amelia and her sisters circled her.

"Will she be okay?" asked Karina, running between trees that lined the village.

"I hope so," said Molly.

"Kayla will be fine," replied Ashley as they made their way to the fence bordering the village.

"She's a fake!" yelled Amelia, her voice echoing throughout the village.

"Find her!" screamed Torhild.

"Shoot! Get to the tree quickly," said Ashley.

The girls quickened their pace to an all-out sprint. Karina had never been that fast, but she raced along like her feet were on fire.

Meanwhile, the courtyard was becoming a mob scene. The girls from the Coven yelled back and forth at one another. Fenrir quieted them, letting out a ferocious roar.

In the distance was a tree very similar to the one that had transported Karina to Vallaborg. Its jagged arms stretched out in every direction. Dense fog hovered around the mystical tree.

Karina glanced back over her shoulder. They had been spotted. "Girls, we have trouble," said Karina.

Hundreds of girls from the Coven charged in their direction, led by Fenrir. His mighty paws pounded the ground as several girls on horseback trailed behind him. A loud shriek echoed throughout the village. Amelia soared through the sky on top of Hábrók.

"Ashley!" yelled Molly.

"I see them," replied Ashley.

As they reached the tree, Ashley stepped forward, shouting, "Taccipere noboss zut Norlandis."

The branches of the tree twisted and stretched around as they reached up toward the sky. An immense light split the tree in half, like it was being ripped open. Within seconds, a large gateway appeared in the middle of the light.

"There's no time!" yelled Ashley.

They were surrounded by Amelia's sisters on horseback. Fenrir growled protectively at their side while Amelia swooped down like a predator closing in on its prey. The rest of the Coven had them surrounded.

"Don't you dare leave!" Amelia yelled, approaching with rage-filled eyes. Her eyes were locked onto the three girls. "This is my kingdom! No one is allowed to leave without me!" Her hands gestured upwards, repeatedly muttering words in Norlandic under her breath.

The earth trembled beneath their feet while flames erupted between the two groups. A gust of wind swept through, fanning the flames and intensifying them. The wildfire spread with frightening speed, threatening to consume everything in its path.

"That's what you think," hissed Ashley through clenched teeth. Summoning every ounce of her power, Ashley snapped her hands forward, sending shock waves through the air, extinguishing the flames. Embers danced in the air amidst the smoke before dying out completely. Amelia's eyes widened in disbelief. She was knocked off her feet by Ashley's spell. Amelia's body crashed against the ground with an echoing thud.

"Now!" yelled Ashley.

Karina moved toward the opening as Amelia's body was magically thrust forward and lifted off the ground. She landed back on her feet and sent a powerful shock wave from her hand.

Molly leaped out in front of Karina, absorbing the force. Molly screamed in agony and fell to the ground. Ashley grabbed her and dragged her toward the tree gateway. Karina rushed over to help with Molly, who was now unconscious.

"Leaving this Realm without me is forbidden!" Amelia shouted, motioning with both hands up to the sky.

The sky darkened instantly. Thunder erupted and echoed all around the madness unfolding. Lightning bolts struck the ground, almost striking Karina and Ashley. The ground split beneath their feet, rattling stones and sending cracks racing like veins through the dirt. Karina stumbled forward, clutching Molly tighter against her chest. Behind them, Fenrir's snarls tore through the night like thunder, each growl reverberating inside her ribcage.

The branches of the tree twisted higher, splintering as light beams sliced through the fog. The portal widened, illuminating the entire area. Karina's eyes watered from the glow, but she pressed forward, heart pounding so hard she thought Amelia must surely hear it.

"Quick!" yelled Ashley to Karina, who was pulling Molly's body the best she could.

Torhild drew her sword, closing in on the girls. "Don't let them leave," yelled Torhild.

Olga and Runa drew crossbows from quivers hidden behind their long blond hair. "Don't make me shoot you," declared Olga. She took aim, her eyes narrowing.

"Down!" shouted Ashley, thrusting her hands forward, muttering under her breath while conjuring a wall of shimmering blue light. In a flash, it exploded toward the Coven. Amelia reacted, sending a blinding red flame toward the blue light. In a deafening roar, the two opposing forces resisted one another until there was a blinding explosion. Sparks shot out in every possible direction like fireworks. A few embers fell on Karina's pants. She tried to shield her face with her arm.

"We gotta go," screamed Karina as both she and Ashley pulled Molly through the portal.

Amelia and her four sisters advanced toward the portal, fury burning within their eyes. A horde of screeching bats appeared out of nowhere and flew towards the fleeing girls. But it was too late. All three of them had made it through the portal in the nick of time, leaving Amelia in utter rage on the other side. The gateway closed behind them, sealing their escape.

Chapter Twenty-Seven

Karina wanted to scream in jubilation. She was no longer a prisoner in Vallaborg. Sunlight spilled across the vast, open field, warming her skin and filling her chest with a rush of hope. Even the air smelled fresher and felt crisper, carrying a faint sweetness from wildflowers hidden among the tall weeds. It was like the first beautiful spring day after a long, cold winter. It was absolutely invigorating.

The three girls were back in Norlandis and safe for the moment. But they had to move quickly. Amelia and the Coven would surely burst through the portal at any moment.

Ashley and Karina carefully lowered Molly onto the ground. She remained unconscious, her chest rising and falling shallowly. Karina bent close, relieved by the faint warmth of her breath against her cheek. Thankfully, she was still alive. Karina hoped she could save her life, as Molly had done for her. Ashley's eyes darted around the field, frantically looking for cover.

"We need somewhere to hide. Like now," said Karina.

"No need. I'll just make us invisible," Ashley replied. She closed her eyes, lifted her right hand, and whispered, "Machora noboss unsinlig."

The air shimmered around them, bending like heat waves on summer stone. And suddenly, they were gone. Not a trace of them lingered in the open field. Karina could still see her own hands, her legs, but to the world, they were nothing but ghosts. It was a strange feeling knowing you were invisible but could still somehow see yourself.

"Are you sure they won't see us?" asked Karina.

"Of course, but it won't last long. It should give us enough time, though, to find somewhere to rest and take care of Molly."

"I'm curious; why didn't you use the invisibility spell to help us escape?"

"It wouldn't have worked. Amelia cast a spell against the use of invisibility in Vallaborg. Here, she doesn't have the power to do so."

"Got it. Where should we hide?"

"I know just the place."

Together, they lifted Molly. Karina held her legs, while Ashley grabbed her shoulders. Luckily, Molly did not weigh all that much.

They hadn't moved more than a few feet before the portal opened wide, spilling white light over the field. Amelia emerged first, followed by her four sisters and a swarm of cloaked girls. Their boots trampled the grass, flattening the delicate wildflowers in their path.

"They couldn't have gone far," declared Amelia, her eyes scanning the meadow.

"Search every possible square inch of this field! I want them in our possession by sundown," Torhild barked, drawing her sword.

"Be calm sister. We will find them," said Runa.

"Easier said than done," snapped Torhild.

The Coven fanned out, sweeping through the waist-high weeds and circling the jagged rocks that jutted up like broken teeth. They scoured every inch of the field and any possible hiding place.

"Maybe they went into the Bamboo Forest," said Olga.

"No way they could have made it there yet," replied Rowan.

Meanwhile, Karina and Ashley did not move a muscle. Molly dangled by her feet and arms. Karina could not hold on much longer. Her arms felt like they were going to give out any second. She noticed Ashley struggling to hold onto Molly as well. They both made eye contact with each other and simultaneously laid Molly gently down in the tall grass, making sure not to make any noise while doing so.

Every passing second felt like hours. The clock was ticking. The Coven combed through the meadow with relentless determination. The girls had to do something if the Coven did not leave soon. Karina's heart pounded as Amelia and her four sisters marched in their direction. Adrenaline started to take over her body as they drew closer. Karina knew it would be just their luck that the spell would wear off at this exact moment.

Amelia stopped a few yards away from the girls, looking directly at their hiding place. Karina could almost feel her breath on her. She pressed a silent hand against Molly's mouth, fearing that any sound would give them away. "They are close. I can feel it," said Amelia. Sweat trickled down Karina's forehead, stinging her eyes. She forced herself not to move, not even to blink.

"Of course they are!" Torhild replied, while storming around. "Check over there!" she demanded, pointing toward the tree.

Several cloaked girls rushed off, their boots thudding against the earth. The rest pressed on. Meanwhile, Ashley and Karina lay silently in the grass. Molly stirred slightly but did not wake. Karina pressed her hand tightly against Molly's mouth.

A rustle came from the nearby brush. Every head turned at once. As a soft breeze blew through the leaves of the trees, a small fox darted out from underneath the bushes, its reddish fur glistening in the sunlight. The entire Coven sighed.

"I'm not going to do this all day," Rowan complained.

"Stop being such a crybaby," said Olga.

"Shut your mouth!" Rowan shouted, shoving her sister.

"You first," replied Olga, pushing Rowan hard to the ground.

"Stop fighting. We need to keep looking. They are somewhere," commanded Torhild.

The Coven scoured until almost every rock and thicket had been overturned. Torhild paced dangerously close, so near that Karina could have reached out and touched the hem of her cloak. Karina held her breath and wondered what would happen if the Coven bumped into them. Would they physically feel them, or would they pass through like a ghost? She hoped she did not have to find out. The Coven was closing in on them. Any second, their spell would wear off.

"I still think they went to the Bamboo Forest," Runa said.

"We need to keep looking," replied Torhild.

"I agree with Runa. Gather everyone immediately," snapped Amelia.

"Are you sure?"

"Yes. They couldn't have gone too far. We can send out the Hábróks and Ratis to inform everyone in the meantime."

"Fine."

Torhild whistled shrilly. Within seconds, the Coven regrouped. Torhild barked out orders and explained the plan, while Amelia approached the jagged tree. Amelia raised her hands, muttering a chant. Light poured from the portal once again. One by one, the Coven scattered back through.

The air grew still. The portal dimmed. As the portal closed, another girl wearing her cloak over her face came from behind the other side of the tree.

"I know you're here," mumbled the girl.

Karina lay as flat as she could while the girl approached them. They were doomed. Karina could not bear to look up.

"Show yourself," said the cloaked girl, approaching the three girls.

Suddenly, the spell had worn off. The shimmer faded, and Karina, Ashley, and Molly were exposed as if they had been pulled into the open by invisible hands.

"Wait until Amelia finds out," the girl muttered, her voice low and sharp.

She leapt forward, landing directly in front of them. Karina pressed her face into the damp blades of grass, her heart pounding in her ears. She couldn't bear to look. The girl towered above them and removed her hood in a flash, revealing her identity.

"Kayla!" screamed Ashley.

"Yes, it's me," Kayla replied quickly. "We don't have long. Once they realize I've left them, they'll come back."

"You're right. But we can't keep carrying Molly. Karina, do you think you can heal her?"

"I'll try," replied Karina, looking down at Molly. She wasn't exactly sure what her actual abilities were, and if there were certain things she wouldn't be able to heal.

Karina's hands shook nervously, placing them onto Molly's head. Cold shot through her arms, her fingertips stiff and numb, as though the life inside her had frozen solid. Panic surged. Were her healing powers gone? What if Molly died here, in her arms? Hannah would never forgive her. And without her abilities, Karina would be useless to the Shadow Embers. Her hands continued to tremble. Molly was still unconscious.

Tears welled in her eyes. "It's not working," Karina whispered, her voice cracking.

"I don't know anything about healing someone. What I do know is that any spell has to be assertive and sincere. There can't be any doubt in your mind. Otherwise, it will never work. If you truly want to heal Molly, it has to be genuine and come from your heart. You can't just go through the motions."

Karina nodded her head, wiping the tears from her eyes. She desperately and truly wanted to save Molly. She placed her hands gently on Molly's head and closed her eyes. An enormous comfort overcame her as her hands became warm. The energy flowed throughout her hands and down through her fingertips. Her fingers twitched as a tingling sensation released into Molly's head.

"Oh my goodness, she's awake," gasped Kayla.

Molly stared back up at Karina with confusion. "Where am I?" muttered Molly.

"You're okay," said Karina, helping Molly to her feet.

"You did it, you really did it. I can't believe it's you," said Ashley.

Karina brushed it off as if it were nothing, even though deep down, she had a profound sense of self-satisfaction. She had saved Molly's life once again. "Come on, let's get moving," said Karina, trying to make it seem like it wasn't a big deal.

"You're right," said Ashley.

The four girls hurried across the field, away from the tree and the portal's lingering glow. Grass whipped against their legs, and the sun was already starting its slow descent, painting the sky in long streaks of gold. Karina glanced back more than once, her nerves prickling, making certain no one was following them. They slowed their pace once they reached a rocky path, so they could stop to catch their breath for a moment.

"What now?" asked Molly.

"I'm not sure. I didn't think this far ahead," replied Ashley.

"We gotta hide somewhere soon," said Kayla.

"I got an idea. Follow me," replied Karina. She surveyed the quiet and peaceful field behind them. Ahead was a rocky path that led to the Bamboo Forest. "We can't take this path. That's where they are going to look for us," said Karina.

"Good point," replied Molly.

"What do you suggest then?" asked Ashley.

Karina looked in the other direction on the path and felt the hairs stand up on the back of her neck. The air felt suddenly colder. She could sense Amelia was coming for them any moment.

Next to the path was a steep and rocky hill leading hundreds of feet down to a river.

"Quick! Down the hill," demanded Karina.

Sensing Karina's urgency, the girls scrambled down the hill.

Karina wondered if the river below was the same one that Jenny, Dana, and Diana had pulled her from.

The sky started to darken as cold winds swept through the woods.

"We need to move faster. They're coming," whispered Karina.

Karina plopped down on the hill and used her feet to start sliding. She knew it would hurt, but it was the fastest way. The other girls followed her lead.

The pounding of the horse's hooves echoed from the path above. Karina stopped herself from sliding and rolled onto her stomach, lying as flat as she could on the hill. She wriggled behind a thicket of trees and shrubs. The other three girls did the same. The four girls hid on their stomachs with their heads faced upwards, not too far from the path. Their pursuers were getting closer.

The ground began to tremble. Karina lay her head tightly on the ground, trying to blend into the brush, praying the Coven would disappear into the woods. Karina glanced out of the corner of her eyes and spotted Amelia leading the charge with her four sisters. Hundreds from the Coven raced behind them on horseback.

Chapter Twenty-Eight

The pounding of the horses' hooves sounded like thunder as they raced down the path, kicking up a cloud of dust. Karina, Ashley, Molly, and Kayla lay hidden on the ground behind the brush on the side of the hill, awaiting their fate. Dust and dirt particles sprinkled down on top of the four girls, making Kayla burst into a coughing fit.

The other three girls whipped their heads toward her, eyes wide, and gestured frantically for her to be quiet. Kayla clenched her mouth tightly, covering it until she got her coughing under control. Karina cautiously peeked through the leaves, eager to see what was happening and hoping no one heard Kayla coughing. Hundreds of girls from the Coven raced around the bend in the path. The earth shook beneath their weight, each hoofbeat vibrating through the soil. Amelia had summoned them all—every single girl in Vallaborg. Karina's stomach turned. Karina never would have imagined that she would have provoked an all-out war between the two sides. She held her ear close to the ground, listening carefully to the vibrations caused by the herd of horses as the dust settled around her. The majority of the Coven were now in the bamboo forest.

A couple of ravens above the hill let out loud raspy caws. Karina lifted her head and spotted the two menacing black birds perched on the ridge, feathers glistening with oil-sheen in the sun. Their beady eyes locked onto Karina. They stared so long she felt her skin crawl until, at last, they spread their wings and took off into the sky. They squawked, reporting what they had just seen.

"They are near," said Amelia, as she and her sisters appeared right above the girls. All five of them dismounted their horses and scoured the area. Karina raised a finger to her lips, pleading with Ashley, Molly, and Kayla to remain silent.

"Find them," demanded Amelia from above.

Rowan and Olga went to the opposite side of the path, searching through the overgrown grass. Meanwhile, Torhild and Runa marched up and down the path before concentrating their efforts along the edge of the bamboo forest.

All four sisters checked every possible hiding place, while Amelia approached the hill where the four girls were hiding. Her eyes were fixated on their hiding spot. "Get over here!" she yelled.

Her sisters swarmed at her call. Within moments, they were descending the hill. "I see them!" yelled Runa.

"Go, go, go!" said Karina, her throat tight with fear.

"Get them!" yelled Torhild.

The girls let go of the branches that had been holding them in place and launched themselves backward. The hillside gave way beneath them, and they slid down the slope on their backs, soil ripping at their clothes, rocks bruising their arms.

Amelia and her sisters chased after them, moving effortlessly downwards. She shouted something at them, and within seconds, the trees uprooted themselves and began to wrap their limbs and roots around the girls, trying to ensnare them.

"Watch out!" yelled Karina as the four girls tumbled down the hill.

Each of the four girls got to their feet, zigzagging and weaving around the tree roots, racing down the massive hill. Karina quickly ducked as a tree root tried to wrap itself around her neck. Molly leaped over a large root that nearly swept out her legs. Kayla shifted hard to her right as a root almost pulled her by her ribcage. Ashley moved from side to side, avoiding a series of tree roots swinging at her.

Before they knew it, the trees started swinging their branches down at them as if they were made of rubber, slinging every which way. Their roots and limbs came at the girls from every possible direction. Karina did not understand how they were doing it, but all four of them were able to dodge anything that came their way. The closer they got to the bottom of the hill, the trees became sparser, making it easier for the girls to avoid their attacks. They had almost made it to the base of the hill and the bank of the river.

Karina dodged two tree limbs that came at her. She seized one of the limbs with both hands, yanked hard, and the wood cracked with a sharp splintering pop.

"There is nowhere to go!" called Amelia. She and her sisters continued to pursue the girls.

"You might as well surrender and face the music," said Torhild.

"Never!" yelled Karina. The four girls had reached the edge of the riverbank.

The sisters closed in, chanting in unison, their voices weaving into a dark incantation that carried on the air like rolling thunder. The hillside answered their call, suddenly becoming a massive mudslide. Rocks, tree limbs, and debris of all sorts came gushing down. Amelia and her sisters stood unfazed, their boots rooted in place as the mudslide washed all around them.

"We need to jump!" Karina shouted, her voice breaking as she watched the mud devour everything in its path.

"Are there any other options?" asked Kayla, nervously looking out at the river.

"We can make this all end," Amelia said as the mudslide intensified.

"What are we going to do?" asked Molly.

"We don't have many options," said Ashley.

"We need to decide quickly," said Kayla.

Karina looked back at the roaring river and knew it was their only option. "Jump!" yelled Karina. As soon as the words left her lips, she sprang from the bank of the river and plunged into the frigid water.

Molly and Ashley jumped in right after her right when the mudslide came gushing down. Karina rose to the surface and noticed that Kayla was still on the riverbank terrified, her knees buckling in fear. Mud covered her legs up to her knees. Amelia and her sisters approached her faster.

"I can't swim!" Kayla cried, her voice cracking.

"Come on! We'll help you!" Karina shouted, thrashing against the current.

Amelia was only a few feet away. She stretched out her hand, but Kayla squeezed her eyes shut and hurled herself forward into the water.

Kayla hit the river like a stone. The current dragged her under, her arms flailing wildly as she struggled to rise.

Ashley tried to swim upstream to reach her, but the current was too strong. "You have to kick your feet and move your arms like this," said Ashley as she tried to demonstrate how to swim to Kayla, who could barely keep her head above water.

"We have to help her," said Karina, glancing back at Amelia, who was now the only one on the riverbank. Her sisters had retreated up the hill, while Amelia stood on the riverbank with her arms held high, reciting something repeatedly.

Suddenly, the river became extremely choppy. The sky instantly darkened as a storm started to brew. Just up the river was an enormous wave, steamrolling in the girls' direction.

"Brace yourself!" yelled Karina as the wave came barreling down on top of the four girls, sucking them underneath the turbulent waters.

Kayla and Molly both slammed against the rocky riverbed, each struggling to swim back up to the surface. They gasped for air, their heads bobbing in and out of the water.

"Watch out! Here comes another one," said Ashley.

Evil laughter erupted from the riverbank as Amelia bowed to the four girls. "Enjoy my fun little water park." Amelia laughed, turning to trek back up the hill.

Another massive wave came crashing down upon the four girls, swallowing them up. Karina jabbed her leg awkwardly against several rocks on the riverbed, grimacing in pain. She swam hard up to the surface while grabbing her throbbing ankle. She tried her best to tread water in the choppy river. "Oh no," gasped Karina.

"Not again," said Molly. Another large wave approached them rapidly.

"Where's Kayla?" asked Ashley.

The three girls searched around frantically for any sign of her while trying to keep their heads above water. In a near panic, Karina spotted Kayla downstream, lying against the side of the riverbank.

"She's over there!" shouted Karina, pointing in Kayla's direction.

"She isn't moving," exclaimed Molly.

Karina, Ashley, and Molly kicked their legs with all their might, determined to reach Kayla as quickly as possible. Right when they were about to reach her, a third wave crashed over them, pulling them underneath the current. Unbothered, the three girls fought through the strong currents and rough waters. Gasping for air, they scanned the riverbank to see if Kayla was safe. To their horror, she was no longer there. Molly pointed at her body floating away downstream toward a dangerous rapid.

Before the girls could even think about what to do to save Kayla, another enormous wave approached them. It was the largest one of them all and continued to grow as it gained speed and intensity.

"Girls," Karina muttered.

Suddenly, the wave split right down the middle as a wooden boat emerged, causing the turbulent water to subside. The three girls bobbed up and down in shock, while the sky brightened and the storm ceased.

The boat was a beacon of light and hope, skimming along the river toward them. Rayna, Jenny, and several other girls from the Shadow Embers had found and rescued them in the nick of time.

"Need a hand?" asked Jenny with a smile as bright as the sun, leaning over the boat and extending her hand.

"Yeah, but we gotta help Kayla first.

"Not a problem," said Rayna. The boat sped away, skimming past Kayla. It pulled around sideways, blocking Kayla from floating away any farther. Moments later, Kayla's unconscious body slammed up against the boat.

Karina, Ashley, and Molly swam as fast as they could toward Kayla, holding onto a glimmer of hope that she would be all right. When they reached her body, they worked together to lift her, while Jenny and Rayna pulled her the rest of the way into the boat. Jenny tried to tend to Kayla as Sophia, Diana, and Dana each helped pull the girls out of the water. Rayna grabbed the helm of the boat and steered it around to continue floating down the river.

"She's not breathing," declared Jenny.

Kayla lay motionless in the boat, unconscious with a bloated face that was starting to turn blue.

"Does anyone know CPR?" asked Ashley.

Everyone shook their heads except for Karina. "I do," she said.

Karina pushed past the other girls and got down on her knees. She immediately started to perform chest compressions and mouth-to-mouth resuscitation. The other girls watched nervously. Molly bit her thumbnail, tears filling her eyes. Dana and Diana covered their eyes, too afraid to watch.

Time passed by in slow motion. All five of Karina's senses became numb. Her vision blurred, and all sounds became muffled. She could no longer feel her arms and felt like she was just going through the motions. Minutes ticked by without a single sign of life from Kayla. CPR was not helping. Karina placed her hands on Kayla's lungs and heart, hoping her powers would be of better use. But Karina felt nothing. She never felt the warm and tingly sensation she had previously felt when she healed others. Karina hated to admit it, but she didn't think she would be able to bring Kayla back to life.

Kayla became more flushed in the face. Karina put her ear up against Kayla's chest to listen, but there wasn't a heartbeat. Her healing powers were useless. Tears started to form in Karina's eyes when he started doing CPR on Kayla again.

Ashley and Molly began to weep. Jenny leaned over to feel a pulse in Kayla's neck. "I'm sorry Karina. She's gone," said Jenny.

Karina tried to ignore Jenny. She was determined not to give up. She continued doing chest compressions and mouth-to-mouth resuscitation. She threw her wet hair back. Sweat started to drip down her face. Kayla's lips were beginning to get cold and rigid.

"It's okay," said Jenny, wrapping her arms around Karina.

"It's all my fault," cried Karina as she finally gave up doing CPR.

"No, it's not," said Molly.

"You can't blame yourself. There is nothing you could have done to save her," replied Jenny as she stood back up.

"I'm the one who told her to jump!"

Ashley put her arms around Karina. They both wept into each other's arms.

"She had no other choice. We both know that. It was an unavoidable tragedy," said Ashley.

"Yeah! And what about my powers? They did nothing. What good am I, if I can't help anyone?" replied Karina, releasing her grip on Ashley.

Rayna turned around as she continued to steer the boat with one hand. "You won't be able to save everyone. Especially for those who have already passed. Once they cross over, there is sadly nothing you can do," said Rayna.

Karina nodded her head, wiping the tears from her eyes. She had never witnessed someone die right before her eyes. She knew Ashley was right, but she could not help but feel Kayla's death was all her fault. Between the three of them, someone could have saved her.

The mood was somber for hours. Ashley and Molly were inconsolable. No one knew what to say, so no one said anything. Everyone was lost in their own thoughts and emotions, as Rayna continued to steer the boat down the calm river.

Chapter Twenty-Nine

As the sun majestically set behind the mountain range, the crisp air sent goosebumps up and down Karina's arms. The scent of rain filled the air, yet not a single cloud could be seen in the clear blue sky. All the girls remained silent. The boat sailed peacefully along the calm river, its wooden hull creaking gently, while the water lapped against the sides like a rhythmic hush.

It was difficult for Karina to see precisely where they were headed. The river appeared to wind its way into the side of the mountain. She desperately wanted to ask someone where they were, but she knew she couldn't break the eerie silence that had lingered since Kayla's death.

Rage began to build inside Karina the more she thought about Kayla's tragic death. She wanted revenge on Amelia and the Coven for what they had done to Kayla. All she had wanted to do was to escape their oppression and find a way home. Kayla innocently wanted a better life, and they took hers away. She had risked her life to save the lives of her friends, and Karina who was practically a stranger.

The more Karina pondered it, the more she felt deep within her soul that there was no way the girls in the Coven were all truly that evil deep down. Molly had anger issues, of course, but even Karina herself did. Sure, Ashley had a rebellious side and was undoubtedly searching for her own identity. But is that not what all teenagers go through? Does that make either one of them a bad person? If Kayla had been evil or wicked in her heart, as Jenny had described girls from the Coven, then there was no way she would have risked her life for others. Karina was convinced Jenny and Rayna were wrong about how fate was decided in the Forbidden Woods. Could some girls actually be evil within the Coven? Maybe? But Karina felt it was more likely that the girls who wound up in the Coven were simply troubled and lost or easily convinced because of their vulnerability and fragile state of mind. Coming to this realization brought a smile to Karina's face.

Karina gasped as she gazed out at the water, which had changed into a wondrous transparent aqua color. Tiny colorful fish swam around the boat, shimmering in the sunlight.

They had wound their way around the side of the mountain, which had a wide opening where the river ran through. The boat slowed down as it approached the mysterious opening covered in vines and overgrown brush.

Karina, Molly, and Ashley were completely awestruck. It was not just an opening or tunnel through which the river flowed, but rather a breathtaking and magnificent cavern that loomed ahead. Several girls waited on the rocky sides of the entrance to the cavern.

The water level was very shallow as the boat entered the cavern. Dana and Dianna threw ropes from each side of the boat to the girls on the shore. They took hold of the ropes and tied them around the wooden vertical pillars to help secure the boat so it could dock.

Once the boat was settled, Rayna, Dana, and Diana jumped from the boat onto the rocky edge of the cavern.

"Welcome to our home, and your new home, that is," said Jenny.

"This is where you live?" asked Ashley.

"Well, for now anyway," replied Jenny, hopping down.

"You'll love it," said Sophia. She jumped down next to Jenny on the rocky shore. The two girls then helped Karina, Ashley, and Molly get down and then led the way inside the cavern.

Karina realized why the Shadow Embers had chosen to live here. Inside the cavern was a gigantic waterfall that cascaded down into a small pond where the river fed in. A stone bridge spanned the pond near the waterfall, lit up by hundreds of lanterns. Soft sunlight filtered into the cavern from the high ceiling, illuminating its natural beauty. Scattered around the walls of the cavern were hundreds of sphere homes, similar to the ones in the bamboo forest.

"Pretty amazing, huh?" asked Jenny.

"This is incredible!" exclaimed Karina, grinning ear to ear.

"So much nicer than Vallaborg," said Molly.

"I bet," replied Jenny.

"Don't tell Amelia," Molly said with a snicker.

"I don't think any of us will anytime soon," Ashley agreed.

As the three girls stood at the edge of the pond in amazement, Jenny motioned for all the other girls from the Shadow Embers to come join them. Suddenly, girls of all different ages flocked to them as if they were heroes. Karina did not understand it at all. They had done nothing to deserve this kind of excitement and greeting.

Karina, Ashley, and Molly introduced themselves to the hundred or so girls who had gathered before them. After Karina declared who she was, she scanned the crowd of girls, hoping to find Hannah, but her hopes were quickly dashed.

Jenny tried to introduce everyone from the Shadow Embers to the three girls, but it all became a blur. She realized the three girls were just nodding along and knew it would be impossible for them to remember any of their names. "You know what, don't worry about learning anyone's names right now. We're so glad you're all here," said Jenny.

It became clear to Karina why everyone was so excited to see them. No one else had ever escaped the clutches of Amelia and the Coven before. They were the first to leave the Coven and Vallaborg of their own free will. Of course, it should have been three of them if only Kayla had not drowned in the river. Karina could not get Kayla's death out of her mind. She racked her brain, wondering how she could have done things differently. Then maybe Kayla would be with them right now, all being treated like heroes.

Karina's thoughts were interrupted as the spotlight was suddenly thrust upon her. She had not realized that Molly and Ashley had taken a few steps back, and everyone was now staring at her and Jenny.

"Karina is finally here! The prophecy is true! She is the one we have been waiting for all these years," exclaimed Jenny. As the words left her lips, the girls charged at Karina as if she were handing out bags full of money, surrounding her like a swarm of bees.

"Please, please, fix my elbow," cried one girl.

"Me first. I can't see out of my right eye," said another girl.

"Karina, please help my leg," wailed an older teenage girl.

A loud whistle came from across the pond, stopping the chaos in its tracks. Rayna stood on the bridge watching the madness before her. The mob of girls backed away from Karina and scattered throughout the cavern.

"Sorry about them. I didn't think they would have all bombarded you like that," said Jenny.

"It's fine. I would have probably done the same if it were me," replied Karina.

"Right. Well, let's get you settled in."

"I honestly don't plan to stay for too long, though. I have to find Hannah."

"And where do you suppose she is?"

"Well, she doesn't appear to be here, and she wasn't in Vallaborg. I'm guessing she's on the Islands of Runa then."

"I think I can help with that," said Molly. She walked quietly over, revealing Amelia's cloth coin purse hidden in her cloak.

"How did you get that?" asked Karina.

"I might have stolen it," replied Molly with an impish smile.

"Might have?" said Karina, joking with Molly.

"Yeah, might have." Molly's eyes twinkled as she laughed at herself.

"Jenny, do you have a fire pit somewhere?" asked Ashley.

"Yeah, of course. I can take you there now. May I ask why?" replied Jenny.

"You'll see."

Jenny led the girls around the pond, passing several sphere homes hanging above, jutting out from the cavern walls. Underneath the homes were picnic tables surrounded by beautiful flowering trees. A few groups of girls sat at the tables talking, stopping their conversations momentarily as they watched the girls pass by.

"Carry on," said Jenny to the girls at the tables.

Karina, Ashley, and Molly followed Jenny quietly, taking in everything that they passed. The cavern became so narrow that they could only walk single file through it. Hundreds of tiny bluish lights illuminated the stone walls and ceiling. Normally, Karina would have been claustrophobic, but the flickering lights made it quite pleasant.

The passageway kept going until it finally opened up to a room filled with plants, trees, and flowers of all kinds, which climbed up most of the walls. The ground was covered in a lush purple and cranberry-red bed of flowers. Across from the girls at the edge of the room was a large fire pit that was already blazing. Directly above the pit was a massive hole in the cavern that led to the outside. Warm sunlight came through the opening as the sun set behind the distant mountain range.

"This is absolutely amazing!" exclaimed Karina. The girls stood at the edge of the room in admiration.

"Oh, my goodness. It's Incredible!" said Ashley.

"Are we allowed to walk on the flowers?" asked Molly.

"Of course," replied Jenny.

Karina, Ashley, and Molly tentatively inched their way toward the flower bed, while Jenny casually strolled across it to the fire pit.

"You won't ruin them, I promise," said Jenny.

"Are you sure? My mom would kill me if I walked across her flowers," said Karina.

"I'm not your mom, am I?"

The girls laughed as they made their way to the fire pit. They circled around the fire. It made a loud popping noise, making Molly nearly jump out of her skin. The girls chuckled.

"So, what do you have to show me?" asked Jenny, trying to get serious.

Molly handed the small coin purse to Ashley.

"She'll show you," said Molly.

Ashley untied the twine holding the cloth together and reached her hand in to grab a small pinch of the metallic dust. She threw it directly into the fire and said a few words under her breath as the girls waited in anticipation.

The fire roared to life. Within seconds, it took the shape of Hannah, who sat all alone on the edge of a very steep cliff, overlooking the sea. Her hands covered her face, while she sobbed into them. Suddenly, she snapped her head back around as someone approached her. She jumped up and left her spot on the cliff.

The fire crackled a few times as it returned to normal.

"Where is she? Where is my sister?" asked Molly.

Karina was a little surprised to see Molly's sincere concern for Hannah's well-being. She not only risked her life to escape Vallaborg, but she truly wanted to find her sister.

"She's somewhere on the Islands of Runa, I'm sorry to say," replied Jenny.

"And how do we get there?" asked Karina.

"Well, there are two ways that I'm aware of," replied Jenny.

"And they are?" asked Molly impatiently.

"We can either travel across the dangerous sea that has the most wicked and fearsome creatures, or we can go through a portal that is heavily guarded by the Coven," said Jenny, exhaling deeply.

"What would you suggest?" asked Ashley.

"I don't know. I haven't done either. Let me speak with Rayna, and we can talk about it in the morning," replied Jenny.

"Okay, but we need to decide soon. I think she's in danger," said Karina, sensing Molly was feeling the same anxiety.

"I understand. Let's grab some food and talk about it more," said Jenny as she left the fire pit, followed by Ashley.

Molly and Karina made eye contact with each other, feeling the urge to stay behind for a moment. The two of them lingered by the fire pit, waiting for Jenny and Ashley to walk a little farther so they could have some privacy.

"We need to find Hannah, no matter what," whispered Molly.

"I agree. I promise we will find her. I don't care who helps us," replied Karina.

They smiled at each other and followed Jenny and Ashley out of the room and back down the narrow hallway.

Chapter Thirty

Karina had probably slept less than an hour, her thoughts consumed with how they could possibly save Hannah. She had tossed and turned all night. There were so many unknowns, and she had no idea what journey awaited her. Everything about Norlandis was still so new and peculiar.

There was no use staring at the walls anymore. Karina was clearly unable to fall back asleep. So, she eased out of her bed, making sure not to wake any of the other girls.

A stone staircase carved into the cavern walls led to the edge of the pond below. Karina descended them silently, her bare feet chilled by the cold stone. The rest of the Shadow Embers appeared to be sound asleep. She made her way to the wooden bridge as sunlight started to filter down through the cascading waterfall. It illuminated the entire cavern with warm, burnt-orange hues.

Karina stood on the bridge facing the splendid waterfall before her, and all she could think about was leaving this amazing place. She would love to stay and explore the caverns and the surrounding mountains. Everything about the caverns intrigued her, and she wondered if she would ever make it back here again. Karina truly hoped she would, but she needed to focus on what was most important. The more she settled into being comfortable and familiar with Norlandis, the less of an urgency she would feel to find her way home. She had to stay motivated and determined.

Karina had no idea what the future held. She had to rely on the Shadow Embers and their advice. But she couldn't follow them around like a sheep; she needed to follow her own intuition and instincts. Karina still didn't know whom she could trust in the Shadow Embers. She had serious doubts about Rayna, who had been acting very cold and distant since the day Karina fell from the bridge.

"May I join you?" Rayna's voice startled her.

"Yeah, of course," replied Karina. "Speak of the devil," she muttered under her breath.

"What did you say?"

"Nothing. I was just talking to myself." Karina gazed up at the waterfall.

"This place is incredible, isn't it?"

"It sure is."

"I found this cavern many years ago when I was all alone, trying to hide from the Coven. It has become our haven ever since."

"Well, this place is awesome," Karina said, her eyes darting around the cavern walls.

"Listen, I came down here to talk to you about the Islands of Runa."

"Okay, and?"

"I know you want to find Hannah, but I can't risk everyone's lives helping you try to save your friend."

"Then I'll go alone, or with whoever wants to join me."

"I don't think you understand how dangerous it is. Amelia doesn't want anyone to leave Norlandis. She will do everything she possibly can to prevent you or anyone else from leaving."

"I don't know what to tell you. I'm going, and there is nothing you can do to stop me. I will not let Hannah die alone on some island."

"We cannot afford to lose you. Too many girls need you here. Don't be selfish. You need to share the gift you have been given."

"Why? Because they all want to use me selfishly to heal themselves? Do you see the hypocrisy?"

"Karina, whether or not you want to hear this, your powers are unique. No one else has the ability that you have. You need to share those powers with those who need help."

"I understand. And what if there are girls on the Islands of Runa who could use my help just as much?"

"I get that. They probably could use your help. But we need you here. Once you settle in, you will see how incredible this place is and the girls in the Shadow Embers."

"It doesn't change the fact that I need to find Hannah."

"Then go! But, I won't be coming with you, and I won't ask anyone to join you on your suicide mission." Rayna turned and marched away from the bridge.

Karina wanted to scream back at Rayna or, better yet, throw her underneath the waterfall. How was she being selfish for wanting to save someone? They had risked their lives to save her, Molly, and Ashley. What's the difference? It did not make any sense. How could she not care about Hannah or anyone else stranded on the Islands of Runa? Karina turned to run after her but was blocked by Jenny, Dana, and Diana, who were approaching her.

"You won't be able to change her mind. She is quite stubborn," said Jenny.

Karina exhaled deeply, trying to calm herself down. "And what about you three? Are you staying here as well?" asked Karina.

"It depends."

"On what?"

"Tell us why we should risk our lives for you?"

Karina glanced back at the waterfall, trying to gather her words. She looked back at Jenny, Dana, and Diana, then at the tiny civilization the Shadow Embers had built within the cavern.

Molly and Ashley descended downstairs as Karina began to get choked up. She tried to push it aside, but she couldn't control her emotions. Her tears started to flow like lava from a volcano.

"Almost my whole life, I've had basically no friends. Everyone back home thought I was weird, strange, or some kind of freak. No one saw me for me. I've always kept to myself. Finally, I became friends with someone who accepted me for who I was. Something deep inside my gut tells me Hannah and everyone on the Islands of Runa are in danger. I need to do everything I can to save them. If it means risking my life to save Hannah and anyone else, then fine. It's a sacrifice

I'm willing to make. I cannot sit here knowing she and other girls could be in danger." As she finished talking, Molly and Ashley walked onto the bridge.

"We're in," said Ashley, as both she and Molly squeezed past Dana and Diana to stand next to Karina.

"I'll take you to the Islands of Runa on one condition," said Jenny.

"And that is?" asked Karina.

"If you follow my lead and do exactly what I say. It can't be like the Bamboo Forest."

"Of course. I promise."

"Then it's settled. I will lead you to the portal by the sea."

"Awesome! And what about you two?" asked Karina, motioning to Dana and Diana.

They both nodded as Karina drew closer to the twins. She studied them curiously before placing her hands gently on Dana's neck. Karina felt a surge from her hands shoot up her fingertips and into Dana's neck. Dana gasped for air as Karina removed her hands.

Dana coughed a couple of times and exhaled sharply. She made a few audible noises barely above a whisper and then swallowed hard. A smile spread across her face. "I can talk again; I can talk!"

Karina smiled approaching Diana. She repeated what she had just done. Within seconds, Diana was gasping for air. "You did it! I can talk again, too, Dana!" Tears streamed down Diana's face. "Thank you so much."

Dana hugged her sister as tightly as she could. They both cried into each other's arms and were soon laughing.

"Get over here!" said Dana, reaching for Karina. As soon as Karina joined the girls, both Dana and Diana wrapped their arms around her, almost suffocating her.

"You're going to kill me," joked Karina.

The twins lightened their grip and burst out laughing. Karina hugged them back.

"You're the best," said Dana.

"I don't know about that," said Karina.

"You have no idea what it's been like, not being able to talk. We will follow you anywhere you need us to," said Diana.

"Just let us know when you need us and we'll be there," said Dana.

"Thank you," replied Karina. The twins excitedly ran off across the bridge and past the waterfall.

"More will follow. I promise you," said Jenny.

"How soon do you think we can leave?" asked Karina.

"Give me about a week to train you three and to come up with a plan."

"Okay. I want you to tell any girl here that I will heal whatever I possibly can if they are willing to join us."

"An incentive! I like it. I'll get the word out now." Jenny rushed off the bridge, yelling for girls to join her.

Girls dashed from every corner of the cavern, descending from their homes and various nooks around the cavern. It didn't take long before they formed a large circle around Jenny, while she explained everything to them.

Rayna watched from above skeptically. Karina noticed her and tried to smile at her. Rayna averted her eyes, pretending not to notice Karina.

Chapter Thirty-One

For several days, Jenny had trained Karina, Ashley, Molly, and several girls from the Shadow Embers to the point of physical exhaustion. During the day, they spent their time doing hurdles and jumping exercises, running, swimming, crawling, and horseback riding. At night, the girls practiced their archery skills and learned some magic. Ashley already knew many spells, so she easily learned more and helped teach the others how to perform them. Karina had always loved archery and was eager to improve her skills. And she was more than ecstatic to learn how to do real magic, finally. Ever since the first time she saw Rayna use magic, she hoped she'd get a chance to use it herself.

Late at night, the girls sat by the fire in the room where they'd seen Hannah in the flames. Jenny went through every detail of their plan of attack to reach the Islands of Runa many times, to the point that everyone knew it like the back of their hand.

Karina had to fulfill her end of the bargain. She was able to heal countless injuries and ailments of the girls, who all promised to join them on their adventure. The girls had a wide range of injuries, rashes, and other medical problems. Karina healed their broken bones, infections, scars, and painful injuries. Still, she was a little skeptical about whether they would all fulfill their promises. Many seemed more eager to fix themselves than to truly help Karina. She noticed many of the girls from the Shadow Embers seemed perfectly fine spending their days in the cavern like they were at an extended camp. Karina didn't understand why they didn't have a sense of urgency to leave this place.

Regardless, everything was coming together. They had a small group of girls who would join them, and there was even talk that Rayna might, as well. Karina had her doubts but seriously hoped Rayna would be there. If the journey to the Islands of Runa was going to be as difficult as Rayna and Jenny said it would be, then they would seriously need the help of Rayna and everyone possible from the Shadow Embers.

With each passing day, Karina became more anxious. They had prepared as much as they possibly could for whatever awaited them, but there were still unknowns that they would never be prepared for. Karina had never trained this hard in her whole life. Physically, she was ready, but she was still a bundle of nerves. She prayed that Hannah was still alive and they hadn't missed their chance to rescue her.

The night had finally arrived before their big journey would begin the next day. The Caverns buzzed with excitement, anxiety, and nervousness. Everywhere you went, it was all that anyone talked about. Karina sat outside with Ashley and Molly at a picnic table far away from all the other girls. Fragrant and gorgeous flowering trees surrounded them, making the girls feel at home. Karina had genuinely enjoyed her time in the caverns with Molly and Ashley. It was amazing how much she had learned about both of them. The three girls shared many laughs together, and also many tears. All three of them had so many mixed emotions about being in Norlandis, journeying to the Islands of Runa, and the possibility of never returning home.

Molly and Ashley were lost deep in thought as Karina let out an enormous yawn. She was physically, mentally, and emotionally drained.

"Are you girls ready for bed?" asked Karina.

"I suppose," said Ashley.

"Yeah, let's hit the hay," said Molly.

"Okay. See you in the morning," said Karina as the girls parted ways.

As Karina made her way toward the stairs, she noticed Rayna alone by the edge of the pond. She really needed to talk to her and finally confront her. This could be her last chance to do so. Karina hurried over, hoping to catch her before she walked away. "Hey, Rayna, can I talk to you for a second?"

"My answer is still no," replied Rayna, gazing out at the pond.

"I'm not asking you to come with us. I know you don't care."

"Then what do you want?"

"I need to know why you're so angry with me and seem to hate me so much."

"I don't hate you at all. I get frustrated with you. There's a difference," Rayna muttered.

"Okay, I guess I can understand that. Then, why did you lie to me?"

"Lie to you! About what?" Rayna turned to face Karina.

"About your powers. You've said from the moment we met that you had limited powers. But I know how powerful you truly are. You have almost as much power as Amelia."

"I did this to test you. I needed to see what you could and could not do, without any of my help. Of course, I could have defeated the giant easily, helped us transport from place to place, and saved you from crossing the bridge."

"Then, why didn't you? I almost died!" Karina blurted.

"I never would have let that happen. I've known for years that you were the one whom the prophecy spoke of. You were too young before, and I needed to wait until you were a little older. Who do you think was manipulating your dreams and trying desperately to get you here?"

Karina's eyes widened. She had always felt like there was some outside force pulling her in, and she'd wondered why her dreams felt so real and vivid. "Then, if you needed me so badly, why didn't you save me or help me get to the caverns sooner?"

"Like I said, I had to test every ability you had" Rayna said. "I had to make sure you were truly the One. I never made any of the other girls here do what you went through. I had a feeling you were the one, which is why I had to test you."

"I understand. I'm sorry I failed you."

"But you haven't. You have healed almost every girl here, and you did something no one else has been able to do in over two hundred years."

"And what's that?"

"You rescued girls from Vallaborg."

"They wanted to leave, though."

"And hundreds of additional girls also want to leave there and are waiting to be rescued from the Coven. You will be the one who sets them free. You see, the prophecy has more to say about you, Karina. You are not just a healer," Rayna assured her.

"I don't understand."

"You will be the one who breaks the curse, rescues everyone from the nine Realms, and helps us all return home. As many of us have said before, we have been waiting for you."

"I don't know what to say. This is all so overwhelming." Karina rubbed her tired eyes.

"This is why I've kept it from you. Sometimes it's best not to know these types of things."

"I totally agree." Karina laughed and exhaled deeply.

"You should go get some sleep. You have a big day tomorrow."

Rayna extended her arms. Karina gave her a hug for the first time, wondering if this would be the last time she would see Rayna again.

"Take care of my girls," said Rayna.

"I will," replied Karina as she walked away from Rayna. She had never felt a heavier weight on her shoulders. She was not only the healer on Norlandis, but the one who had to break the curse so everyone could return home.

Chapter Thirty-Two

B eyond the caverns, on the far side of the river, a sprawling stable nestled in the valley between two towering mountains. The scent of hay and leather lingered in the early-morning air. Karina approached her horse, a magnificent creature with a coat as white as fresh snow, glistening faintly in the dawn light. She adjusted the quiver of arrows strapped to her back and felt the now-familiar weight of her bow as she slung it over her shoulder.

Karina ran her fingers through her horse's soft mane, feeling the steady, warm breath of the animal beneath her. Across from her, Dana and Diana were helping Ashley and Molly climb up onto their horses, whose rich, dark-chocolate coats shone in contrast to the pale-blue sky. Karina was particularly worried about Ashley and Molly. They had done well with swimming and all the exercises over the last few days. But they had never ridden a horse or fired an arrow until a week ago, and now they were riding into a potential battle. At least, Ashley was very good at magic; her skills had only grown stronger this past week, which might just be their saving grace.

After Ashley and Molly were steady on their horses and secured their quivers, Dana and Diana mounted their horses with ease. The girls galloped away from the horse stables and onto a dirt path that wound around to the top of the hill. The sun was beginning to rise, filling the sky with gorgeous shades of orange and pink. Waiting for them at the top of the hill were Jenny, Sophia, and a small group of girls on horseback.

"Where is everyone?" asked Karina.

"I'm sorry, but the others decided to stay," said Jenny.

"Why?"

"They didn't think the risk was worth it."

"Who cares! We don't need them," replied Ashley confidently.

"Right. Well, let's get going then," said Jenny.

"We can do this!" exclaimed Karina.

Jenny gave her muscular black horse, who was far superior to all the other horses, a swift kick with her heels. They bolted down the mountain toward the rising sun, while everyone else followed. Ashley, Molly, and Karina brought up the rear.

Karina's stomach was in complete knots thinking about what awaited them near the portal by the sea. Just thinking about all the horrible and vicious creatures protecting the portal made her queasy. On top of that, the Coven guarded the portal day and night, while a flock of Hábróks was on constant alert, circling the sky. Thankfully, Karina had some time to gather her strength and courage. It would take them a couple of hours to reach the portal if they were lucky. She feared the worst, but she would rather die trying to do what was right than hide away in the caverns like a coward.

The girls rode in silence. Everyone was on high alert and lost in their own thoughts making their way through the mountains. The path was no longer visible, having been overtaken by very tall grass and weeds. By the looks of it, the route had not been traveled for many years. Karina wondered how many of their friends, neighbors, family members, or former classmates might be stranded on the Islands of Runa. For girls who were supposed to be pure in heart and good and honest people, there were not many who dared to stand up against evil.

They all slowed to a halt as Jenny raised her hand, signaling to move no farther. On the horizon, the sun sparkled above the calm and peaceful sea. The early morning sunlight shimmered across the water like scattered diamonds. The salty air was cool against their cheeks. The gentle hush of waves mingled with the distant cries of seagulls.

"Let the horses rest for a moment," said Jenny as she dismounted.

"And don't forget to water them," said Dana.

Everyone followed Jenny and Dana's lead. The horses grazed on the thick weeds as a few girls tended to the horses, giving them water from buckets that seemed to appear out of thin air.

Jenny walked over to Karina, Ashley, and Molly with a concerned face.

"Something isn't right," said Jenny.

"What do you mean?" asked Molly.

"Well, I don't see anyone or anything guarding the portal. It should not be this easy."

"Right."

Karina squinted, her eyes straining to see past the piercing rays of sunlight that scattered across the landscape, bouncing off the water and nearly blinding her. After a few moments, the rocky coastline came into focus.

Jenny was right. There wasn't a single soul in sight. No creatures lurked among the rocks, and there were no girls from the Coven anywhere. It was eerily silent, except for the crashing waves, which usually brought Karina much peace. For some reason, she felt the sea was warning her.

"Maybe it's a trap," said Karina.

"I agree. Amelia is very cunning. I wouldn't be surprised if she is hiding somewhere with her sisters," said Ashley.

"Should we go back to the caverns?" asked Molly.

"No! We have come this far. We aren't going to turn back yet. I, too, want to see the Islands of Runa and find my sister," replied Jenny.

"Your sister?" muttered Karina under her breath.

"Yes, my sister disappeared a few years before me until I finally worked up enough courage to search for her in the forbidden woods."

"Then, we will find her, too," said Karina.

Jenny nodded, her eyes fixated on the shoreline. "We all need to be extremely careful and be ready for anything and everything," she said, then strolled away, talking quietly to the different groups of girls who stood around waiting.

"I don't like this one bit. Amelia is ready to strike. As soon as we get down to the sea, she'll try to ambush us and catch us off guard," said Ashley.

"Maybe there is another way," said Molly.

"If there is, no one knows about it. Just be ready. Remember who we are doing this for," replied Karina.

Molly nodded as Jenny called out, "Girls, mount your horses!"

Karina swiftly mounted her horse and trotted over to Jenny, who was already mounted on hers.

"Do you mind if I say a quick word?" asked Karina.

"Go ahead," replied Jenny.

Karina tightened her grip on the reins, maneuvering her horse to face the determined group of girls, who were ready to charge forward. She carefully studied their faces, almost all of them anxious and worried.

"Girls of the Shadow Embers, thank you for joining me on my journey to the Islands of Runa. I know that you may be afraid of what might come. But I want you to know and hear this well: You have more courage and strength than all the other girls sitting comfortably in the caverns right now. It is an honor to ride beside you and fight with you. You chose to risk your lives for something even greater. You, too, may have friends, family, and loved ones on the Islands of Runa who need you. I need you! We will no longer cower in fear and hide in the shadows of the caverns, letting Amelia and her Coven rule Norlandis. We must reclaim our freedom and fight for what we believe in. I want you to think about all the years you have been stuck on Norlandis, while your friends and family back home worried about you, cried for you, searched endlessly for you, and ultimately grieved for you because they thought they would never see you again. Here is your chance to be part of something amazing, find your loved ones, find our way back home, and defeat our enemy!" said Karina as she raised her fist in the air.

The girls erupted with a thunderous roar of enthusiasm, their spirits ignited by Karina's words.

"If that doesn't encourage them, then I don't know what will," said Jenny.

Karina locked eyes with Jenny. "I meant every word." Her horse carried her around the group of girls to join Ashley and Molly.

"Be ready for anything that might come," said Jenny, kicking her heels into the sides of her horse.

Jenny galloped away down a small hill toward the sea. Everyone followed her down in groups of twos. Karina rode beside Molly, who showed worry in her eyes.

"Have no fear. You are the bravest young warrior among us. We won't let anything happen to you," said Karina.

"I can fight for myself. They have no idea what I'm about to unleash," Molly vowed.

They rode down the rest of the mountain in silence. Karina's eyes darted around, double-checking to make sure no one was hiding behind any rock or tree they passed. There were no signs of danger. But her gut told her otherwise. She could sense the presence of the Coven lurking nearby, sending a shiver down her spine. Evil was close.

Chapter Thirty-Three

As the salty breeze filled Karina's lungs, a soothing peace washed over her. The waves crashed down upon the shore and up against an archway carved out of the rocky cliff, which jutted out into the sea by the shore. Sunlight flickered through the archway, beckoning Karina. The portal and her path to finally finding Hannah were right before her eyes.

Jenny turned around and motioned for everyone to slow their pace. Karina pulled hard on her reins, trying to coax her horse into easing up and slowing down. She approached the shore carefully, expecting something to happen any moment. They were so close, Karina could taste it.

Suddenly, the wind started to howl off the sea and the temperature dropped rapidly. The sky darkened, and the sun almost completely vanished behind the menacing clouds. The ground beneath the horses' hooves started to rumble.

"Take cover!" yelled Jenny.

The ground shook violently as the horses circled, stomping their hooves. The ground started to ripple like a wave toward them, knocking some of the girls off their horses. Karina and Molly veered quickly to opposite sides. The ground rattled and shook, creating a large crack that extended all the way down to the sea.

"Quick! To the portal!" yelled Jenny.

Karina kicked the horse with her heels and started to move down the hill, until she noticed a girl hanging through the crack in the ground. She pulled hard on the reins, bringing her horse to an abrupt stop. Karina dismounted and rushed over. Sophia grasped onto the edge of the ground for dear life as her body dangled down into a dark abyss.

"Take my hand," said Karina, reaching out.

"Please don't let me go," Sophia replied, clenching Karina's hand.

As Karina tried with all her might to pull Sophia up, Ashley came over and supported Karina's back with one arm, while pulling Sophia's arm with her other. The two of them were able to bring Sophia safely back onto solid ground.

"Thank you," said Sophia, gazing at the girls who squeezed her hands.

"Let's go!" said Ashley

Sophia climbed onto the horse with Karina as Ashley mounted her horse. They rode only a few more feet when a large flock of Hábróks appeared above them.

Amelia, her four sisters, and several other girls from the Coven swooped down from the sky on top of the Hábróks. Before they knew it, Amelia shot lightning bolts down at them, striking a couple of girls from the Shadow Embers who now lay motionless on the beach. Amelia shot another round of lightning bolts at girls still trying to make their way to the portal. They narrowly missed Karina's horse, which got spooked. It lifted his front legs high into the air, knocking Karina and Sophia to the ground. The horse galloped away in the opposite direction.

Both Karina and Sophia were able to leap to their feet just as Amelia and the girls from the Coven jumped down from their Hábróks onto the shore. They moved toward the girls from the Shadow Embers, ready to strike.

Jenny, Dana, Diana, and a couple of other girls had already made it safely to the beach. They dismounted their horses and ran toward the water. Amelia caught sight of them and instantly shot ice from her fingertips, making the sea around the portal turn into an ice-skating rink. The girls tried to step carefully onto the ice but immediately slipped and fell onto their backs. A couple of girls Karina didn't really know managed to get to the sea, but Amelia retaliated by conjuring roaring flames in their direction, causing the ice to crack. The girls slipped through a hole that suddenly broke open. Amelia's four sisters approached the two girls and used a spell to seal up the cracks in the ice, trapping the two girls underneath.

"Don't you dare try to save them!" yelled Torhild, wielding her sword and approached Jenny, Dana, and Diana. The two girls trapped underneath pounded their hands and kicked their feet desperately, trying to break free.

"You're going to kill them!" yelled Diana.

"So what?" replied Torhild as she and her three sisters approached. The trio backed away slowly on the slippery ice, their bows drawn back and aimed at Amelia's sisters.

The two girls' muffled screams from under the ice dissipated as their bodies became stiff as a board. Tears began to stream down Dana and Diana's faces watching the horror unfold. Jenny pulled back on her bow, ready to release an arrow. "You will pay for their deaths," said Jenny as Torhild held her sword ready to fight.

Suddenly, another large flock of Hábróks swooped down from the sky, and more girls from the Coven appeared beside Amelia.

Karina, Ashley, Sophia, and Molly had reached the shore amidst the chaos. Amelia spotted them from the other side of the beach across the crack in the surface. In the blink of an eye, she transported herself to the other side of the beach and was now blocking the way toward the portal for the four girls.

"Thought you could get away so easily, huh?" asked Amelia.

"We were just going for a swim," joked Molly.

"Don't mock me!" yelled Amelia.

Karina and Ashley reached for an arrow in their quivers.

"Don't you dare think about it!" replied Amelia with intensity in her eyes.

"Leave us alone. You don't need us," said Ashley.

"Don't tell me what I need!" Amelia snapped as she approached the girls, who backed away from her. "Who should I kill first? Tough decision, tough decision. You know what? You decide."

Karina stepped out in front of Ashley, Molly, and Sophia. "You can kill me or take me back to Vallaborg. I'll do whatever you want. Just let them go," said Karina.

"No thanks," replied Amelia, thrusting her hand forward, sending shock waves directly at Sophia, knocking her to the ground. Sophia gasped for air, and within seconds, she was no longer breathing.

"Get away from us!" Karina yelled, slamming her hands down by her side, sending shockwaves back at Amelia, causing her to fall.

Amelia got right back to her feet with fire raging in her eyes. "You think you can learn a little magic and defeat me?"

Suddenly, a roar of thunder shook the ground. Arrows rained down all around them, almost striking Amelia. Rayna and many girls from the Shadow Embers appeared on the beach.

"Get out of here, Karina. I'm sorry we didn't come sooner," said Rayna.

The girls from the Shadow Embers fired a series of arrows at Amelia's four sisters, halting their advance toward Jenny, Dana, and Diana, joining their defense.

Karina, Molly, and Ashley hesitated. They knew this was their chance to leave but felt like they needed to help Rayna.

"Go!" yelled Rayna.

"They are not going anywhere!" screamed Amelia.

Amelia tried to block Karina from moving, but Rayna shot fire from her hands, making Amelia retaliate by shooting ice to stop the fire from hitting her. The two of them were locked in a fight as the Shadow Embers fought with the Coven.

Karina motioned for Ashley and Molly to follow her. They scurried away from the battle toward the sea that was no longer ice. Jenny, Dana, and Diana were waiting for them by the portal. Karina looked back over her shoulder to see Torhild and Runa sprinting toward them.

Arrows whizzed past Karina toward Torhild. Karina turned back around and moved as quickly as she could through the choppy water. Jenny, Dana, and Diana shot arrow after arrow toward Torhild and Runa, giving Karina, Ashley, and Molly time to reach the portal.

"If you leave this Realm, you will never be able to come back!" yelled Torhild.

Jenny ignored Torhild and put all her focus into saying the spell to open the portal.

Bright light radiated from the archway as Dana and Diana ran through. Jenny stood guard with her bow drawn toward Torhild and Runa, allowing Ashley and Molly to go through the portal. Karina looked back at the fighting on the shore. Amelia and Rayna continued to fight with each other. Rayna made eye contact with Karina, and she heard Rayna's whisper inside her head. "Everything will be all right. Go and find your friend."

Karina and Jenny stepped through the blinding light and into the portal. Instantly, Karina felt a rush of sensation as if her spirit and soul had left her physical body. Bright light consumed her very being as cool air engulfed her. Then, only darkness.

Chapter Thirty-Four

K arina's five senses slowly returned. She rubbed her fingertips together, running them along the palms of her hand, feeling the various lines, wrinkles, and scars. She wiggled her toes in the warm, soft sand, feeling each individual grain against her skin. It was a strange sensation at first, being able only to touch and feel things, until the overwhelming smell of the beach consumed her. After the initial aroma of salty air and sand, the faint smell of meat roasting made Karina's salivary glands go berserk. She could practically taste the barbecued meat in her mouth. As she imagined feasting on the food, sounds of crashing waves and laughter filled the air. Gradually, the brilliant light diminished, making it possible for her to see clearly.

They had made it to the Islands of Runa, while the Coven and the rest of the Shadow Embers were still on Norlandis. Would the Coven come after them again? Karina wondered. She hoped Rayna and the rest of the Shadow Embers were okay and hated that she and her group left during the epic battle. Too many girls had been injured and killed, which brought immense sadness to Karina. She prayed that if they could find a way to break the curse, then perhaps the girls would never have truly died. No one had any idea what their mortality meant on Norlandis.

Karina had to be strong and push these thoughts aside. Ashley and Molly approached Karina with the biggest smiles she had ever seen. Dana and Diana jogged along the shore, playfully dodging the crashing waves. They were like little kids on vacation. You wouldn't have thought that minutes ago their lives were in danger as blood was spilled all around them.

Jenny appeared tense and worried, her eyes nervously scanning the shoreline and unfamiliar surroundings. Karina and Jenny both stared at the dense jungle of tropical trees right off the shoreline. Other than the white sandy beach, trees appeared to cover the entire island. In the distance was a large mountain range covered in vegetation with storm clouds hovering over the tallest peak.

"What do we do now?" asked Karina.

"Should we split into two groups and meet back here later?" Ashley asked, wiggling her toes in the sand.

Dana and Diana stopped running along the shore and joined the group, trying to hide their excitement.

"Let's stick together for now. We have no idea what or who is on this island?" replied Jenny.

"We also have no idea if Amelia and the Coven will come searching for us," said Ashley.

"I agree," said Karina as the rest of the girls nodded.

"Let's not stand around here then," said Jenny.

The girls walked along the beach toward the overgrown jungle of palm trees and thick brush. As they approached, shadowy figures moved from tree to tree on the edge of the jungle. Karina could not tell if she was seeing an animal, a human, or possibly some other strange creature.

"Something is moving in there," said Karina.

"Maybe we should try another way," said Molly.

"It's going to be okay," said Ashley.

"Girls, be ready," added Jenny.

As the girls drew nearer, the trees shook even more violently, and loud grunting noises came from the shadowy figures.

"Who are they?" whispered Molly.

Before Karina could answer, three older teenage boys jumped down from the banana trees, landing on the beach with ease. All three of them were shirtless, their chiseled bodies glistening in the sun. The boy in the middle had long, wavy brown hair and carried a sharp spear. With a frown, he eyed the girls as the other two boys drew knives from their belts.

"What are we going to do?" Molly and the other girls backpedaled toward the crashing waves, while the three boys approached.

"Please don't hurt us," said Karina.

"Maybe we will, maybe we won't," said the boy carrying the spear. His eyes wandered from one girl to another, and the other two boys remained silent. "Where did you all come from?"

"Norlandis," said Jenny.

"Norlandis? Impossible!" replied the boy.

"We just got here," said Ashley.

"From Norlandis?"

"Yes, Norlandis. We've been there for many years," replied Jenny.

"And we both escaped Vallaborg," Ashley said, pointing at Molly.

"Vallaborg! Now I know you're lying. No one escapes from there," replied the boy.

"Well, we did. I was with them as well," declared Karina.

The boys eyed the girls, while they circled them, holding their weapons at the ready. "We're not here for a fight," said Karina. The boys eased up, pointing their knives and spears at the ground.

"Tell me something about Vallaborg that only someone who has been there would know," replied the boy with the spear.

"Amelia has an eight-legged horse," Karina snapped.

"A horse with eight legs. Interesting. And what is this horse's name?"

"Sleipnir," replied Molly.

"Well, I have no idea if you are lying or telling the truth. Mainly because I don't know much about that wretched place, but it sounds legit, I guess."

"Told you we weren't lying," said Ashley as she brushed her dangling hair from her face.

"My name is Finan. To my right is Michael, and to my left is Isaiah," said Finan.

The girls all introduced themselves to the boys, who were now admiring a few of them. The older four girls blushed, fighting back smiles.

"May I ask how you got here?" asked Finan.

"Through the portal," said Karina.

"Portal? What portal?"

Karina turned to point in the direction of the beach but realized she had no idea where the actual portal was that led back to Norlandis. Was it only a one-way portal? Were they now stuck on the Islands of Runa? "I'm not sure where it went, but it's how we got here."

The rest of the girls looked frantically over their shoulders, searching for the portal. "Where did it go?" muttered Ashley.

"We used magic," said Jenny nervously.

"Magic! You know magic?" asked Finan.

"Yes, of course. Would you like me to show you?"

"Absolutely!" said Finan as the boys anxiously watched Jenny.

"Do you mind if I show them?" said Ashley, moving in front of Jenny.

"Nope, go ahead." Annoyed, Jenny rolled her eyes.

"Schokoladaa," said Ashley under her breath as a bar of chocolate appeared in her outstretched hand.

"Chocolate! My favorite," yelled Finan. He broke off a big piece of the chocolate and devoured it. Isaiah and Michael split the rest of it, stuffing the chocolate in their mouths.

"Holy smokes! This is amazing," said Isaiah as chocolate saliva dripped from his mouth.

"I know, right?" said Michael.

"Been way too long," said Isaiah.

"She can give you more if you can help us out," said Karina.

"Oh, what do you have in mind?" asked Finan.

"We're looking for a few girls," continued Karina.

"Aren't we all," joked Michael as he playfully shoved Isaiah.

"Do you happen to know a girl by the name of Hannah?" asked Karina.

"Hannah? I think there are a few," replied Finan.

"She looks like an older version of me," shouted Molly.

"The one with the nose ring?" asked Isaiah.

"Yes! That's probably her."

"Yeah, I know her. We can take you to her if you can give us more chocolate. It was so good. Almost makes my teeth hurt," said Finan.

"Probably because you haven't had any sugar for years," said Karina.

"Maybe," replied Finan.

"It's cool. We will happily fight through the pain," laughed Michael.

Ashley smiled and quietly said the spell again. Three bars of chocolate appeared in her hands. Ashley handed them to each of the three boys, who beamed and engulfed the chocolate, like a kid after trick-or-treating on Halloween night.

"This is incredible," said Michael.

"My teeth hurt." Isaiah was laughing and mimicking Finan.

"It's probably because you haven't had sugar for years," declared Jenny with a smile.

"It's well worth the pain," said Isaiah, joining in the fun.

"Almost as sweet as you girls," smirked Finan, finishing his last piece of chocolate.

"I'm glad you enjoyed it," said Ashley, beaming with delight.

Karina rolled her eyes. She didn't have time to watch them keep flirting. She was so close to finally finding Hannah. "So-o-o-o, can you show us the way?"

"Of course," replied Finan. He kept his word, leading the group along the beach by the edge of the jungle and up a sandy dune. The three boys talked the whole way with the older girls, telling them how long they'd been on the Island of Runa and what they missed most about home. Karina and Molly walked behind them, both lost in thought and anxious to hopefully find Hannah.

Not too far from the shore was an island covered with tropical trees and an enormous looming cliff. Various rock formations jutted out here and there up the face of the cliff. Four tall pillars made of rock towered at the edges of the island, reminiscent of a castle.

Finan led the girls to the edge of the sea facing the island with the cliff. The water was relatively calm and clear blue, stretching across the horizon. Other than the imposing cliff ahead, there was nothing else around. No seagulls, boats, or people.

"And this is the end of the road for us," said Finan.

"What do you mean? You said you would take us to see Hannah!" said Karina angrily.

"We can't cross the sea. This is our island, and that is the girls' island. You all shouldn't even be here right now as it is."

"I thought you saw Hannah. How would you have seen her if you couldn't go onto each other's islands?"

"We can go in the water together, but we can't venture to each other's islands."

"I see," replied Karina as she craned her neck, trying to see if she could spot any girls on the other island."

"You promise us she's up there?" asked Molly.

"Of course," replied Finan.

"Will we have any trouble crossing?" asked Ashley.

"Shouldn't be a problem. The water isn't very deep this time of year," replied Finan.

"Do you have a boat by any chance?" asked Jenny.

"Yes, but we can't give it to you," replied Michael.

"We understand. Guess we're swimming then," replied Jenny.

"Good luck!" said Finan.

"Thanks, Finan. I hope to see you again soon," said Jenny.

"My pleasure. Perhaps we can go for a swim together sometime."

"I'd like that."

"Me too," replied Ashley.

"And us too," giggled Dana and Diana

"I'm sure we'll see you soon enough," said Isaiah.

Karina and Molly made their way into the warm, clear water while the other girls continued to flirt with the boys. They had already walked about a hundred feet from the shore before the other girls finally entered the sea. Karina did not have time for boys right now. She had already been through too much and was not going to let anything distract her at this point.

They made it about halfway across on foot until the terrain became too difficult. Karina dove into the cool water, propelling herself forward. She came up for air, while Molly swam behind her. Just as their arms began to tire, they made it to the shallow part of the sea. Thankfully, they could walk the rest of the way. The water was calm and very peaceful.

Once they reached the shore, two teenage girls suddenly appeared from behind a large boulder, each wielding a sword.

"What are you all doing here!" demanded the shorter girl with golden brown skin, pointing her sword directly at the girls.

"We are looking for my friend, who is also her sister," replied Karina, pointing to Molly.

"Looking for my sister as well," said Jenny.

"Okay, and who are you looking for?" the girl asked.

"Hannah," replied Karina.

"And Madison," said Jenny.

"Where did you come from?" the girl asked.

"Norlandis," replied Karina.

"Norlandis! Follow me then."

The six girls followed the island girls who carried swords toward the rocky cliffside. Behind the overgrown brush hanging off the rocks was a wooden platform used as an elevator, which had ropes running up the cliffside.

"I can take two of you at a time," said the shorter girl.

Karina and Molly stepped forward and onto the platform before the other girls could even think about it.

"Be careful not to move too much," said the short girl as the elevator slowly ascended high into the air. It wasn't long before they were a couple of hundred feet in the air. Karina turned around to catch sight of the breathtaking sea and the boys' island that was covered with trees and mountains. The closer they got to the top, the slower the elevator moved.

Karina turned back around when the elevator came to a stop. They had finally reached the top of the cliff, which was covered in lush grass and thick with trees. Small tents were pitched here and there with girls bustling about.

"Welcome to our sanctuary," said the shorter girl, motioning toward the tents. The scent of salt and sea mingled with the fragrance of the island's tropical flowers, creating a sweet aroma. "My name is Maria, and this is Chloe," she said, pointing to the other girl who had remained silent.

"Nice to meet you. I'm Karina, and this is Molly." They stepped off the lift, looking around. Girls of various ages were scattered throughout the camp, some cooking over fires, some practicing with swords or bows, and others sitting around talking.

The girls smiled back at them. "Wait here," said Maria.

Several girls on the island stopped what they were doing as their eyes locked onto their new visitors. Maria walked away toward the girls on the island and spoke quietly to them, pointing back at Karina and Molly. She then walked away with two of the girls and disappeared. The other girls on the island continued to stare at Karina and Molly without saying a word.

A very tall and muscular teenage girl stopped cutting wood and approached Karina and Molly, her axe in hand.

"Why are you two here?" asked the tall girl.

"We're just here to see Hannah. Nothing else, I promise."

"And what do you intend to do with her?"

"Well, I'm not sure yet," Karina said.

"We've come all the way from Norlandis to find my sister," said Molly.

"You won't be taking her, if that's what you think," said the tall girl. She continued toward the girls, twirling her axe.

"I understand," replied Karina. She and Molly waited for what seemed like an hour. Ashley, Jenny, Dana, and Diana had joined them on the island with the other guard from the beach. The tall girl with the axe circled the girls from the Shadow Embers, sizing them up. Other girls from the island stood by, yielding swords, axes, and daggers.

Karina noticed the sharp contrast between the two islands. The boys had been so welcoming compared to the girls. They were like innocent little boys, especially when they got to have their chocolate. Karina wondered why the boys had spears and were ready to attack whoever was on their island. They must have been scouting the island as they hid among the trees. Meanwhile, on the girls' island everyone seemed on edge and ready for some kind of battle. They were less than welcoming and seemed irritated that visitors had shown up. Karina needed to know more about what was going on in the Islands of Runa and how she could try to save them.

Suddenly, Hannah came sprinting through the trees. She stopped when she spotted Karina and Molly.

"Molly! Karina!" yelled Hannah as tears streamed down her face.

"Hannah!" yelled Karina and Molly in unison as they ran toward Hannah.

Molly practically leaped into Hannah's arms, both of them with tear-filled eyes. Karina threw her arms around Molly and Hannah.

"How did you find me?" asked Hannah.

"It's a long story," replied Karina.

"Very long story for sure," laughed Molly.

Jenny gasped as her sister appeared from a nearby tent. She was a little older than Jenny and was a mirror image of her, with slightly darker red hair and freckles. The two ran toward each other and jumped up and down in excitement, before wrapping their arms around each other. Tears of excitement and laughter filled the air.

Karina didn't know whether to smile or cry. She had finally found Hannah after weeks of searching and everything she had been through. Karina had had doubts about whether she would ever see her friend again. Her adventure through Norlandis, Vallaborg, and now to the Islands of Runa had all been completely worth it. She wished it had never come to this. But she was here, and she knew her purpose. Karina had no idea what the girls were going to do now, how she would break the curse, and most importantly, how everyone would make it back home.

Their journey was far from over. It had truly just begun.

Epilogue

At the back of an enormously long room, an imposing figure sat on a wooden throne with intricate engravings. Amelia. She was surrounded by a pack of coyotes lying on the floor. An emerald-green carpet ran down the center of the room between several stone pillars and tall arched windows which lined the length of the room on both sides. The scent of burnt sage lingered in the dark room. Amelia had always found the smell to be relaxing and thought-provoking.

The Coven had eliminated or captured most of their enemy. The victory had been sweet. The battle with the Shadow Embers was over for now. Many of the girls were taken as prisoners. Amelia relished the opportunity to take back Norlandis. Sure, there were still some Shadow Embers left to defeat, but she would soon deal with them, and Norlandis would be hers alone. Once everyone from the Shadow Embers was locked away, the only thing left to do was to venture to the Islands of Runa and capture Karina and the other girls who had escaped.

The door at the opposite end of the room creaked open. Torhild ventured inside, her head bowed. Amelia snapped her fingers as Torhild approached, causing the candles hanging from the pillars and on the chandelier to illuminate the castle room.

"Have you secured the prisoners?" asked Amelia.

"Of course," replied Torhild, approaching the throne.

"Good. How many did we get this time?"

"Twenty-one."

"That's it? I thought we had significantly more than that."

"No. Unfortunately, some got away during your battle with Rayna."

"Very well. Please bring her to me."

Torhild stopped in her tracks in the middle of the room. "She, uh… "

"Out with it!"

"Rayna escaped."

"What do you mean, she escaped?" yelled Amelia. She rose from her throne and stalked toward Torhild.

"I don't know how it happened. All four of us were dragging her into the dungeon when she vanished between our fingertips."

"Impossible! No one can use magic inside these castle walls and on Vallaborg. No one except us."

"That's what I thought too."

"Must I do everything myself!"

"No, of course not. I will find her."

Runa, Olga, and Rowan burst into the room.

"She's gone! We can't find her anywhere!" shouted Olga.

"I'm well aware of it," replied Amelia.

"What should we do?" asked Torhild.

"Find her!" yelled Amelia.

The four sisters scampered out of the castle room, while Amelia turned to face her throne. She screamed at the top of her lungs, causing every candle to blow out simultaneously. The room darkened as Amelia's hopes dimmed.

THE END

About the Author

Jason B. Whittier

Jason B. Whittier is a writer and teacher based in Massachusetts, where he lives with his wife and seven children. Jason earned his B.A. in German with minors in History and Slavic Studies from West Virginia University, his first M.A. in German Studies from the University of Georgia, and his second M.A. in Education from Arizona State University. He has written and produced the horror film *Waterfront Nightmare* and co-written and co-produced the psychological thriller *The Secret Village*. Jason has a few feature films in active development with different producers. Over the years, he has optioned multiple screenplays and created several short films. While balancing the busy rhythm of family and professional life with his creative pursuits, Jason also enjoys traveling, sports, and gardening. He currently teaches ESL at both the middle school and adult education levels. Jason recently completed his debut young adult novel, *Forbidden Woods – Adventures in Norlandis.*

Howling Wolf Press

www.howlingwolfpress.com

Stories that howl through the night...

At **Howling Wolf Press**, we publish bold, imaginative fiction with heart.
From whimsical fantasy to haunting adventures, our books are crafted
to enchant and endure.

JOIN THE PACK

Discover unforgettable stories or share your own.

HowlingWolfPress.com

Follow the call